SHARED BY TWO

JON ATHAN

For more information on this book or the author, please visit
www.jon-athan.com. General inquiries are welcome.

Facebook: https://www.facebook.com/AuthorJonAthan
Twitter: @Jonny_Athan
Email: info@jon-athan.com
Instagram: @AuthorJonnyAthan

Cover illustration by Pedro Bianchi Guerra
Book cover typography and logo by MiblArt: https://miblart.com/
Proofreading provided by Karen Bennett: kbennett4653@gmail.com

Thank you for the support!
ISBN: 9798370123603
First Edition

This book is about horror writers and readers, so it's only right that I dedicate it to the genre and the people who support it—who have been supporting me, and authors like me, with their kindness and generosity for years.

Thank you to Mellisa Butler, Andy and Brandy Carroll, Travis Davis, Tony Dellafiore, John Dugan, Joe Elliot, Samantha Hawkins, Tara Losacano, Carrie Shields, Judith Sonnet, Nancy Sienna Sundquist, Don Taylor, John Tomlinson, Markus Tremel, Michael Watson-Tate, and the thousands of you who continue to read my work every month—in the US, Germany, UK, Canada, anywhere and everywhere. I can't name everyone, I might have overdone it already, but I wish I could thank you all individually. Maybe someday. Until then, enjoy the book!

WARNING

This book contains scenes of intense violence and some disturbing themes. Some parts of this book may be considered violent, cruel, disturbing, or unusual. This book is not intended for those easily offended or appalled. Please enjoy at your own discretion.

TABLE OF CONTENTS

1

THE BOY

TWELVE-YEAR-OLD HARRISON HAMMER AWOKE WITH A racking cough, spasming on a thin, sheetless mattress. He lay under a threadbare quilted jacket, using it as a blanket. Only his head and bony legs stuck out from under it. To his right, cracks between the broken blinds let in slits of pale light. Although the window was closed, he heard a man yelling in a language he didn't understand outside and, far in the distance, he could hear dogs barking.

"Harry!" his mother called out to him from another room in the home.

Harrison opened his mouth to answer but he was immediately interrupted by a coughing fit. He groaned as he sat up in bed, a hail of dandruff falling from his shaggy brown hair. The jacket fell onto his lap. He was wearing a tank top with a brown spatter stain, which looked like drips of coffee or chocolate or blood. His striped boxers were loose, one size too big. Like his legs, his arms and torso were alarmingly skinny. Every bone jutted out against his ghostly skin.

He reached over and turned the knob on his bedside lamp. It made a clicking noise but it didn't turn on. He didn't bother to try turning it on again because the power often went out in his home. He pushed himself up to his feet, then wobbled across the room like a drunk. The floor was flooded with trash—snack wrappers, empty water bottles, crumpled paper, broken toys—and dirty laundry. He opened the door, then leaned against the jamb to catch his breath.

"Ha–Harry!" his mother hollered again.

Her voice, loud but choppy, came from a room down the hall to his left. To his right, he heard plates and silverware clinking and clacking along with some unintelligible grumbling and whimpering. He followed his mother's voice, shambling past a storage closet, a bathroom, and a nursery. The door at the end of the hall opened up to the master bedroom. The floor, like the rest of the home, was covered in trash.

Vera, his mother, lay on the king-sized bed under two blankets with her head propped up on three pillows. Newspapers covered the mattress under her, drenched in urine and smeared with semi-liquid feces. There was a cadaverous pallor to her sunken face. She was thin and malnourished like her son. Thick green and purple veins squiggled across her temples, neck, hands, and arms.

Harrison shuffled over to her, trash rustling around his feet with each step. On the nightstand next to her, he saw a lamp, a bottle of whiskey, a mound of crushed bloodstained tissue paper, and a lit gas lantern.

"Yes, Ma?" Harrison asked as he approached her.

Vera grunted to clear her throat but it didn't help much. In a wet, guttural voice, she said, "Please fetch... me a plate."

"A plate?"

"Din... Dinner, honey. You didn't... eat yet?"

"Oh. No, I think I fell asleep."

Vera frowned and said, "That's why he's been screaming. That man... That stubborn man has such a short temper. Go. Apologize. Then please..." She coughed a spritz of blood into the tissue in her hand. Her voice softer and wetter, she said, "And please bring me a plate and... and some water."

"Yes, Ma."

As the boy reached the foot of the bed, Vera said, "And light some candles. It'll be dark soon."

Harrison looked over his shoulder and nodded at her, then he exited the room. He walked to a console table in the hallway, opened one of its drawers, and pulled a box of matches out. He lit a match, then used it to light the candle on the table. Next to it, there was an uneven stack of envelopes. The one on top had a *Past Due* stamp on it.

He turned on a lantern on the floor next to the storage closet door. He ended up in the living room. He lit a candle on the end table between two sofas. The wide archway to his left led to the dining room. The kitchen was around the corner, beyond a counter. The soft yellow glow of candlelight already illuminated those rooms.

Cheryl, Harrison's fifteen-month-old sister, sat on a highchair at the dining table. She was eating meat sticks off a small pink plate on her tray. His father, a large brawny man named Irwin, stood at the other end of the table. With a spatula, he transferred a slab of burnt meat from a pan to the plate in front of him.

Like his son, the man wore a tank top. It was tucked into his black jeans. Unlike Harrison, however, his chest and arms were muscular and hairy. He was bald on top with graying brown hair on the sides. There was an unkempt mustache on his lip and stubble on his jaw. His Coke-bottle glasses magnified his cold eyes.

"Where have you been, boy?" Irwin asked as he walked into the kitchen.

"I, um... I think I fell asleep," Harrison answered.

"You *think* you fell asleep? Well, did you or didn't you?"

"Sorry, I meant, uh... I fell asleep. I'm still sick."

"You're lying to me again, aren't you?"

"No, I swear. I–I'm cold and my head hurts and I have a sore–"

Irwin threw the pan into the sink. Harrison recoiled in fear. The loud *bang* made Cheryl whine. There was a suppressed whimper in the kitchen, too.

The man grabbed an open can of beer from the counter and took a big swig.

He held it out in front of him, wagged it at his son, and said, "*You* should have cooked dinner. *You* should have made that damn table. I called *you* a dozen times even though I should never have to say your name more than once. *Never,* boy. And now you come here with that stupid look on your face and you tell me you were *sleeping* this whole time?"

"It–It's true, Dad. I think I'm really–"

"*Stop* thinking and *start* working! I don't want to hear your bullshit excuses again. You're sleeping when *I* call you but when your cunt mother says your name, you jump out of bed and run to her side? Hmm? I hear what's going on in this place. I'm not stupid. I'm not deaf. So, don't give me any more shit. *Don't.*"

Harrison bit his bottom lip to stop himself from talking back. He knew better than to argue with his father.

He lowered his head and said, "I'm sorry, sir."

Irwin returned to the dining room with a pot and a ladle. With the ladle, he drizzled a red liquid on the meat on the plates. He poured extra on his—the extra-large serving.

Harrison said, "Mom wants her food."

"She's not eating at the table? Again? What the hell's wrong with that woman?"

"She's still sick."

"Oh, for fuck's sake. You and your mother are

always 'sick,' huh? She can't get her ass to work. You can't go to school. Both of you are useless. And you know what happens when an animal is sick and useless? Do you?"

"Yes, sir."

"Then tell me."

"You... have to put 'em down."

"So, you're not as dumb as you look. You better hope you're not as useless as you've been actin', too. Take her damn food. Tell her to enjoy it. I cooked it special just for her and you."

"For me?" Harrison asked, head cocked to the side.

Irwin brought the pot and ladle back to the kitchen. He threw the kitchenware into the sink. Cheryl bawled louder, clenching a meat stick in each hand while bouncing in her seat. Irwin cracked open another beer and muttered indistinctly. Harrison approached the dining table and examined the plate next to his sister.

There was a thick slice of meat on the plate. It was overcooked—charred in some places—and covered with drizzles of a dark red liquid, like strawberry syrup on a pancake. The red juices puddled under the meat. It didn't look like anything special to him. He took some silverware, the plate, and the glass of tap water next to it.

"Your good-for-nothing mother should have cooked this shit," Irwin muttered as the boy left the dining room. "Not me. No, I'm not your damn slave."

In the master bedroom, Harrison pushed the heap of used tissue paper off his mother's nightstand. He put the plate down, then handed her the glass of water.

"Drink," the boy said.

Vera's arms trembled, muscles contracting and fingers twitching. Like a washing machine, the water sloshed and splashed in the cup. A drop landed on her white nightgown. Harrison put his hand on the bottom of the glass to stabilize it. His mother could only muster the energy to take a sip.

"Thank you, honey," she said.

"You want me to cut the meat for you?"

"No, no, I can... do it myself. I'm feeling a little better already. You should eat something."

"I will," Harrison said with a nod.

As the boy walked over to the door, Vera said, "Oh, and honey... please feed Luka. Poor boy needs to eat, too."

"Yes, Ma."

Harrison returned to the dining room. Irwin was now sitting at the end of the table. There was a bottle of whiskey and a shot glass next to his plate. He took a shot, then poured himself another.

"Hey, Cherry," Harrison said as he approached his baby sister. He kissed her cheek, then asked, "You still hungry?"

"*Hey, Cherry,*" Irwin repeated in a mocking voice while sneering in annoyance. "Stop being a little sissy boy in front of your sister. We don't need your '*sickness*' to rub off on her now, do we? Get your brother, then sit your ass down and eat. You're washing the dishes and cleaning this place up when we're done."

"Mom wants me to feed Luka."

"We're all outta dog food."

"I'll give him some of mine."

Raising his voice, Irwin said, "*I* did *not* cook for an animal. *We* eat first, boy. Dogs get the scraps. Now stop giving me lip and get your brother."

Harrison clenched his jaw, bottling his desire to scream. He exhaled loudly through his nose, then asked, "Where is he?"

"He's being punished. I had to break him to fix him."

"Oh..."

Harrison didn't have to ask why or how his brother was being punished. He knew where to find him. He walked into the kitchen and opened the cabinet under the sink.

Andrey, Harrison's nine-year-old brother, was crammed into the cabinet—back hunched, knees against his cheeks, arms hooked around his shins. The boy, wearing only pee-stained tighty-whities, was shuddering and sniveling. Three house spiders skittered through his short black hair while cockroaches crawled across his legs and arms. He was scared of insects, small spaces, and the dark, so this was how their father broke him.

"C'mon," Harrison said softly. "It's time to eat."

He swiped the spiders and cockroaches off him, then grabbed his brother's arm and helped him out of the cabinet.

As he struggled to his feet, Andrey whispered, "I tried to stop him."

"Stop him? What did he–"

"Get in here and start eating before your damn food gets cold, you pansies," Irwin snarled from the dining room. "I didn't bust my ass in that kitchen for nothing."

Harrison led his little brother to the dining table. He sat him down in the seat across from Cheryl so he could put some distance between him and their father. He didn't want his brother to have to suffer through more abuse. Harrison took the seat directly to Irwin's right and stared down at the dark meat on his plate. It emitted a musky odor.

"Eat," Irwin said before shoving a forkful of meat into his mouth.

The stench of alcohol on Irwin's breath was so strong that it masked the scent from the meat for a minute.

Hesitant, Harrison stuttered, "Wha–What is it?"

"Meat."

"What kinda meat?"

"*Meat*," Irwin repeated sternly.

Seeing the unadulterated rage in his father's eyes, Harrison nodded. With his knife and fork, he cut a piece of the meat and put it in his mouth. When it touched his tongue, his taste buds cramped and his face crumpled in a grimace of disgust. The metallic flavor of the red liquid reminded him of blood. With the first bite, goosebumps rashed out across the nape of his neck as well as his arms. It was tender but a little gristly with a strong, earthy flavor. It tasted familiar yet foreign.

Andrey followed his brother's lead. He took a small bite of his meat. Tears fell from his face and plopped in the red juices on his plate. Cheryl held a meat stick close to her mouth like a microphone. Her red face was scrunched up with concern. She was too young to understand everything, but she could sense when something was wrong. She felt her brothers' pain and fear. She felt her father's anger and hatred.

Like the frequent power outages, there were persistent blackouts of love in their home.

"Dad, what is this?" Harrison squeaked out.

"Goddammit, boy," Irwin said, his mouth full. "What's the matter with you? How many times do I have to tell you? It's *meat*. You didn't sit there and ask your mother that question whenever she cooked for you, did you? You ate the crap she made with a shit-eating grin, didn't you? Now I expect you to do the same for me. Believe me, you don't want to let it go to waste. It's good food. Fresh. Delicious."

Irwin stabbed his slice of meat with a fork, then sawed into it with his knife. Stalling, Andrey only used his fork to cut into his meat, leaving his knife on the table. Echoes of Vera's harsh coughs reached the dining room.

Tears standing in his eyes, Harrison said, "Dad, I'm sorry, but... It's too hard to eat. My, um... My throat hurts a lot. It's really hard to swallow. Maybe I need to go to the doctor."

Irwin gulped down a mouthful of meat, then said, "Look at your mother, boy. Does it look like we have money for a doctor?"

"Can I have some soup instead? I think I saw a can in the..."

He stopped speaking as his father slid the shot glass towards him. He looked at it, then up at his dad, then back at the alcohol.

"Drink," Irwin said. "It'll make your throat feel better. Trust me."

Harrison wrapped his fingers around the glass. It wasn't the first time his father offered him alcohol. He hated it. It made his head hurt, his nose run, and his body warm. But his father could make him feel the same whenever he disobeyed his orders, too. The only difference was, Irwin usually used his fists and belt to get the job done.

Harrison wasn't looking for a fight. He only wanted answers. He took a swig of the alcohol. Throat burning, he coughed into his elbow.

Grunting with each pause, he asked, "Can I... go feed... Luka now?"

"My God, boy," Irwin laughed. "You're just as *stubborn* and *stupid* as your mother."

"Can I... go?"

"Boy! You're not feeding that damn dog! Get that through your head! That dog's feeding you!"

"What?"

"He–He killed him, Harry," Andrey cried with his head down. "He killed Loo–Loo... Luka. I couldn't stop him."

"No," Harrison said. "No, no, no."

The boy sprung out of his chair and lurched into the kitchen. Irwin shook his head and continued eating. Harrison planted his palms on a counter, jumped, and leaned forward to peek out a window. In the small backyard, he saw Luka's ramshackle doghouse. A rusty dog chain snaked across the overgrown lawn. But the German shepherd was nowhere to be found.

Harrison lowered himself as he gagged. He cupped his hands over his mouth and sobbed. He was struck with a sudden bout of nausea and lightheadedness. Heartbreak left him short of breath with his chest aching. Upon hearing the screech of a fork scraping a plate, he looked daggers at Irwin.

Face red with fury, Harrison marched up to his father and yelled, "Why did you do that?! Why did–"

"Watch your mouth, boy."

"–you kill Luka?! He was my best friend! We loved him! I loved him!"

"Shut your fucking mouth!"

Cheryl wailed at the top of her lungs. Her high-chair teetered as she bounced in her seat. A meat stick rolled off her tray, followed by another.

"Stop it," Andrey pleaded. "Please stop. Puh–Puh–Please."

Voice strained from all his crying, Harrison shouted, "I hate you! I fuckin' hate you! I hate you so much! You're a monster! You... You... *You fucker!*"

Irwin slammed his fist on the table and yelled, "Who the hell do you think–"

Harrison snatched the table knife off his plate and thrust it at his father's chest. At the last second, Irwin pushed the boy's arm away. The blade grazed his shoulder. Irwin backhanded the boy. Harrison fell on his ass, blood dribbling out of a small cut at the corner of his mouth. The knife slipped out of his hand, falling in a pile of trash behind his father.

Irwin stood from his seat. Towering over his son, he jabbed his finger at him and said, "I killed that dog to teach you a lesson, you ungrateful son of a bitch. You should have listened to me when I called you. Hell, you should have done your damn chores without me having to tell you to do them in the first place."

"I was sick!"

"And so was Luka. So is your mother. And you know what happens when an animal is sick and useless."

"I'm telling mom! She's going to call the police and you're going..."

His voice faded away and his eyes widened with fear as a disturbing realization dawned on him: His mother was eating Luka.

Scrambling to his feet, he shouted, "Mom!" He reeled towards the master bedroom and yelled, "Mom! Ma! Don't eat the meat!"

Andrey ran around the table and grabbed Cheryl's chair, stopping it from tipping over.

Tackling the door with his shoulder, Harrison barged into the master bedroom. Vera was coughing into another piece of tissue. She was surprised by her son's sudden appearance, but she didn't have the energy to show it. On the nightstand, half a slice of meat lay in a puddle of red juices on the plate. Her glass was empty.

"What's... wrong?" she asked.

Harrison slid to a stop next to the bed. He grabbed the plate and hurled it to his left. It hit the closet door, shattering upon impact.

Propping herself up on her elbows, Vera said, "Christ, Harry, what's gotten into you?"

"You have to call the police," Harrison blurted out as he grabbed his mother's arm.

"Calm down, honey. You're scaring me. What happened to your lip? Did that bastard hit you?"

"He killed Luka, Ma," Harrison said, speaking rapidly. "Dad killed Luka. He–He... He cooked him and–and... and made us eat him. He's crazy, Ma. I–I don't know what to do. How do I call the police? How do I–"

"You don't," Irwin interrupted from the doorway. *"You won't."*

The boy turned his head to glare at him. Vera had to fight the urge to retch. Severely dehydrated, she cried but no tears came out.

She asked, "Is it true?"

"It is," Irwin said matter-of-factly.

"You... You killed our Luka?"

"I did."

"And you... you cooked him? And you fed... Jesus Christ, you *fed* him to us?"

"I did."

There was a moment of awed silence.

Vera asked, "What the hell is wrong with you?"

"The boy had to be punished," Irwin replied. "He didn't deserve that dog. No way. No fucking way. He ignores his chores. He skips his classes. Fails 'em, too. He corrupts his brother and sister with his bad behavior. This kid, your precious little 'Harry,' is a goddamn brat. And you've been too soft on him. Enough is enough. No more coddling. No more games. No more disrespect. From him *and* you."

Vera said, "You must have lost..." A violent coughing fit seized her for about ten seconds. Then, with a rough, gurgly voice, she continued, "Lost your mind... you nasty, old bastard."

"Watch how you talk to me, woman."

"Get out... of my house."

"Your house? Who do you think's been paying the rent for this dump since you quit your job?"

"I was..."

While Vera coughed up another mist of blood—Harrison patting her back gently—Irwin said, "You don't have any savings and you haven't earned a dime in over a year. You don't work, woman. Just like your little nancy boy son, you do *not* work. You're no good. Sick. Useless. You're lucky I loved ya once upon a time 'cause if I didn't... Just count your blessings and stay in your place. You hear me?"

"Laid off," Vera said, finally finishing her sentence. "I was laid off. I don't have any savings because... you stole it all."

"I didn't steal a thing. It was *our* money."

"It was 'our' money then, but now... now you pay the rent with 'your' money? You're nothing but a... but a dirty, good-for-nothing rat."

"Don't push me, Vera," Irwin said, stepping forward while thrusting a finger at her.

"You're like... your mother."

"*Vera.*"

"A thieving... sadistic... abusive... cunt."

Irwin lunged at her, effortlessly forcing himself between his son and the bed. Harrison lost his footing but caught himself on the nightstand. Irwin grabbed Vera's neck in one hand and slapped her with the other

—palm, backhand, palm, backhand, *palm*. Her pale cheeks flared red and a string of mucusy blood hung from one of her nostrils. The cut at the corner of her mouth matched the one on her son's lip.

Vera's vision doubled. Waves of stinging pain rippled across the left side of her face. The pain worsened as she screamed. Her cheekbone had been fractured.

Yet, no tears came.

"You ungrateful bitch!" Irwin growled as he continued beating on his wife. "Who do you think you are?!"

Harrison hit his father's legs and back with the bottom of his fists. Thanks to his firm muscles, Irwin felt like someone was poking him. Harrison knew it was unwise to poke a bear, but he could only think about defending his mother. He was willing to sacrifice himself to save her. He grabbed the empty glass off the nightstand, then jumped up and swung it at his father's face. It made a *clanging* noise but it didn't shatter—didn't even crack.

The attack hurt Irwin's ego more than his head.

The man shouted, "You trying to kill me?!"

"Get off her!" Harrison responded.

"You trying to kill your own dad?!"

Irwin grabbed the bottle of whiskey off the nightstand and swung it back at his son. The bottle shattered on Harrison's face. His temple tore open, leaving a piece of his skull exposed in the fleshy crater. Blood raced down the left side of his face. Shards of glass cut the bridge of his nose, his forehead, and his left cheek. Before he could shut them, fragments of glass dusted his eyes and clung to his long eyelashes.

The boy fell unconscious, landing on a black garbage bag in front of the closet. He sank into the trash, as if he were sitting on a bean bag.

Ears ringing, Harrison's eyes flickered open to a blur. His head throbbed, matching the swift rhythm of his heart. His face burned and tingled due to the alcohol in his cuts. He felt like a colony of fire ants was walking across his face, each one biting him with every step. He couldn't tell if a minute, two, or ten had passed. His vision began to focus and the ringing in his ears started to quieten after a few seconds.

"You killed him!" his mother was saying.

"Shut up!" Irwin barked.

Harrison's father was now on the bed. One blanket was on the floor and the other was next to Vera on the mattress.

"You killed him!" Vera cried while struggling under her husband. "Oh my God, you killed my baby!"

There was genuine sorrow in her voice. She truly believed her son was dead.

"Ma... Mom," Harrison said meekly.

Vera couldn't hear him. Irwin tightened his grip on her throat. He lifted her head from the pillow, then slammed it back down.

Slamming her head with every pause, he said, "I'll

give you... another baby... if you're going to miss... that brat... so bad."

With his free hand, he pushed her nightgown up, then pulled her underwear down. Vera was dazed, so she couldn't fight back or scream. Then he dropped his pants. His penis was already erect. Violence aroused him. He thrust his cock at her crotch, but he had trouble penetrating her. He took the slimy blood from her nose and slathered it on his dick, then he rubbed the glans against her vulva, making sure to share the 'natural' lubricant. He thrust into her.

With the penetration, Vera felt a surge of adrenaline blast through her. She slapped Irwin's face and chest while floundering under him. Yet, the man kept thrusting into her.

"Stop it," Irwin said. "Don't make this worse for yourself."

Vera threw a flurry of aimless punches—at his chin, his nose, his forehead, his chest, his shoulders—but she couldn't hurt him. In fact, she hurt her bony hands more than she hurt his rugged face. So, she clawed at his cheeks, shoulders, and neck. The thin cuts stung, so he stopped thrusting but he stayed inside of her. Then one of her fingernails nicked his left eye. He slapped his hand over it and screamed.

She seized the opportunity and went for the other one. She tried to press her finger against his right eye, but she wound up thumbing his cheek.

Irwin grabbed the broken bottle. He glassed her

with it, stabbing the side of her neck. Her face knotted and she ground her teeth, which aggravated her smashed cheekbone. She grabbed his forearm, but she couldn't stop the saw-like glass from eating away at her throat. The jagged shards severed a jugular and pierced her windpipe. Blood sprayed out of her throat in spurts. It filled the bottle, then poured out of its orifice in a steady stream.

Weak from the loss of blood, Vera released her grip on his arm. Her hands fell to her chest, palms up. Irwin felt her vagina tighten around his cock as she convulsed under him.

"That's how I like it," he said, smirking as he resumed his thrusting.

Tears blurred Harrison's eyesight. Blood had entered his left eye, turning part of his vision red. He couldn't summon enough strength to get up and fight. He didn't even have the energy to scream. He could only sit in the trash and watch his father rape his dying mother. His eyes began to roll up while his head bobbed like a sleepy toddler's. It all went black. But for a few seconds, he could still hear his mother gargling her own blood and his father's groans of pleasure.

Then he fell unconscious again.

2

CORRESPONDENCE #1

Subject: **Greetings!**
From: Butterfly <admin@splattersociety.com>
September 16, 2022, 10:07 AM
To: Nestor Castle <info@nes-castle.com>

Long time no see, Nes!

You might not recognize me because of the new email address. Real official, huh? Figured if I'm running a real fan club, I should have a real website. Anyway, it's me, Butterfly. It's been a while since we last chatted, so I wouldn't blame you if you forgot about me. I was a BIG fan of your extreme horror. Still am, as a matter of fact. I've read all of your books, and re-read some of them recently. *Hooks & Hookers* is my all-time favorite. I even have some signed copies of your old books, including some that you removed from circulation. They're my prized possessions.

We used to talk about criminology and true crime and stuff like that. I have a degree in Criminal Justice like you. I wanted to be a cop, but I guess you could say I ended up in the private sector. I hope this rings a couple of bells. Would love to start where we left off, but if not, I'm always happy to start anew and chat some more. Actually, that's kinda why I'm contacting you now. If you remember me, then you remember that I run your 'unofficial' fan club. (Still waiting for you to make us official when you get the chance. A little shoutout on your socials would do the job, I think.) I'm even thinking about starting up a fan club for you in Russian, Polish, and German. I speak a little of all of the above and I have some connections. I'm sure you know this already, but they love extreme horror over there. In the meantime, I'd love to have you join our group for a live Q&A. I know you don't like public speaking, so if that's too much for you, me and you can record something privately. No pressure, of course. :)

.   .   .

I also heard about your upcoming appearance at the Worldwide Splatter Festival 2022. I'm guessing that means you're finally returning to extreme horror? Don't ask me how I know, but I heard a rumor you might be announcing a new book. (Ok, ok, I might have some other friends in the industry. Haha) I've read your newer stuff. The thrillers are pretty good. You've still got a knack for writing violence. Not the biggest fan of the fantasy stuff, but I can see why fantasy readers enjoy it. You remember that book you wrote, *The Demons We Inherit*? You said you were going to write a sequel to it. Any chance we'll see that in the near future? I need to know what happens next. I have some ideas, but I need to see it in your words. Still waiting on the 'spiritual successor' to *Pin Pals* as well. That one was sick! If you're really coming back to the horror world, I'm glad you were able to turn over a new leaf. You'll be making a ton of people happy with this move.

By the way, before I let you go, I know I'm late but congrats on the baby! I saw the pictures you posted of her before I went away. She's a cutie. Your wife is Japanese, right? I've always found Asian women to be very attractive. So kind, so smart, so classy, conservative and traditional but still open-minded. You, sir, have got yourself a keeper. Unfortunately, I couldn't find a good woman like yours because of some circumstances beyond my control. I have what some people would consider 'a troubled past.'

You know, you and I are at different points in our lives —different careers, different homes, different families —but we're more alike than you may think. We can talk about that at another time, though. Let me know what you think about making an appearance in our fan club. And good luck with the Worldwide Splatter panel. We'll be watching!

Thank you for reading and have a wonderful day!

Sincerely,
    Butterfly (your biggest fan)

P.S. If you remember me, you might remember I sent you a list of book recommendations. Did you ever get around to reading them? If it slipped your mind, let me know and I can send you the list again. No problem!

3

THE ANNOUNCEMENT

CENTER STAGE, NESTOR CASTLE SAT BEHIND A LONG table, looking down with his eyes on the black table-cloth. In front of him, two of his novels—an extreme horror story titled *Not for Children Under 3 Years Old* and a fantasy book titled *The Last Fairy Tale*—sat on plastic display stands facing the audience. A tabletop gooseneck microphone was pointed at his face.

Three other panelists sat to his left and two to his right, all authors like himself. And like him, they each had two of their books on matching displays in front of them. Omar Hughley, the panel's moderator, stood behind a lectern at one end of the table. Candace Davis—Nestor's full-time agent, part-time assistant, and occasional confidant—lurked behind a curtain stage left.

Resembling horror movie posters from the 70s, worn and grungy banners hung on the wall behind the panelists. The banners depicted gory murders, screaming victims, and hands holding bladed weapons. At the top of each banner, in red font with a yellow outline, a message read: *Welcome to the WORLD-WIDE SPLATTER FESTIVAL 2022.* The horror convention was being held at a hotel.

Nestor lifted his gaze to study the room. His throat tightened and his mouth dried up for the umpteenth time that evening. Rows of folding chairs stretched across the banquet hall. Over a hundred people were in attendance, but to him, it looked like he was facing *thousands.* Although he knew they weren't all there to see him, he felt like everyone was staring at him.

He picked up a water bottle from the floor next to his seat. He was about to unscrew the cap when he realized the bottle was already empty. Big beads of cold sweat trickled down his face. He was tempted to lick it off his lips just to moisturize his mouth a little. But his mind was tortured by what-ifs.

What if someone takes my picture right when I'm licking my lips?

What if they think I'm doing something sexual?

What if I look stupid doing it?

Despite all of his fame and success, he was as anxious in his mid-thirties as he was in his early teens. He had a mop of thick, wavy black hair. He kept his jaw covered in stubble. His hazel eyes glowed with a child-like innocence. He had slaughtered hundreds of people in his books, but he had never thrown a punch in real life. He was tall and fit, but fragile and timid on the inside.

He heard a muffled voice, but he couldn't make out the words. He didn't think much of it since he had been trying to block everything out since the panel began. Then he heard his name from another stifled voice. It sounded like it was coming from the back of his head, but he didn't want to cause a scene by looking over his shoulder all of a sudden.

He heard his name once more, but this time, he recognized the voice. He glanced to his left and saw Candace pointing at him with both her index fingers from behind the curtain while mouthing: *You're up. You're up.* Now he could hear the curious chatter from the audience. He saw the other authors peeking over at him.

"Nestor?" Omar said wonderingly. "We're ready for that special announcement when you are, buddy."

Nestor cleared his throat, then said, "Right. Sorry about that. I just wanted to make sure I didn't forget any–"

"Can you move a little closer to your mic, please?"

Nestor smiled at the moderator and leaned forward. An awkward silence filled the banquet hall. On the left side of his face, the corner of his mouth, his cheek, and his eyelids twitched slightly. He could only hope it wasn't noticeable from afar. He had to clear his throat again, then he took a deep breath through his nose.

You can do this, he told himself.

He said, "So, as you may have heard, I've been teasing a new project for a while now. I'm happy to report that I've now made enough progress to share some details of this new story with you today. I can't share a title or a release date because we're still discussing all that behind the scenes, but, uh... Um... Yes, the book is a grimdark fantasy novel inspired by the Roman Emperor, Nero Claudius Caesar... Augustus Germanicus." He laughed nervously, then said, "Now that's a mouthful, isn't it?"

There were a couple of chuckles in the audience.

Camilla North, another panelist, said, "That sounds freakin' amazing."

"Uh, thanks," Nestor said apathetically, unmoved by the compliment. "Anyway, I don't want to share *too* much because I don't want to spoil anything or make any promises I can't keep. But it's going to be like... How should I put this? Well... I guess it would be like if you blended my old splatterpunk work with my recent stuff. It's going to be really, really dark. At the same time, it's going to be an... an *epic* adventure. It's something new from..."

He flinched as a door slammed at the other end of the room. A couple of gasps came from the audience, followed by confused murmurs. A faint scream and a banging noise penetrated the double doors behind the audience. Nestor's chair screeched as he pushed himself away from the table and leaned down. The first thought to spring into his agitated mind was: *Mass shooter*. He was ready to hit the floor and scramble to cover.

"Looks like someone couldn't hold their bladder," Omar said with a reassuring smile. "Sorry about the interruption. So, Nestor, you were saying this new novel is a departure from your previous work."

"Ye–Yeah," Nestor stuttered, returning to an upright position.

"That's exciting stuff. We'll take questions from readers in a minute, but as a fan and an aspiring writer myself, I've got one for you. Don't worry, it's not a curveball or anything like that."

"Yeah, sure. Go for it."

"According to surveys from several popular horror magazines and social media groups, a lot of readers were expecting you to return to horror—*extreme* horror, to be precise. I guess you could say you're throwing a curveball to some of those readers with this announcement of a grimdark epic. How do you decide what you're going to write next? And how do you deal with the pressure of expectations?"

Keeping an eye on the double doors, Nestor answered, "I think I've said this before, but, um... Look, although this isn't an all-out horror novel, it is part of the genre in many ways. Like I said, it shares a lot of the... the *DNA* of my old work. You know what I mean? As far as expectations go, by now, I thought most readers would notice I like to buck the trend. I've never liked being in a box, being pigeonholed, in the first place. I hope you'll all give this new book a shot. I'm confident it will feel right at home with the rest of my work. It's a Nestor Castle novel at its core."

Some of the audience members clapped.

Nestor smiled and waved at them while constantly glancing at the double doors. Although he didn't see who had stormed out of the room, he couldn't stop thinking about the angry exit. It could have been an audience member, someone from the convention's crew, a hotel employee, or a guest who had mistakenly stumbled into the room and had to make a swift exit. Regardless, he believed the departure was directly related to his announcement. He couldn't shake the sense of impending doom looming over him.

Camila answered a question from one of the audience members. Nestor didn't hear any of it, but he chuckled along with the others just to keep a semblance of normality.

"I'm telling you, that went *incredibly* well," Candace's voice came out of the SUV's speakers.

Nestor sat in the driver's seat, hands at ten and two. The sunset painted the darkening sky with dark shades of orange and red. Trees and shrubs lined the street. The lake houses to his right were separated by swathes of trees and hedges and other greenery. There were more large, luxurious houses to his left.

"That's what you get paid to say," Nestor said—half-joking, half-serious.

"Believe it or not, flattering clients is not part of my job description. You really killed it out there today. I know you don't like making public appearances or speaking in public, but you should consider doing it more often. You're good at it. And I know you won't believe this, either, but your readers want to see you in person. You're more than just a name on a book cover."

"I know, I know. But this whole 'Worldwide Splatter Festival' thing, it was just a favor for you. I'm not saying I'll never do it again, but conventions are just a little too much for me. I'm still up for the book signings, though."

Candace said, "You did yourself a favor, too, Nes. Readers are buzzing about your next one on social media. You got the ball rolling. That next book should have a strong launch and we should be seeing a surge in sales for your backlist."

Nestor could see her intentions were pure. He knew she was only trying to help his career. His success benefitted the both of them after all. He didn't really like all of the praise, though. He never did. He spun the steering wheel and took a right into a sloped driveway.

"Hey, I'm just getting home," Nestor said.

"All righty. I'll call you in a couple days about that meeting. You have yourself a good night."

"You too."

The call ended. Nestor grabbed his laptop bag from the passenger seat, then climbed out of the vehicle. He followed the bluestone walkway—fringed with bushes—from the driveway to the porch. He checked the mailbox next to the front door.

Empty.

He entered the house, set his bag down on the bench next to an umbrella basket to his left, then hung his coat from the rack hanging on the wall above it.

"Hey," Mina said, waving back at him from a three-seat sofa in the living room. She turned her attention to their one-and-a-half-year-old daughter, Melody, who was sitting next to her. She said, "Look who's home, sweetie. Hey, look who's home. It's daddy. It's da-da, honey."

Melody ignored her. She giggled and bounced as if she were playing on a Hoppity Hop. They were watching an episode of *Doraemon*, a Japanese anime, on TV. Mina's parents had sent her a collection of *Doraemon* DVDs and manga comics—as well as a variety of other baby gifts—from Japan.

Mina's hair was dyed brown. It touched her shoulders when it wasn't tied in a bun. She passed her dark brown eyes down to her daughter. In black ink, tattoos of two roses blossomed from the base of her left palm. The roses' thorny stems ran down her forearm like veins, stopping a few inches away from the crook of her elbow.

"Melly," Nestor said as he took off his shoes. "Hey, baby, daddy's home."

Melody kept her eyes glued to the blue robotic cat on the TV.

"She's really into it," Mina laughed.

As he approached the sofa, Nestor looked at the TV and said, "The girl can barely say hi and mama and dada, so how is she going to understand any of this if it's all in Japanese?"

"She can say a little more than that. Plus, this is supposed to be some, you know, audio-visual stimulation for her. I think she just likes the sound of Japanese, too."

"Might confuse her, no? She could end up speaking 'Japanglish' or whatever they call it?"

"Or she could end up bilingual. That would help her quite a bit in the future."

"Yeah, I guess," Nestor said. He ruffled Melody's short, wispy black hair before leaning over the sofa and planting a big kiss on the back of her head. In a soft voice, he said, "Love you, baby."

Grinning, Melody glanced over at him and said, "Daddy."

Then she unleashed a stream of incomprehensible baby talk as she pointed at the TV. Only one other word out of her mouth made sense to Nestor: '*Cat.*' Mina grabbed her cell phone from the end table. She played a video and showed it to her husband. It was footage from the panel. It was shot by someone standing to the left of the seating area.

"I see the announcement went well," she said.

Nestor gave a half-hearted smile before walking over to the kitchen and saying, "Candace sent that to you already, huh?"

"She knew I didn't want to miss it. I really wish I could have seen it live."

"Yeah, well, it wasn't anything special."

Although he wasn't hungry, Nestor opened the refrigerator and looked inside. He only wanted to get as far away from Mina's phone as possible so he didn't have to hear his voice. Mina lifted Melody from the sofa. She couldn't follow Nestor to the fridge or Melody would start wailing, so she stopped at the kitchen bar so her daughter could continue watching TV.

"You looked really cute," Mina said, sounding kittenish.

Without looking back, Nestor huffed and raised a hand, as if to say: 'Yeah, yeah, whatever.' Despite the cool breeze from the refrigerator hitting his face, his cheeks flushed a pale red like a boy trying to speak to his crush for the first time. It was partly because he enjoyed his wife's flirting but also because he felt embarrassed being the subject of conversation.

Shifting to a serious tone, Mina said, "And you looked healthy up there, too. I'm proud of you, babe."

Nestor said, "Thank you. I guess it wasn't as..." He stopped and narrowed his eyes. He glanced over his shoulder and asked, "What was that?"

"What was what?"

"The–The... The slam. *The bang*. In the video."

"What are you talking about, Nes?"

Nestor hurried to her side. She put her phone down on the kitchen bar. He rewound the video and raised the volume. The camera caught the sound of the person slamming the door during his book announcement. However, due to the angle, the culprit wasn't visible in the footage. He rewound the video and played it again, watching unblinkingly.

"He must have been sitting in the back," he whispered.

Mina asked, "Nestor, what's wrong?"

"It's, um... It's probably nothing. Someone... *left* during my book announcement. I mean, they *left*. They walked out and slammed the door. They made sure everyone heard them."

"Oh. Well, that could have been anything. Maybe someone had to go pee. Or maybe someone had a family emergency—or *any* type of emergency—and they had to run out."

Laughing tensely, Nestor said, "I know, but I–I don't know. That doesn't make sense, does it?"

Melody giggled along with her father, although she was laughing at the TV.

Mina said, "I think I get what you're saying. You

don't know for certain, so you don't know at all. You need the absolute truth."

"*Exactly*," Nestor responded. "And look, you can't hear it in this video, maybe you can if you use headphones, but we heard this person screaming after he left the room. And it sounded like he hit something."

"There are so many different possibilities, though. Maybe it *was* someone from the panel. Or it could have been some guy having a bad day, yelling at someone on his phone. Maybe it was an employee who dropped something. But I bet you already thought of all of the possibilities with that wild imagination of yours."

With her free hand, she stroked the stubble on his jaw. She had a way of comforting him with her soft touch and her genuine, understanding smile.

She said, "Don't get worked up over this. Trust me, you'll forget about it as soon as you get back to writing. For now, go hit the showers, champ. I'll clean up down here."

"Yeah, you're right," Nestor said. He kissed her, kissed their daughter, then said, "You're always right. I'll come help you out in a minute."

Nestor went to the bathroom upstairs and took a shower. He came back down in his flannel pajamas and house slippers, his hair still damp. Along with his wife, he fed Melody thinly sliced apples with a dab of peanut butter. Then, using her stacking blocks, he played with his daughter in the living room and skimmed through one of the *Doraemon* manga comics with her.

When she got tired, they took Melody to the nursery upstairs and laid her gently down on the toddler bed in the corner of the room. The master bedroom was at the end of the hall within earshot.

Nestor sat in bed with his back against the headrest, his laptop on a throw pillow on his lap. He stared at the screen, eyes slitted in curiosity behind his glasses. The toilet flushed in their attached bathroom.

"You're writing? Now?" Mina asked as she walked into the bedroom.

Captivated by his laptop, Nestor didn't answer. He blindly reached for the water bottle on his nightstand, unscrewed the cap, and took a swig.

Mina jumped into bed, leaned in close to him, and asked, "New idea?"

"Huh?" Nestor responded. He looked at her as if he had just realized she was there. He shook his head as he stared back at his laptop. He said, "Oh. No. It's an email. It's from a reader."

"So?"

"I don't know. It's kinda strange."

"How?"

"It's... aggressive in a way. Like passive-aggressive, y'know? Look."

4

CORRESPONDENCE #2

Subject: **Feedback**
From: Butterfly <admin@splattersociety.com>
September 24, 2022, 9:12 PM
To: Nestor Castle <info@nes-castle.com>

HELLO NESTOR,

Everyone's talking about your latest announcement in our group. Sorry to be the bearer of bad news, but a lot of us are disappointed. After months and months of you promising a 'dark' and 'disturbing' epic like your extreme horror book *The Nature of Violence*, we were gutted to hear you're writing ANOTHER 'period piece' (or whatever you call them). If we're being honest, it's just going to be another soft, generic drama like your newer stuff. The darkest thing in it is probably going to be the ink on the page.

I think you need a reminder of what made your old work special, so I want to give you some feedback to jog your memory. You probably get enough of this from all of those one-star reviews you have, but you should hear the truth from a REAL fan. Your book, *In the Bad Place*, is full of some of the most brutal deaths I've ever read but when it came time to torture and kill the little girl in the end, you wussed out and 'left it to the reader's imagination.' That's bullshit, man. I don't buy books so *I* can write them in my head. You should have let her get raped with the jackhammer. You didn't have to stop before getting to the action.

You did something similar with one of your last splatterpunk books, *Cannibal Island*. You had the main guy survive so much, but then when he escapes the cannibal camp, he gets bitten by a snake. You say he goes unconscious, then he wakes up in a hospital. To be honest, that was such a lazy, abrupt ending. It felt like you just got tired of writing and you didn't want to kill off the main character. Maybe you just ran out of ideas. That's probably why you switched genres all of a sudden.

· · ·

For a while, we were worried that you let the 'woke mob' get to you. You can't let people like that censor you. Real artists aren't afraid to express themselves. You're a real artist, aren't you?

Even though it still has some issues, like typos and shit (cuts don't 'form,' man, maybe a lump or something, geez), your old stuff is a lot better. I had to force myself through some of your new thrillers. I mean, I guess they're enjoyable if you turn your brain off, but they could be much better with more suspense and more violence. Even the John Wick movies have more violence than your books these days! I hope I'm getting my point across to you. You should be careful about turning your back on your original fans and the horror genre.

I didn't mention this before because I didn't want to sound like I had ulterior motives or whatnot, but I'm a writer myself. I self-published some stuff a while ago. I took it all down, though. (I think I got most of it but maybe you can find something?) I'm getting ready for a comeback of my own. My book is a 500,000-word splatterpunk epic. There's nothing else like it. It's my magnum opus and it's going to change the genre. I can send it to you if you want.

· · ·

Maybe you can learn something from me. And hey, as I mentioned before, I admire your earlier work. If you could get back to that headspace, maybe you can teach me a few things. I've always felt like we had something special. I know money is a factor in what you write, you have to pay the bills and all that, but please don't let it change you for good. Your fans are here to support you when you're ready to support *US*. You scratch our backs, we scratch yours, ay?

Your fan,
    Butterfly

5

NATURAL HABITAT

NESTOR SAT IN HIS ROLLING CHAIR AND GAZED DUMBLY at his iMac's display. The email from Butterfly was open on his web browser. He wasn't reading it anymore, though. He was thinking about the sender. He had been asking himself the same question since he first read the message: *Who are you, Butterfly?* His gut told him that the email was sent from the same person who had marched out of the banquet hall during his announcement at the horror convention.

"And here's the writer in his natural habitat," Mina said as she entered Nestor's home office. "Getting some good work done?"

Nestor's desk was under a window overlooking the backyard and the lake outside. On his desk, there was his trusty iMac, two notebooks, a stack of index cards in a small box, and a stainless steel thermal mug full of coffee. He used the notebooks to continue his work whenever his hands cramped up from all his typing. The index cards were used for story-boarding his novels. Framed posters of his favorite movies—the ones that inspired him to write—hung from the walls.

Larry Clark's *Kids*. Mary Harron's *American Psycho*. Pascal Laugier's *Martyrs*. Bob Clark's *Black Christmas*. Francis Ford Coppola's *The Godfather*.

A short bookcase hugged a wall. It was filled with novels he was currently reading, planned on reading soon, and hoped to re-read eventually. His awards—from local and national organizations—stood atop the bookcase. He didn't like seeing them, but Mina insisted on him keeping them there. Behind his desk, on the other side of the room, a recliner faced a TV. When-ever he couldn't get any work done due to brain fog, finger pain, or headaches, he would take a nap or watch something on TV.

"Good work?" Nestor repeated with a hint of disap-pointment while keeping his eyes pinned to the email. "No, not really."

"Writer's block?"

"I wouldn't call it that. Where's Melody?"

"Napping," Mina responded. "So, if you're not writing and you don't have writer's block, what *are* you doing?"

"Emails."

Mina strolled over to him and peeked over his shoulder. She said, "Wait a second. That's the same email from last night, isn't it? You didn't respond, did you? You said you never respond to negative–"

"I didn't," Nestor interrupted.

"Then why are you wasting your time reading it again? It was a bunch of bullshit. They were just trying to get under your skin."

Nestor looked at her, then back at the monitor. He wanted to tell her his theory, but he didn't want her to worry about his mental state. He had a tendency to get obsessive and overthink. Mina could see he was preoccupied.

"What's on your mind?" she asked while rubbing his shoulder.

Nestor sighed, then said, "I think this was sent from a, uh... a disgruntled reader. It's possible that this was sent from the same person who left the room during my announcement."

"But you've never met this reader before, right?"

"In person? No, I don't think so. No one ever introduced themselves as 'Butterfly' during any of my book signings. I think I've read this person's messages before, though. Maybe he sent me a package once, too. A long, long time ago. If I'm remembering correctly, it was a handbound journal. I'm not even sure if I have it around here anymore."

"And you didn't see a 'disgruntled' reader *actually* walk out of the room at the convention, right?"

"See it? No, I guess not," Nestor said, shaking his head.

"So, there's still no evidence that any of the audience viewers walked out in protest. It sounds like you're just trying to find a connection. You know, you've got two pieces to a puzzle and you're trying to mash 'em together and make 'em fit. But, really, you're not sure if they're from the same puzzle in the first place. You're just overthinking it."

"Yeah, I guess... that could be it."

Mina leaned over him from behind, wrapped her arms around his neck, and whispered, "Or maybe —*maybe*—you're just looking for a reason to procrastinate."

Nestor made a *tsk* sound, then said, "Yeah? And how's that painting going?"

"Let's just say that it's a good thing your books are still selling so well."

They laughed. Years ago, Mina worked as a bookkeeper for a chain of local restaurants. Initially, she had taken an unpaid sabbatical to support her husband and pursue her own art career. She sold her paintings to family and friends, neighbors, and local businesses. She decided to quit her job after she became pregnant with Melody. And she still used her free time to paint.

She said, "I'm going to take Melody over to Chelsea's house. She has a playdate with Kaylee."

"I can go with you."

"Oh no, it's fine. I'll text you when I get there. You

just focus on your writing. *Writing*, okay? No more reading emails."

"Yeah, of course."

"*Nestor*," Mina said with playful seriousness.

Laughing quietly, Nestor closed the web browser and said, "Writing. I got it."

As she walked to the door, Mina asked, "You need me to pick anything up on my way back?"

"No, I'm good."

"Okay. Love you."

"Love you, too."

Mina exited the room, shutting the door behind her. Nestor listened to his wife's footsteps until they died away in the nursery down the hall. He shimmied in his seat to find a comfortable position. He drew a breath, took a sip of his coffee, then cracked his knuckles. With a click of his mouse, he brought his Microsoft Word window up from the iMac's Dock. His manuscript—a file titled NERO (FIRST DRAFT)—was already open.

The word count at the bottom read: *77480 words*. He was expecting it to end up close to 200,000 words long —his longest manuscript. He outlined all of his stories, and he wrote his first drafts *in* the outlines. He simply saved it as a new file and changed the filename. He had already finished writing sixteen chapters out of the forty-two he had outlined. So far, although it was tentative, he had only written the title of the seventeenth chapter: *Playing with Fire*.

He stared at the blinking cursor under the chapter title. He rested his fingers on the keyboard. He typed: *Nero.* He hit the spacebar once, then curled his fingers back towards his palm and stared at the blinking cursor for another long moment. With his mouse, he jumped back to the previous chapter, then back to the fifteenth chapter. Both of them started with the word 'Nero.'

Variety, he told himself. *Spruce it up, man.*

He deleted the word from the seventeenth chapter and replaced it with a quotation mark. While thinking about what his character should say, he pulled his lips into his mouth and tapped the keys on his keyboard without pressing them. He drew a blank, though. No words came to mind. He deleted the quotation mark, then typed: *Emperor Nero.*

"That's... better?" he murmured questioningly.

His mind wandered back to the email from Butterfly. He was supposed to be writing a horror-fantasy epic, but he started thinking about the extreme horror genre.

"Raped with a jackhammer," he said with a small smile. "I can outdo that."

He took a pen out of a drawer on his desk, then flipped open one of his notebooks. On a blank page, he jotted a few notes while sneering and cringing.

Jackhammer down a throat.

Sounding with a toothbrush.

Nails removed with a box cutter, fingers dipped in

rubbing alcohol, then forced to drink the bloody rubbing alcohol.

"Inspiration comes from the strangest places," he whispered. "And the strangest people. Thank you, Butterfly."

Nestor went for a sip of his coffee but his mug was empty. He headed down to the kitchen for a refill. Aside from the hiss and gurgle of the coffee machine, the house was quiet. The author leaned over the counter and scrolled through his social media apps while waiting for his coffee. He heard a *tap* from the window over the sink but paid it no mind. Ten seconds later, there was another *tap*. Prying his eyes off the video of a dog playing on his phone, he cast a brief look at the window.

There was nothing there.

He checked on the coffee machine, then looked back at his phone. In the video, a dog tipped over his food bowl, causing the kibble to spill across a kitchen floor. As he laughed, Nestor heard two *taps* on the window and saw something move from the corner of his eye. The smile was wiped off his face. He put his phone to sleep and set it down on the counter. Holding his breath, he inched towards the window with his shoulders hitched up to his ears. He was expecting someone or something to leap out from the bush under the window, like a jump scare in a horror movie.

There was no one out there.

Nestor went to the front porch and took a look

around. It was a sunny, normal day. Their SUV was parked in the driveway. Mina had taken Melody to her friend's house in their minivan.

"Mina?" he called out in just under a shout.

He didn't want his neighbors to hear him. There was no response. He walked backwards into the house. He took one final glance around, then shut the door and checked the locks twice.

6

CORRESPONDENCE #3

Subject: **HELLO??**
From: Butterfly <admin@splattersociety.com>
September 29, 2022, 3:13 AM
To: Nestor Castle <info@nes-castle.com>

WHAT'S YOUR DEAL? YOU'RE TOO GOOD FOR YOUR FANS now? Are we just talking wallets to you? I know you saw my last two emails. I can see the read receipts. You opened them just to ignore me? What the hell did I do to you? You would be NOTHING without your original fans. Readers like ME boosted you up. We shared your work for free. We were in all the Facebook groups talking about you, we posted reviews on Instagram, we tweeted about your books, we made fucking TikToks for you, man! We did everything you asked us to do.

We built your platform. We made you. I should have known better than to waste my time with you. I revisited your older books recently and I was dead wrong. You've always been overrated. I thought if I patted you on the back enough you'd grow up and become a better writer. I saw potential but you never rose to it. You squandered it. You threw it all away for money. Your writing is repetitive. Same themes, same characters, same shit over and over and over. How many times are you going to write about revenge? You even do it in your crappy thrill-less thrillers. We get it, 'an eye for an eye' and 'the real world is a dark place.' Wow, so deep... NOT! I don't know, couldn't you have done any of those themes with a little bit of subtlety? Or maybe some better plot twists and some actual character development? Even the violence started to get boring fast. Let me guess, you're going to kill another kid or a baby in your next book? Cheap shocks as usual. I see now why you switched genres. But it's not like you're doing much better in fantasy. You'll never be like George R. R. Martin. You're never going to write the next Lord of the Rings. Your writing is too immature. You don't have the vocabulary, the command of language, to compete with your peers. They see you for what you are: a fucking imposter, a phony looking for quick buck, a writer on his last cartridge of ink. I see why you're ignoring me, too. You don't want me to come in and take your place, do you? You don't want your old fans to see that you were a fraud. My story is going to SHIT on your legacy. And you know it. That's why you don't want to read it. You sad, pathetic man!

We had something special. We were more than just friends. We had a bond. We shared more than we probably even realized. We had a real connection, man. But you're sabotaging it. You're going to regret it in the long run.

Butterfly

Sent from my iPad

7

OPTIONS

SEATED IN FRONT OF HIS WRITING DESK, NESTOR STARED down at his keyboard. Through his wireless over-ear headphones, he listened to Candace's voice. They were having a video meeting. She was droning on about conversations with film agents in hopes of optioning one of Nestor's stories to a producer. She had connections throughout the entertainment industry. She wanted to sell one of his old horror stories or early thrillers because she thought they would be cheaper— and therefore less risky—to produce.

Nestor didn't care about that side of the business. That was one of the reasons he had decided to stop self-publishing his work to pursue a career in traditional publishing. He only wanted to focus on his writing. Yet, even with Candace's help, he couldn't avoid the distractions that came with being a public figure. He couldn't forget the incident at the Worldwide

Splatter Festival 2022, and he was disturbed by Butter-fly's latest messages.

There was so much on his mind that he didn't notice the ten seconds of silence during the video call.

"Well?" Candace said. "Nestor? Neeeeeh–stor? Hey, can you hear me? Ah crap, did we lose connection? I don't see you moving and I can't hear you if you're speaking. Hello? Should we hang up and reconnect?"

Nestor finally looked at the screen. Candace was in her office. She was fiddling with her phone, checking to see if the internet was working.

"I can hear you," the author said, his voice dull and uninterested.

"Oh," Candace replied. "Is... something wrong?"

"No. Why?"

"Most authors would be ecstatic at the mere possi-bility of landing a movie deal. I figured you'd be at least somewhat happy. I know I said the first payment isn't going to be massive, but if we get something signed—and I've got a good feeling about this—you could have a blockbuster movie under your name and you could get paid blockbuster money. But if you don't want me to pursue this, we could stick to books."

"No, no, that's not... Listen, I want you to keep doing what you're doing. I know you're only trying to help and I appreciate everything you do."

"So, then what's up with you? You seem out of it."

Nestor slid the headphones down to the nape of his neck and looked at the door. It was closed. Mina and

Melody were downstairs. He didn't want his wife to hear his worries because he didn't want to share his torment with her. He put the headphones back over his ears and turned to face the monitor.

Lowering his voice but speaking loud enough so Candace could hear him, he said, "I've been getting hate mail from a reader who calls themself Butterfly."

Candace stared deadpan at him for a few seconds, then she smiled and shrugged. She said, "Nestor, that's part of the job, isn't it? Even *I* get hate mail from your readers. Every fandom has its fair share of toxic fanboys—or as they sometimes call themselves, '*stans*.' I think they might have misunderstood that song but I digress. The point is: this is, unfortunately, normal. You can't let these people get under your skin. You are an excellent writer and a genuinely good person. You have a loving family and more supporters than haters. And many of your readers *love* you. You have a career people would *kill* for. And other writers would *kill* to have your fanbase, too. What else do you need? Want me to tell you you're handsome, too?"

Nestor uttered a small laugh in appreciation. Candace was always very helpful and sincere. But the compliments weren't enough to alleviate his anxiety.

He said, "This is different, though. You have to... to see it for yourself. I'll send you the emails. Read them and you'll see what I'm talking about."

While Nestor forwarded two of Butterfly's messages to her, Candace asked, "Are you sure you should be sending any personal emails to me? They should be private, no?"

"They should be, but... It's not like there's some sort of doctor-patient confidentiality thing between authors and readers. And you have to read this or you won't understand what I'm talking about. I'm serious."

"*O*-kay."

The emails—titled *Fw: Feedback* and *Fw: HELLO??* —hit Candace's mailbox. She took a minute to read them. Her facial expression shifted from neutral to amused to irritated to amused again and then disgusted. She closed her mailbox, then brought her undivided attention back to the video call.

She said, "Sounds like an unhinged fan—*a troll*. Ignore him and everything will be fine."

"That's it? You want me to just sit here and do nothing?"

"No. I said *ignore* him. Block his email address. Make sure his messages don't even get to your spam folder. If he makes a new email address, block that one, too. Don't give him the satisfaction of a response. That's what he wants. It's what trolls feed off of. In all likelihood, this is a jealous writer who expected you to boost them up just because they shared your work a few times. Seriously, they practically spelled it out in one of the emails. 'You scratch our backs, we scratch yours.' More like 'I bought your book, now help me build my career.' *The gall.*"

"Yeah, I... I guess that makes sense."

"Just look at how he mentioned his 500,000-word 'magnum opus.' Not once, but *twice*. He's really trying to push that book onto you. He was probably going to ask you to pass it onto me or to a publisher. It's not the first time I've seen someone try something like that. But 500,000 words? Who the hell's going to publish a story like that from a no-name author in today's market? I'm not even sure he could self-publish something that size. Sorry, I'm just rambling now. But seriously, just ignore him and forget him."

Nestor sat silent with downcast eyes. For a brief moment, Candace wondered if the internet had cut out.

"It's not that easy," Nestor said. "I don't mean to put all of this on you, but there's more to it."

"Yeah?"

"A few days after that last message, I got another email. It came from a different address, but I have this feeling—this strong hunch—that it was sent from the same person. It didn't have a subject and the only text read: 'Hey.' A six-second video of a person was attached to it. It's a man, I think, sitting in a dark room. There's some bluish flashing light, probably coming from a muted TV. I don't know if he has the camera on a tripod or if someone else is holding it, but this person, um... He slits his wrists with a box cutter. Horizontally. It didn't look too deep, but it was bloody. There was a picture, too. It showed that he sliced that same wrist four more times."

"Jesus."

There was a minute of stunned silence.

Candace said, "Send it to me."

"No," Nestor said, shaking his head. "I wouldn't want you to see that. Besides, I deleted it right after I saw it. Deleted it from the 'trash' folder, too. It looked real. And that's too much even for me."

"I understand. However, next time you get a message like that, please forward it to me so I can look into our legal options. In the meantime, I say you should just continue ignoring messages like those and blocking people like them. And if it is from the same person, we'll see what we can do about it. I know this sort of thing can be traumatic, so if you need any assistance, let me know. We have professionals that can help."

"I'll be fine," Nestor said with an empty smile, lying through his teeth. "I feel better just getting this off my chest already. I'll let you go now. Let me know how those movie talks go."

"I will. Don't hesitate to call me if you need anything. Have a great night."

"You too."

Nestor took off his headphones as the video call ended. On his iMac, he pulled up his web browser and opened his mailbox. He searched for the emails from Butterfly. There were three so far. He opened the latest message, then navigated to the 'More Actions' menu at the top right. The mouse cursor hovered over the *Block [sender]* option. He sat there with a thumb tucked under his chin and index finger over his lips. He blamed his curiosity for his hesitation.

He found no comfort in the idea of sweeping his problems under a rug. Turning his back to a stalker didn't mean the stalker would turn his back on him. It only meant he wouldn't see him coming. He sought to put a face to the nickname.

Who are you, Butterfly? he asked himself.

His thoughts were interrupted by Melody's laughter. His wife and daughter were in the nursery now. Although he was tempted to respond to his stalker, he chose to put his family's safety first. He clicked the *Block [sender]* option, then closed the web browser.

Nestor took the rest of the day off and spent it with his family. The next day, he got to work on his manuscript, finishing up the seventeenth chapter and taking down notes for the next one. During the weekend, the Castle family visited a zoo and had a picnic at a park. On Sunday night, they sat down in their living room and watched Pixar's *Cars* together, which Mina and Melody adored.

During the movie, there was a knock at the front door.

"Can you get that?" Mina asked.

Nestor looked over his shoulder at the entryway. His face tightened, his neck stiffened, and butterflies swarmed in his stomach. People knocked on doors every day, but his overwrought mind was giving him a dozen reasons explaining why it wasn't normal for his family. They didn't receive many uninvited visitors. If someone was planning to visit, they always informed the Castles first. It wasn't a normal residential neighborhood either, so they didn't see many door-to-door salespeople out there.

He sidestepped over to the front door and peeked out the sidelight. He caught a glimpse of a postal truck on the street just as it drove off. He rolled his neck to get a good look at the porch, making sure no one was waiting to ambush him. The coast was clear. He opened the door and took a cautious step out, then froze up. There was a package—a small, normal box with a shipping label slapped onto it—on the floor next to the door. He was afraid he was going to find a severed head inside. He leaned over and inspected it for any bloodstains.

"Who was it?" Mina asked.

Startled, Nestor gasped and staggered out of the house. Wide-eyed, he looked back at Mina and said, "Holy shit, what are you doing sneaking up on me like that?"

"Sneaking?" his wife repeated while keeping one eye on Melody. "I called out to you twice."

"Seriously? I didn't hear a thing."

"Oh, I think that's my package," Mina said as she scooped up the box. "Hurry up and join us. You're missing the movie."

Mina set the package down on the kitchen bar,

then returned to her daughter's side on the sofa. Nestor breathed a sigh of relief. He opened the mailbox. Amidst the bills and junk mail, he found a brown document-sized envelope. On the return address, he saw it was sent from a John Doe in Florida. Walking back into the home, he kicked the door shut behind him and secured the locks. At the kitchen bar, he opened the large envelope. He pulled a stack of papers, which were stapled together at the top left corner, out of it.

The first page appeared to be the title page of a short story. It was titled: *The Castillo Family Murder*. And the story was authored by Butterfly.

From the sofa, Mina asked, "What is it?"

So as not to alarm her, Nestor said, "It's paperwork. From Candace. I'm going to go look it over in my office."

"You're not going to finish the movie with us?"

"I wish I could, but this is... It's urgent. I'm sorry."

"It's okay. It's not that big of a deal. Are you at least going to eat dinner with us?"

"Yeah, yeah, of course. I'll be back in a jiffy."

8

CORRESPONDENCE #4

The Castillo Family Murder
By Butterfly

OUTSIDE OF A LAKE HOUSE, THE LURKER CROUCHED under a kitchen window. Dressed in black from head to toe—a jacket, jeans, and boots—he was hidden by the darkness of the night. Except for his eyes, a balaclava covered his face. His light blue irises seemed to glow in the dark. His ecstatic eyes revealed the grin under his mask.

As he peeped into the home, he caressed the windowsill with his gloved hand and whispered, "My beautiful family."

Over the kitchen bar, he could see the Castillo family sitting on a three-seat sofa in the living room. Rodolfo sat on one end of the sofa and Daniela, his wife, sat at the other end. Elisa, their baby daughter, sat between them. They were watching an episode of *Doraemon* on their gigantic, bulky rear-projection television.

As the episode came to an end, Daniela carried Elisa upstairs. Rodolfo stayed seated and channel-surfed.

"Bedtime?" the Lurker whispered.

He ducked down upon hearing the purr of a car engine. He saw a Tesla Model Y cruise down the road in front of the lake house. He waited until he couldn't see the vehicle before moving a muscle. He crouched his way to the back of the home. The lake down the hill was calm and quiet. Lights from the other lake houses penetrated the surrounding trees.

The Lurker walked quietly onto the back porch. Blue light from the living room television flickered through the window next to the back door. He lifted his jacket a little, revealing the claw hammer tucked into his waistband. He drew the tool and raised it over his shoulder, ready to swing at a moment's notice.

With his free hand, he grabbed the doorknob. Nodding with each number, he counted down in his head.

Three.

Two.

One.

He turned the knob slowly. To his disappointment, the door was locked. He stuck the hammer's handle back into his waistband and snuck off the porch. He had been casing the house for months, so he had backup plans. He scratched the easy way off his mental list and proceeded to Plan B. He climbed up the tree in the backyard.

Near the top, he wormed his way onto a thick, sturdy branch; his limbs wrapped around it like a koala hugging a tree. The wood groaned and creaked under his weight. He stretched an arm out in front of him and touched a windowsill. He slid the window up, inch by inch. He paused only when he heard muffled footsteps and voices in the house.

As soon as it was big enough to fit his body, he grabbed the windowsill with both hands and pulled himself through the opening. He planted his palms on the floor, crawled forward a little, and then let his knees drop. Although it was dark, he could tell he was in a bathroom on the second floor.

He cupped his hand over his mouth to suppress his snicker of excitement. It was hard for him to believe it was *that* easy. He took off his boots and hid them behind the toilet. A ray of light from the hall sliced into the darkness in the bathroom as he cracked the door open. He stuck his head out a little and caught a glimpse of Daniela as she walked down the stairs at the end of the hall.

"She's sleeping like a log," the woman said.

Rodolfo responded but the Lurker couldn't make out his words.

The intruder shuffled out of the bathroom, barely

lifting his feet with each step. He noticed the door across the hall was left slightly open. He took a peek inside.

Sitting on a short bookcase in the corner of the room, a rabbit-shaped night light emitted a dim white glow. One of the baby blue walls was painted with fluffy white clouds while the parallel wall had a dazzling sun. A padded floor mat—decorated with caricatures of otters—covered the center of the room. In the middle of the room, there was a baby jumper as well as some stacking blocks and plushy toys.

The Lurker crept over to the cradle to his left. Next to it, there was a rocking chair with a pillow on the seat. A small blue blanket was draped over the chair's backrest. He stared down at little Elisa in the cradle. His smile was so big now that his mask molded around his freakish features. He caressed her face, sweeping the thin black hair away from her forehead with the back of his fingers.

"My beautiful girl," he whispered on the verge of cackling.

Arms up as if she were being arrested in her dreams, the baby was fast asleep in her blue blanket sleeper pajamas. She smacked her lips while making some grunting and gurgling noises. Every once in a while, her little fingers twitched and her shoulders jerked. She was a deep but fidgety sleeper.

The Lurker pulled the claw hammer out of his waistband. He lowered it into the cradle until it hovered a few inches above the baby's head. He tapped her small, button-shaped nose with the face of the hammer. She didn't react, so he did it again. She whined and swiped at her nose. The intruder put his hand over his mouth as he giggled like a child.

Eyes glittering with hope and love, he said, "So, so precious."

He leaned over the cradle, raised the hammer over-head, then swung it down with all of his might. The hammer pulverized her nose before sinking *into* her face with a crunchy thud. He struck her with so much force that the soft spot at the top of her head—the anterior fontanelle—burst open. Gooey blood welled out from the wound like yolk from a cracked egg.

The baby's eyelids were partway open, revealing the whites of her eyes. Due to all of the broken bones across her face, her upper lip descended into her mouth so it looked like she had a severe underbite. Some of her fingers curled inward while her arms shook. A rattling noise came out of her mouth.

The Lurker knew what was coming next. The cradle had made a clattering sound during the attack. He was sure one of the parents was on their way to check up on Elisa. He grabbed the pillow from the rocking chair and removed the pillowcase. He let the pillow fall to his feet. Then, in a chillingly casual manner, he shoved the dead baby into the pillowcase.

He carried it over to the corner of the room. He stopped next to the door, just far enough so that it wouldn't hit him when it swung open. He laughed softly while shaking his head, as if in delighted disbelief. Blood soaked through the white pillowcase. The rattling noise from the baby faded away. It was replaced by the occasional hiccup.

The Lurker raised his clenched fist up to his mouth and held his breath upon hearing the footsteps in the hallway. The door opened at a snail's pace. The yellow light from the hallway invaded the nursery, clashing with the white glow from the night light.

Daniela poked her head into the room. She squinted at the cradle and listened for a few seconds. The silence was unusual—and *awful*. Ever since Elisa's birth, quiet moments were rare in the Castillo home.

Daniela hurried to the cradle. Upon finding it empty, she let out a little gasp and staggered. Her mouth hung open as wide as humanly possible and she dug her fingers into her chest, as if she were having a heart attack. Her upper body swaying in every direction, she looked like she was about to collapse.

She hurled herself forward, headfirst into the cradle. She wanted to believe that her eyes were playing a trick on her, that she only needed a closer look, that Elisa wasn't gone. The bloodstain on the fitted sheet looked black in the dim light. She pulled the sheet off the bed, as if she were expecting to find her baby underneath it.

"Eh–Eh–Elisa," she stammered in a hushed voice,

struggling to draw enough air to scream. "Ro–Rodolfo, Elisa is..."

Her voice trailed off as she heard the door close. A chill ran down her spine and panic sent her mind into a tailspin. She was scared to look but more afraid of losing her daughter. As she turned to face the door, she saw the intruder at the periphery of her vision. He looked like a shadow standing against the baby blue wall.

"Pillow fight," he said, tittering.

He swung the pillow at her. The dead baby hit her face like a twenty-pound dumbbell, straining her neck and launching her off her feet. She yelped and hit the floor hard, floorboards rumbling under the padded mat. The blow to the head made her dizzy. She felt herself spinning, like a disc in a CD player.

The Lurker swung the pillow at her again. The dead baby hit the side of her abdomen, knocking the wind out of her. Upon impact, another squirt of blood sprayed out of the infant's head. He swung the baby at her a few more times, hitting her directly on her bony hip, then her thigh, and then one of her knees. With the last hit, a bone *popped* in her leg.

The pillowcase got bloodier and bloodier.

"Stop," Daniela cried. "Please... Please, I–I only want my baby."

"Daniela!" Rodolfo hollered from downstairs. "Everything okay?!"

He was still in the living room, relaxing on the sofa

with his feet kicked up on an ottoman. He lowered the volume on the television and gazed at the stairs.

"Daniela?" he said.

Up in the nursery, the Lurker opened the pillow-case, gave it a shake, and said, "One baby, coming right up."

The dead baby dropped to the floor between his feet. Elisa's pajamas were spattered with blood. Her small head resembled a rotten tomato. She was unrecognizable.

Yet, Daniela knew she was staring at her daughter. Her mouth moved as if she were speaking, but she couldn't find the words to express her intense grief— her sadness, her fear, her confusion, *her rage*. She screamed and threw a stacking block at the intruder, then a stuffed dog, and then another stacking block.

While laughing, the man raised a hand to shield his face and said, "Hey, stop that. You're playing too rough. You wouldn't like it if I played rough with you, would ya?"

The Lurker lunged at her with his arms outstretched in front of him, fingers splayed out as if he were going to strangle her. Before he could reach her, Daniela kicked him. She missed his genitals, her bare heel landing in his pubic region. He teetered back to the corner of the room, simpering under his balaclava.

From the bottom of the stairs, Rodolfo shouted, "Daniela! Need a hand?"

Daniela scrambled forward and picked up Elisa's

corpse. She didn't bother checking on her injuries. Despite Elisa's lack of movement and noise, she was sure she could save her daughter as long as she got her away from the intruder and to a hospital as soon as possible. She lurched to the door.

Just as she pulled it open, the Lurker swung the hammer at the side of her head. The claw penetrated her skull. A splash of blood lashed out, whipping the intruder's face.

With the hammer sticking out of her head, Daniela crashed into the doorway to stop herself from falling. Pulses of pain—fiery, debilitating pain—radiated through her skull. Her stomach was a bundle of knots and her legs were like noodles. She could see the hammer's handle at the corner of her eye, but she couldn't identify it.

She had no idea she had been hit with a hammer in the first place, so she didn't know what was happening. It was as if the hammer had scrambled her thoughts. Her survival instincts took over and told her to run. She stumbled into the hallway. From under the hammer's head and above it, two streams of blood jetted out of her scalp and hit the wall to her right.

Four steps away from the top of the stairs, Rodolfo saw his wife. She was holding Elisa's corpse upside down, feet between her breasts. A chunk of brain prolapsed from the hole at the soft spot of her head.

"Oh my God!" Rodolfo shouted, bug-eyed.

He ran to Daniela just as she dropped to her knees.

He grabbed her arms to stop her from toppling over. Elisa slipped out of her hands and landed on her thighs. The woman's vacant gaze went right through her husband.

"Oh my God!" he repeated.

The Lurker stepped out of the nursery. He held the night light in one hand and its cord in the other.

He said, "Don't you know this is a hazard for toddlers?"

"Who... What do you... We–We need... I need..."

Rodolfo couldn't finish a sentence. The Lurker rushed towards him. Rodolfo wasn't fast enough to get to his feet. The intruder punted his face, making his teeth *clink*. Rodolfo lost his balance, the back of his head slamming into the wall behind him. Daniela crumpled to the floor on top of her dead daughter.

The Lurker pounced on Rodolfo. He wrapped the night light's cord around his neck and tugged on it, strangling him as he dragged him down the hall.

"How about a house tour?" the intruder asked. Without relaxing his grip on the cord, he shouldered the door to his left open. He said, "Oh, that's the bathroom. I've already been in there. Let's see... what's behind... Door Number Two."

He continued dragging him down the hall. Rocking from side to side, Rodolfo kicked the floor and the wall and a console table as he was pulled away from his family. He raked his fingernails across his neck, trying desperately to slip his fingers under the cord to no avail. Thick veins bulged from his forehead while his mouth hung open in a soundless scream.

The Lurker opened the next door to his left. Although the lights were off, silvery moonlight helped him see. At the other end of the room, a desk was installed under a bay window overlooking the lake. A typewriter, stacks of paper, and a small basket with black and red pens sat atop the desk. Filled with text-books, journals, and novels, bookcases covered the walls.

"This must be... your writing den," the intruder said while dragging Rodolfo into the room. "Every writer... needs a writing den."

Near the desk, he released his grip on the cord and let the night light fall to the floor along with his captive. The back of Rodolfo's head bounced off a floorboard. He kept clawing at his neck. He felt like his throat had swollen shut. His mind was sent into a frenzy of fear. The alarms in his head were telling him that he was going to die if he didn't take a big gulp of air soon.

The lack of oxygen rendered him lethargic, too. He didn't have the energy to get up and run. He could only squirm and cough and gasp for air.

The Lurker took a knee on his victim's chest, pinning him to the floor. Holding a crisp sheet of paper in one hand, he grabbed one of Rodolfo's arms and pulled it towards him. He held it tightly at the wrist, thumb pressed against his palm. He slid the edge of the paper under his index finger's fingernail, then swiped it like a credit card, slashing the thick skin underneath it open.

Rodolfo groaned weakly. A drop of blood dribbled out from the bright pink wound. The Lurker tightened his grip on his arm to stop him from pulling away. He turned the sheet of paper and pressed another edge of it under his middle finger's fingernail. With another swift swipe, he gave him a second paper cut.

The cut bled *under* his fingernail, spreading towards his cuticle like a blot of red ink. The intruder continued to his ring and pinky fingers. But, due to the victim's trembling, he only managed to slice his pinky's fingertip. The sharp, burning pain rolled through Rodolfo's fingers in waves. He could feel it in his knuckles.

"You're moving too much!" the Lurker hissed.

He took his knee off him, then straddled his chest. He pushed his palm against his face and pushed his head down. Then he swiped the edge of the paper across his neck. The thin cut stretched from his Adam's apple to his jugular. It didn't bleed, though. So, he slashed his neck a few more times with the paper. Each cut stung more than the last.

The Lurker wondered how long it would take him to behead his victim with paper cuts. A few days? A few weeks? A few months? A few years? But he grew bored after the twenty-fourth slice. They were horizontal, vertical, and diagonal. Some were parallel to each other, others crossed in Xs.

As he got to his feet, the intruder said, "Let's get to the point, shall we?"

Rodolfo continued twisting and turning on the floor, massaging his sliced throat in an attempt to soothe the pain. The Lurker walked over to the desk. He picked up the mechanical typewriter and lugged it over to his victim. Rodolfo had his eyes clenched shut in agony—physical and emotional—so he didn't see it coming.

The Lurker swung the twenty-five-pound typewriter at Rodolfo's face, opening a deep cut at the center of his forehead. His body stiffened. His fingers involuntarily curled into his throat. He looked like he was strangling himself. His legs shook violently, feet banging on the floorboards. His eyes appeared to be spinning under his sealed eyelids.

The intruder raised the typewriter overhead, then brought it down to Rodolfo's face a second time. The victim's forehead was split open down the middle from his hairline to the bridge of his nose. His cracked frontal bone, glazed with blood, was visible in the deep, fleshy gash. Foamy blood spumed out of his mouth. He had bitten the tip of his tongue off.

The Lurker hit him a third time with the typewriter. Rodolfo's muscles relaxed. Blood kept frothing past his lips and his legs continued twitching. But he was no longer breathing.

"That's 'the end' for you," the killer said as he set the bloodied typewriter down next to the victim's head.

He walked around the room, scouring the bookshelves. He smiled and pointed at some of the books' spines, as if to say: *Oh, I've read that one before! And this one! And that one!* He was attracted to one of the shelves closest to the desk. It was filled with novels by an author named Rodolfo Castillo.

He glanced over at the dead body in the room and said, "That's you, huh? You know, you used to be my favorite writer. Now you're my favorite victim."

He giggled and shook his head, amused by his own words. He returned to the desk and found a stack of papers with plastic spiral binding. It was a manuscript.

Murder Your Idols
By Rodolfo Castillo

"I like the title," the Lurker said, grinning under his mask. "It's appropriate, isn't it?"

He flipped through the first few pages, skimming through a couple of paragraphs and notes written in red ink. Towards the middle of the manuscript, he tore five pages out. He walked out of the room. Daniela hadn't moved a muscle, face down with her ass up. He entered the bathroom and turned on the light. He pulled his pants and underwear down, then sat on the toilet.

While shitting, farts echoing through the house, he

bent over and put on his boots. The feces came out of him like brown snakes, so long that parts of the shit disappeared down the drain. The stench drifted out of the restroom, filling the hallway and reaching the staircase. He wiped his ass with a page from the manuscript. He crushed it into a ball, then let it fall into the bowl.

He repeated the process four more times—wipe, crumple, drop. He simultaneously stood from the toilet and pulled his pants up. He touched the flush handle but stopped before he could push it down. An amusing thought sprung into his mind: *Let it marinate.* He left the bathroom without flushing.

He towered over Daniela and Elisa, marveling at his work. It was a masterpiece. He grabbed the hammer's handle and pulled on it. He heard Daniela's scalp *crinkle.* Blood dripped out and plopped on a floorboard under her. He stepped on her upper back, then gave the handle a good tug. The hammer came out of her skull, threads of slimy blood and strands of hair hanging from the claw.

"Thank you for holding this for me," the intruder said.

He lunged over the dead bodies, then made his way downstairs. The TV was still on. A news report about an increase in prowler incidents was playing at a low volume. He went into the kitchen. After setting his hammer down on a counter, he opened the refrigerator and browsed his options.

He took out a Tupperware container with leftover lasagna inside it. It was his favorite. He heated it in the microwave, then pulled his mask up to his nose and scarfed the food down with a fork he found in a drawer. He left the empty container in the sink, as if he were expecting someone to wash it for him.

But he wasn't finished yet. He still had time for dessert. He opened the freezer and found a tub of ice cream.

"Lucky me," he said, noticing it was his favorite flavor—peanut butter.

He popped it open, took a spoon out of a drawer, and ate until he was full. He was unfazed by the violence—and the reek of shit spreading through the home. With a little bit of ice cream at the bottom, he left the tub on the counter. After finishing his meal, he pissed in the kitchen sink. His urine had a strong smell of ammonia. It was more noticeable in the kitchen since the scent of feces wasn't as strong as it was in the bathroom upstairs.

Hammer in hand, he exited the house through the front door. He didn't bother closing it behind him. He wanted someone—*anyone*—to find the massacre. With a happy-go-lucky attitude, he strolled up the driveway while juggling his hammer and whistling a joyful tune.

9

HELP

"WE NEED TO DO SOMETHING ABOUT THIS!" NESTOR shouted, thrusting his index finger at Candace.

He was pacing around the small office. His agent sat at the other side of the desk, a cup of yogurt parfait in one hand and a plastic spoon in the other. She sat motionless while blinking excessively with surprise. The story by Butterfly, pages creased and bent, was on the desk beyond her keyboard and monitor.

"Well, hello to you too, Nes," Candace said.

"I don't have time for formalities, damn it!"

"Nestor, you need to calm down and lower your voice. You don't want everyone around here thinking you're going postal."

The author stopped between two armchairs. He was screaming because he was scared and frustrated. He knew she was right, though. He wasn't there to cause a scene. And yelling wasn't going to solve his problem or expedite the conversation. Shaking his head and frowning with great concern, he agonized over what to say next.

"Help me," he said.

Candace saw the helplessness in his eyes. She shoved her spoon into the parfait, then set the cup down on her desk. She walked over to the door behind Nestor. A chorus of unintelligible voices, complimented by a soundtrack of ringtones from phones and computers, rose from the other rooms down the hall. She closed the door, then returned to her seat behind her desk.

"What's the problem?" she asked.

"It's... The, uh... Just read that. Pay attention to every detail and you'll get the picture."

Candace grabbed the manuscript. Running her eyes over the title, she said, "It's a story?"

"More than that."

While his agent skimmed through the pages, Nestor went back to pacing. He nibbled on his fingernails while sifting through his options in his head. He considered taking a sabbatical to wait out his stalker. *They'll get bored eventually,* he told himself. Then he thought about ending his career to appease Butterfly. He figured the reader was angry about his writing. He even considered moving to a different country and changing his name.

"Nestor."

Candace's voice snapped him out of his contemplation. He stopped pacing and turned to look at her. A quizzical smile broke on her face.

She asked, "Why is there, like, two paragraphs of this guy taking a shit? Did you write this?"

"Look at the title page."

"By Butterfly? Butterfly... Why does that sound familiar?"

"It's the same person who's been harassing me with those emails I showed you."

"This is from a reader?" Candace asked. She put the manuscript down on her keyboard and said, "You can't tell anyone you showed me this. You know I don't read unsolicited material. These guys start thinking we stole their ideas. Next thing you know, they're trying to torch our offices and–"

"It's not just a damn short story," Nestor interrupted. "It's a message. *A threat.*"

"A... A threat?"

"You read it, didn't you?"

Candace cast her eyes down at the manuscript. She flipped through the pages again with skepticism written on her face. Nestor's frustration grew. He had only read the story once, but he memorized every detail. *Did I lock the bathroom window?* he asked himself. He thought about calling his wife to check on her. He felt like he was running out of time. Despite less than a minute passing, he wanted to say: '*Can't you read faster?*'

Candace said, "I can tell you what I'm reading. It's a

very, very grotesque story. It feels like... like you, like an imitation of your writing style, like your old extreme horror stories. I can see that, yeah. I know this person emailed you this story–"

"It was in my mailbox," Nestor corrected.

"–but I'm not really seeing a threat to you."

"It was delivered to my *mailbox* at *home*, Candace."

"Okay, I hear you. But what's the threat exactly? Unless I'm missing a page, I don't see any personal messages to you. I don't think I saw your name once in here, actually."

Nestor sighed, head down and shoulders slumped in defeat. He wasn't getting anywhere with her. Candace was more concerned about Nestor's mental health than the short story. She knew him well, so she didn't want to feed his paranoia by agreeing with his theory. At the same time, she didn't see a good reason to push him away. She cared about him and his family after all. She figured it was best to listen to him—to let him speak so he could hear his own thoughts out loud.

"Sit down," she said. Nestor hesitated. Candace said, "C'mon. Paint the picture for me. Show me what I'm missing."

Nestor breathed deeply, then he sat in one of the armchairs. He took a short, quiet moment to organize his thoughts.

Avoiding eye contact as if in embarrassment, he said, "It's called *The Castillo Family Murder*. The victims' last name is Castillo. I thought that sounded familiar so I looked it up. It's a Spanish surname that means Castle. I'm sure you don't need me to connect those pieces for you."

"I understand what you're saying."

"There's more, though. The Castillo family is very similar to mine. They live in a lake house. They have a baby daughter. Dad's a writer. You might say it's different because there's no mention of the mother being an artist or because I don't use a typewriter, right?"

Candace responded with a half-shrug.

Nestor continued, "Right. But it was the little things that made it all click for me. There's a scene in this story where the family is watching an episode of Doraemon. It's a Japanese anime. A cartoon, you know? Mina just started showing Melody that show a few weeks ago. Then there's the car. The Tesla. My neighbor drives one of those. I'm pretty sure it's the exact same model." He leaned forward in his seat and, in a stern voice, said, "They can't all be coincidences."

While Candace digested the information, the room was dead silent—no footsteps in the hall, no ringtones in the other offices, no chatter from the other employees.

The agent said, "This person obviously knows where you live. You mentioned this cartoon. How do you think someone could know about that? Do you believe someone has been lurking outside of your home? You believe someone's been watching your family?"

"It's a possibility."

"I guess it's also possible that this person made a lucky guess or maybe Mina posted about that show somewhere on social media and he saw it, right?"

Nestor shrugged. He considered telling her about the other commonalities between his life and the story, such as his favorite food being lasagna and his favorite flavor of ice cream being peanut butter. He didn't have a reasonable explanation for those coincidences, though. He didn't want to tell her that he was starting to believe his stalker could read his mind.

Candace asked, "Other than this story, have you noticed anything unusual around your home? Any prowlers?"

"I guess not."

"Okay. So, what would you like me to do about this?"

There was another ten seconds of silence.

Nestor said, "I think we should cancel that book signing at The Hidden Door. I probably shouldn't be walking around with a target on my back."

Candace's lips curled in a little smile. She sank back into her seat as a sense of relief swept through her.

"What?" Nestor asked. "Why're you looking at me like that?"

"Is that what this is all about? You don't want to do

public appearances anymore? I know you only do them for your fans, but this is a little much."

"What? Wait, you think I sent this to myself? I have an envelope at home with this person's return address. The name's obviously bullshit but there *is* an address on there. And I didn't send all those emails to myself. I can't believe you'd even suggest that. It's ridiculous and–and... and *offensive*."

He got up from his seat and began pacing again.

"Let's calm down here," Candace said. "There's been a misunderstanding. I'm not suggesting you faked anything, okay? I simply feel like it's possible that you're blowing this out of proportion to get what you've wanted for a very long time: An exit from the limelight. You can't really blame me for considering that possibility when you've tried to cancel appearances multiple times in the past. And I get it. It's stressful, especially for introverts like yourself. But you're incredibly talented and respected and fortunate, Nestor. I know I say this a lot, but it's true: There are a ton of authors who would *kill* to be in your position. And all I want to do is help you keep that spot—as your agent and as your friend. You're wellbeing is important to me."

Nestor knew she meant well. Although he couldn't admit it to her, she was also partially correct. He was worried about the stalker, but he did see the situation as an opportunity for him to get away from the public eye.

"I'm sorry," he said as he stopped behind one of the armchairs.

"It's fine. Listen, I'll talk to our legal department and explore our options. In the meantime, forward any messages or suspicious mail from Butterfly or John Doe—or *whatever* he wants to call himself—to me. I'll deal with it."

"What do you think about involving the police?"

Candace said, "Like I said, I'm going to follow any advice the legal department gives me. I can't stop you from calling them yourself, though. So, if you feel like you're in danger, you should do it. Be on the safe side, y'know? But, Nestor, if you *are* going to call the cops, you need to be sure about everything. If it's nothing, Mina might start worrying about that... 'issue' from back in the day. I'm no medical expert but..." She paused for much longer. Walking on eggshells, she didn't know how to finish her sentence. She said, "Just take care of yourself. Don't let this stress get to you. Once it does, it can snowball out of control."

Nestor nodded slowly in agreement. Although he believed he was right about the stalker, he could feel his psychological wounds reopening deep in his mind. He wasn't ready to revisit his past.

He said, "Please keep me updated."

"I will," Candace replied. As the author reached the door, she said, "Nestor, everything's going to be okay. I promise."

He didn't say another word.

10

A CORNERED ANIMAL

THE SECURITY GUARD WAS A SHORT, ROUND MIDDLE-aged man. Greasy locks of grizzled hair stuck out from under his cap and beads of sweat clung to his horse-shoe mustache. Thumbs tucked into his waistband, he gripped the front of his utility belt as if he had anchors in his pockets and he was fighting to stop his pants from falling. He leaned against a tall, sturdy bookcase and breathed hard, although he hadn't moved in several minutes.

Nestor side-eyed him from his table. He could see most of the pockets on the guard's utility belt were empty. The guy was only allowed to carry a flashlight and a radio due to the strip mall's policy prohibiting weapons. His patrols usually didn't extend into the strip mall's stores unless he was called out to monitor suspicious customers, but he was assigned to stand guard over the book signing thanks to a request from Candace.

But the pudgy guy spent more time staring at the floor than checking on Nestor or the customers. He looked bored, tired, and uninterested.

This is what they call 'security'? Nestor thought.

In front of him, stacks of his books stood in towers of varying heights at the other end of the table. Covers facing out, more of his novels were displayed across the bookcase behind him. His table was at the back of the store. There was a wide-open space in front of him, plenty of room to breathe and move. But he didn't like the location because he couldn't see the entrance or any of the emergency exits.

He felt like a cornered animal.

The line of fans moved forward with an unsynchronized step.

"Nes," Candace called out to him from beside the table, trying to get him to focus.

Nestor pried his gaze away from the inattentive security guard and forced a smile. A young woman approached his table. She held a hardcover edition of his book, *The Last Fairy Tale.* They exchanged pleasant greetings. She asked a couple of questions about his work and he rattled off a few answers. He signed her book, then got up from his seat and took a picture with her while keeping her at arm's length.

He didn't trust anyone. Appearance didn't mean anything to him. Everyone in that store was capable of squeezing a gun's trigger or plunging a knife into his chest.

The line surged forward.

A young guy, bald by choice, approached the table. Nestor ran his eyes over him while signing another copy of *The Last Fairy Tale*. Since he had never seen him before, he didn't have a clear image of Butterfly in his head. He only assumed his stalker was unhinged. So, he inspected his readers for any eccentricities and, since he wasn't reassured by the guard's presence, he kept his eyes peeled for any weapons.

Another reader, a redheaded woman with a nose ring, stepped up to the table. She had an old paperback of his horror novel, *Not for Children Under 3 Years Old*.

"Oh my God, I can't believe this is finally happening," she said. "I'm your biggest fan. Seriously, I own all of your splatterpunk books. I've been *dying* to get one signed. I think I sent you, like, a million messages about getting an autograph. If I could have, I would have brought a whole cart full of all of your books."

Nestor's eyes darted to the security guard. The guard was staring at the reader—not vigilantly but *lasciviously*. His eyes were stuck on her ass. The author glanced over at Candace. She gestured at him, as if to say: '*Go on, don't be shy.*'

"Tha–Thank you," Nestor stuttered. "I appreciate it."

"The pleasure's all mine," the redhead said. She

handed him the book and said, "I brought this from home. I'm going to buy another one of your books, I had my eye on your new one anyway, but I was hoping you'd sign this one for me. It's my favorite."

"No problem."

As Nestor signed the book, the reader asked, "Any chance you'll write another cannibal horror book in the future? Like those throwbacks to *Cannibal Holocaust* and *Cannibal Ferox* and all those classics? I loved your takes on that genre."

"If the pieces come together, I wouldn't be opposed to it."

"I'm so happy to hear that. Do you mind if I get a picture, too?"

As he closed the book, Nestor saw the tattoo on her chest. He didn't have the best eyesight, so it took him a few seconds to make it out. At first, he thought he saw a butterfly. Then he noticed it was an upside-down dagger with an angular pommel. The blade extended down between her breasts. By the time he finished identifying it, he realized it looked like he was leering at her cleavage.

He handed the book back to her and said, "I'm sorry about that."

"Huh?"

"About the... I–I wasn't... Your tattoo. I was looking at your tattoo."

"Oh. Yeah, it's totally fine. I didn't even notice," she said with a laugh.

She did notice, though. She felt the guard's eyes on her body as well. However, she could tell the difference between the author's inquisitive gaze and the guard's leering. When people stared at her, she usually stared back. She would have done the same to the guard if she wasn't busy meeting her favorite author.

The redhead gave her cell phone to Candace, then went to Nestor's side. He stood next to her with his arm around her shoulders. Candace took two pictures of them, then gave the phone back to the fan.

"Thank you," the redhead said while waving goodbye to him. "Can't wait to read your next one!"

Nestor drank some water before the next reader approached the table. The blond guy was dressed like he had just left the beach—tank top, shorts, flip flops.

"What's up?" he said with a nod.

"Hey, how's it going?"

"You're that Nestor guy?"

The author stared at him, his face expressionless. Posters with Nestor's name were plastered on the storefront windows. A banner with his name *and* face hung from the table in front of him. The answer was obvious. He suspected the customer was playing dumb to get closer to him, so he kept his guard up.

"Yeah," he responded.

The blond man said, "Cool, cool. I think my sister likes your books." He grabbed a random novel from the table and asked, "Sign this one for me, yeah?"

"Sure."

Nestor signed the book while constantly glancing up at the customer's face. He noticed a large, asymmetrical mole on the guy's cheek. *Is that shaped like a butterfly?* he asked himself. And with each glance, it did, in fact, look more and more like a butterfly. As he handed the signed book to the customer, his eyes went directly to the mole.

The blond man furrowed his brow and asked, "Is there something on my face?"

"Yes," Nestor said without thinking. Then he shook his head and said, "I mean no. No, it's nothing. I just thought you looked familiar."

"Really?"

"No. I mean yes. I mean... I mean I thought we might have seen each other before. Why are you surprised? Have you seen me before?"

"I was in a commercial once. It was for a local mattress store. Maybe you've seen it. I'm going to do another one for a clinic soon. It's local, too, and it doesn't pay, but you know how it is. Listen, I don't have an agent—*yet*—but I'm a professional. If you're thinking about making a movie based on one of your books, whatever it is, I'm up for it. I got headshots in my car if you wanna–"

"I'm sorry but we have to keep the line moving," Candace chimed in.

She stepped in and escorted the customer away from the table. Realizing she was Nestor's agent, the blond guy rambled on about his acting experience.

Nestor took a swig of his water and glanced over at the line. No matter how many books he signed, it didn't seem to get any longer or shorter. Like walking, talking mannequins, every customer started to look the same —faces warping into featureless masks of skin—but with different clothing.

A terrible feeling of claustrophobia gripped him. He saw the surrounding bookcases sliding towards him. The ceiling began to descend and the floor started to rise. He breathed in long, raspy gasps. He felt a presence behind him. He glanced back while pulling on the collar of his shirt. There was no one there.

"Are you okay?"

He heard the voice circling his head, as if he were listening to it through a surround sound system. He couldn't tell where the question came from or who had said it. The voice was unusually slow and deep. He saw Candace walking towards the table.

"What's wrong, Nes?" she asked.

"I, um... Everyone is..."

Nestor stopped talking as he looked at the line. The customers' faces had returned. They looked back at him—some baffled, others inattentive.

Frowning, Candace said, "You're pale. What's wrong?"

"I need to use the restroom."

"Yeah, sure, of course."

Candace walked over to the line of eager fans and announced the break. Nestor stumbled away, massaging his throbbing temple with his fingertips. He walked past the guard. The roly-poly guy yawned. Nestor scoffed at him. He went down an aisle to his left. In front of the restrooms, there was a sign that read: *We love your enthusiasm, but please don't read unpurchased books on the toilet.*

He entered the men's restroom, then shut the door, leaned back against it, and heaved a sigh. The room was small—three urinals, two stalls—but he felt like he had more space in there than in the store. He went to a sink and splashed some cool water on his face. It calmed him a little. Then he went to a urinal and peed.

Mid-stream, he heard a snicker from one of the stalls behind him. A jolt of fear shot through him. He imagined an eye with a light blue iris—just like the Lurker's from Butterfly's short story— watching him through a crack in the stall. *He's here,* he thought. Then his mind went blank. Next thing he knew, he was shoving his dick back into his underwear and racing to the door.

His urine left a dark spot on the crotch of his khakis. It got on his fingers and dripped on the floor, too. He was about to reach for the door handle when he felt his mind reactivate. He regained control of his body. He stared at the door's keyhole. Since the door wasn't locked and there were plenty of people in the store, he convinced himself that he was safe.

I can outrun him, he rationalized. *If not, they'd hear me scream.*

Another laugh emerged from the stall.

"You think this is funny?" Nestor asked.

The room was quiet.

Nestor approached the stalls and said, "It's you, isn't it? Butterfly?"

There was a splashing sound, then another chuckle.

"*Answer me,*" the author said, raising his voice but not quite yelling.

The laughing stopped.

"Are you talking to me?" a man responded from the stall.

"You're Butterfly. You've been stalking me for weeks. Don't play dumb now. Don't you dare. You didn't think I'd have the guts to confront you, did you? People like you use fear to try to control others, but you never expect your victims to fight back. Well, *I'm* fighting back. You're going to jail."

"What are you talking about, man?"

The man in the stall grunted in annoyance. Nestor heard the sound of toilet paper tearing three times, then the toilet flushing, then a belt buckle click. He walked backwards to the door, making sure the handle was within reach in case he had to make a hasty escape. He searched for a weapon, too, but there was none in sight.

The stall door opened. A black man with green eyes stepped out. Bluetooth earbuds were plugged in his ears. Nestor cocked his head and squinted at him.

The man's appearance didn't match his image of the Lurker. He didn't spot any butterfly-related symbols on him, either.

"What's your problem?" the man asked. "I'm in there listening to a video, trying to take a shit in peace, and you start yelling about butterflies and stalking. And you wanna *fight* me? What the hell did I do to you?"

Nestor was at a loss for words. He still wasn't sure if he was facing his stalker or a regular customer. *The Lurker could have just been a fake persona to throw me off,* he thought. *Butterfly could be anyone, so I can't trust anyone.* Nevertheless, he was afraid if he escalated the situation and he was wrong, he would end up in hand-cuffs for harassment or sued.

The black man narrowed an eye and asked, "Did you piss yourself?"

Nestor pulled the door open and ran out of the restroom. He dashed down an aisle. At the end of it, Candace walked into his path.

She said, "Nestor, what's going–"

He juked around her, then sprinted down another aisle. He heard her calling out to him but he ignored her. He exited the store through the main entrance.

11

RECOVERY

MINA STOOD IN THE DOORWAY TO NESTOR'S HOME office. Her husband sat at his desk, staring absently at every writer's worst enemy: A blank page on a monitor. Only the light from the screen illuminated his still, tired face. The rest of the room was swallowed by an ominous darkness. It reminded Mina of when she used to be afraid of the dark as a child.

Although it was already cracked open, she knocked on the door and said, "Nestor?"

He didn't react to her voice. He was as still as a statue. His eyes were bloodshot and a thick vein ran down the center of his forehead. Mina glanced over her shoulder, as if she were expecting someone to be standing behind her in the hall. She pushed the door open all the way. Light from the hallway flooded into the office.

"Nestor," she said, louder this time.

The author turned his head slowly until his eyes settled on his wife.

"Hey," he said.

"Why are you sitting in the dark?"

"I'm... writing."

From the doorway, Mina had a clear view of the blank page on his monitor. She flicked the light switch next to the door. The light fixture on the ceiling turned on.

She said, "Staring at that bright screen in the dark is bad for your eyes."

"Yeah, I guess so," Nestor replied. "I didn't even notice it was dark already. Time flies when I'm working."

As his wife walked into the room, he minimized his Microsoft Word document to hide his lack of progress. She stopped next to his desk, arms folded over her chest with unease.

"Something on your mind?" Nestor asked.

"Candace called. She told me about the 'situation' at the bookstore."

"The situation?"

"She said you ran out of the store after–"

"I walked *briskly*."

"–an encounter with someone in the restroom. She didn't get into the specifics. She just wanted to know if you were okay. I want to know, too."

Nestor huffed and rolled his eyes. He opened his email. He found the regular spam, newsletters, and messages from business associates and readers. He skimmed through some of the messages. He was hoping to find an email from Butterfly—more hate mail, a taunt, a threat, anything to confirm his suspicions of being stalked at the bookstore. He was afraid he was going to lose his grip on reality if it was all a figment of his imagination.

"*Are* you okay, Nestor?" Mina asked, placing a gentle hand on his shoulder.

"I'm fine. Candace is blowing it out of proportion because she wanted me to stick around all day. I left because I was tired. I felt a migraine coming on, too. You know how they are. I can barely keep my eyes open when they hit. That's all there is to it, really."

"Honey, you... you haven't been the same since that convention. You're here but you're not. I'm worried you're falling back into the... the 'dark place' in your head. Have you thought about giving Dr. Bates a call?"

"I'm not crazy," Nestor responded sternly, his eyes meeting hers.

"I never said you were. There's nothing wrong with seeing a psychologist. I was seeing a therapist before Melody was born. If you need help, you have–"

"Did you hear me ask for help?"

"Hey, c'mon, don't be like that."

"Then drop it."

Nestor marched out of the room. Mina followed him down the hallway but she stopped at the top of the stairs. Melody was sleeping in the nursery. Mina didn't want to leave her on the second floor unsupervised. She went back to the nursery to get her. Nestor went to the kitchen and prepared the coffee machine. While the machine hissed and gurgled, he looked out the kitchen window.

Through a cluster of trees beyond the lawn at the side of the house, a pair of headlights pierced the night. The shrubs under the trees shifted with the breeze. It was quiet.

"Are you watching me?" Nestor whispered.

Mina carried Melody downstairs. She put her down in the playpen in the corner of the living room. The toddler was fussy after being awakened from her nap but she found some joy in her stacking blocks.

As she walked up to the kitchen bar, Mina said, "We're not finished."

"There's nothing else to talk about," Nestor answered, keeping his back to her. "I don't need a psychologist. I don't need more stress from you. I only need to finish my book."

"I can't force you to see a psychologist. That's your decision to make. But I need you to talk to me. What's going on in your head?"

"Words. There are only words swirling around in my head, Mina. I need to pick them out and put them together to construct meaningful sentences. That's what I do. I'm a writer."

"Why are you lying to me? I saw that blank page. I know you've been having trouble writing. I know how you get when you do. What's wrong? What happened in that restroom?"

Nestor turned around and shouted, "Nothing!"

Startled, Mina jumped. Melody started crying. She could see her father from the playpen but she didn't recognize him. She had never heard him scream before. Mina went to the playpen and scooped her up. She cradled her in her arms and shushed her gently.

The coffee machine beeped, signaling the coffee was ready to serve.

Nestor sighed, disappointed in himself. He wasn't in denial. He knew Mina was right about everything. He was only trying to push his wife away because he didn't want to drag her into his mess. He was trying to maintain a semblance of control. He walked into the living room.

"I'm sorry," he said. He ran his thumb across Melody's cheek and said, "I'm sorry, sweetie."

"It's okay," Mina responded with a trace of reluctance.

"The bookstore... It was a misunderstanding. I thought someone was laughing at me in the restroom for some reason. I exchanged some words with the guy, then I left. Nothing else happened. But by then, I was already tired of everything. You know how I get during these public events. The stress, the pressure, it eats away at me. So, I left. It wasn't the best move, but I could only think of one thing: Home. I just wanted to go home."

Mina nodded as if to accept his explanation, but she didn't believe every word out of his mouth. The fear and pain in his eyes exposed his lies. She wanted to press him to tell her more, but she was afraid he would lose his temper and yell again. She didn't want their daughter to fear him.

She said, "Why don't you take a break from work? Spend some time with us?"

"Yeah, I guess I can do that. You have any plans?"

"It's going to be a sunny weekend. We can book a beachside hotel."

"Like your favorite?" the author asked, smirking.

"Yes, but it would be for all of us. No work for you. No housework for me. Just the three of us together."

"That sounds very nice. Let's do it."

"Really?" Mina asked. "I'm not trying to push this onto you. I don't want you to feel like you have to do it. If you think it's going to mess with your deadlines, we can just–"

"Mina," Nestor interrupted, still smiling. "It's fine. I want this. I need it."

They kissed. Nestor planted a kiss on Melody's forehead, too. Mina took Melody back to the nursery upstairs. After putting her to sleep, she went to her bedroom and booked a room at her favorite hotel, then she started packing for their upcoming stay. Nestor stayed downstairs and drank a mug of coffee. The caffeine didn't affect him so much anymore. He drank it because he liked it.

After finishing his coffee, he went upstairs. He stopped by the nursery to check on Melody. She was in a deep sleep, drool pouring out of her mouth. He grabbed a napkin from a neighboring table and used it to wipe her face. He gave her another kiss on the forehead before leaving the room. He made another stop in the bathroom across the hall. He didn't have to use the toilet, though. He checked the window's lock, then he gave the window a few tugs for good measure.

With his short story, Butterfly had planted seeds of paranoia in Nestor's mind. And his paranoia was blossoming into full-blown obsession.

Nestor went to the master bedroom. There was an open suitcase on the bench at the foot of the bed. Mina was already packing clothes for their trip. She came out of the walk-in closet with a casual dress.

"I've got good news and bad news," she said as she continued packing.

"Yeah?"

Mina said, "The good news is, I booked the room. We can check-in tomorrow morning. The bad news..." She pulled a white lace thong out of the suitcase and held it up with her thumbs hooked around its waistband. She said, "I can't find your favorite underwear. You know... that little... pink... G-string that you like so much. Sorry, babe, but this will have to do if we're going to have any 'adult' playtime."

"It's not in the dirty laundry?"

"Aww, are you disappointed?"

"No, no. I mean, *yeah*, but I'm just wondering."

"Well, no. It's actually been missing for a while. Probably dropped it somewhere behind the laundry machine or maybe Melody got her hands on it somehow and hid it."

Nestor knew she liked to air-dry the laundry. It was something her family did back in Japan. She felt like it kept their clothes fresher.

"You see anything weird around the house recently?" he asked.

"Like what?"

"People. Weird people doing weird things."

"You mean like a... prowler?"

Nestor shrugged.

Mina said, "Maybe this is a bad idea."

"No, no, no. It's not that serious. I was just spitballing," Nestor said. He walked up to her and grabbed her hands. Gazing into her eyes, he said, "I'm fine. Really. Well, I'm *heartbroken*—absolutely *devastated*—about that missing underwear, but I'll recover."

"At least you'll always have your memories of them."

"Might have a video or two of you in them, too."

"You better not," Mina laughed.

"Maybe it was just blown away in the wind. You should really start drying the laundry inside. That's why we bought that dryer."

The Castles went on a little vacation. Nestor was able to play it cool during their stay at the beachside hotel. He spent time with Mina and Melody. He called Candace and apologized for his erratic behavior at the book signing. And he jotted a few notes down on his phone for a new book idea—a slasher set in a resort.

Yet, every night while Mina and Melody slept, he snuck out of bed and checked the locks on the door. He couldn't shake the feeling that he was being watched.

The family returned to the lake house after three nights away. Mina raced inside with Melody to change her diaper. On the way home, the toddler had soiled herself. The girl was all smiles and giggles. Nestor trailed behind them, rolling their suitcase up the walkway. He opened the mailbox and reached inside. But before he could pull anything out, terror paralyzed him.

He saw a brown document-sized envelope inside. He pulled it out carefully, as if he were expecting it to trigger some sort of booby trap. The return address showed it was sent from a man named John Doe in Michigan. From the thickness and weight of the envelope, he knew it was another short story.

Butterfly, he thought.

Envelope in hand, Nestor turned around and scanned the area. Only the family's cars were parked in the driveway. There were no suspicious vehicles on the street. He couldn't see anyone lurking in the hedges or among the trees surrounding the property. Despite the peace and quiet, he expected someone to run up on him and stab him.

He retreated into his home with the large envelope while dragging the suitcase behind him. He walked to the trash can in the kitchen and stepped on the pedal at the foot of the bin. The lid flew open. He looked at the return address once more. Although he was tempted to open it, he threw the envelope into the trash can, then took his foot off the pedal.

12

VISITOR

Type. Delete. Type. Delete. Type. Delete.

Nestor was stuck in this endless loop on his latest manuscript. He wrote a few words—maybe a sentence or two—read them aloud a few times to get a feel of the flow, and then deleted it all. He even deleted chunks of his work from previous days. He was supposed to be on the eighteenth chapter of the story, but now he was back on the seventeenth.

The more he read his story, the more he hated it.

He thought about switching over to a different project. He was attracted to his idea of a slasher set in a resort. Slashers were fun to write. They weren't too grim so they didn't take a major toll on his psyche. They didn't require extensive research. They also gave him the opportunity to devise some creative, outrageously violent death scenes.

He unlocked his cell phone to check his notes, but the countdown widget on his homepage stopped him. His deadline for his Nero project was fast approaching.

"Shit," he murmured. "Write, Nestor. You can make it better in the second draft. Just write, damn it."

He turned his attention back to his iMac and returned to the loop.

Type. Delete. Type. Delete. Type. Delete.

He only decided to take a break after realizing he had deleted more than half of the seventeenth chapter. He went down to the kitchen for a fresh mug of coffee. He turned on the television in the living room and flipped over to a news channel. He had always found inspiration in the real-life horrors of the world.

And something terrible was always happening.

Every day was the worst day of someone's life.

The problem was, Nestor wasn't writing about his neighbors. He wasn't writing a traditional horror story, either. He was writing a period piece with elements of horror.

He started pacing furiously between the kitchen and living room, muttering indistinctly to himself. A minute passed before he slid to a stop. The trash can was slightly open, the lid pushed up by an empty carton of milk. Behind the carton, he saw a corner of the brown envelope. It was calling to him.

Read it, a voice in his head said.

"No," Nestor said through his clenched teeth.

He threw his mug into the sink, hot coffee splashing onto the counters, the wall, and the curtains over the window. He pulled the garbage bag out of the trash can and exited the house through the side door in the kitchen. He tied the bag up while making his way to the driveway. He tossed the garbage into a trash bin, then lugged the bin up the driveway to the curb.

Lost in his thoughts, he attempted to open the front door. It was locked. He laughed at himself, remembering that he had exited the house through the side door. But his smile evaporated faster than it had materialized. He saw movement on the sidelight. The rational part of his mind told him that it was only a reflection of his robe swaying in the wind. The paranoid part—the *louder* part—told him that an intruder had broken into his home.

"Hey!" he yelled as he ran off the porch.

He sprinted back to the side of the house, feet sliding on the wet grass. The side door was closed but unlocked. He barged into the kitchen, then slammed the door behind him and turned the deadbolt. He took a quick glance around. There were no intruders in the kitchen or living room. The news was still playing on the TV.

It was a local report on a suspected serial killer targeting the city's homeless community.

Although he didn't see anyone, a sense of foreboding crawled up Nestor's spine. Something was afoot, but he couldn't put his finger on it. He dug his hands into his robe pockets and groped about for his cell phone, prepared to call the police, but he couldn't find it. He remembered putting it down on his desk.

Head on a swivel, Nestor sidestepped through the kitchen. He grabbed a chef's knife from a knife block on a counter next to the stove.

"I know you're here," he said. "I'm not afraid to defend myself. If you show yourself... I'll let you walk out of here."

There was no answer.

Nestor said, "I know it's you, Butterfly. I'm warning you, I'm armed. If I have to hurt you, I will. I promise you that."

Again, no answer.

Holding the knife in the icepick grip, he walked around the first floor. He checked around the sofas, behind the curtains, and his daughter's playpen. There was no one in sight. He turned off the television, then went to the bathroom under the stairs. There was nowhere to hide in there. Still, he had to fight a strange urge to check the medicine cabinet.

No one can fit in there, no one can fit in there, no one can fit in there, he repeated to himself silently.

He crept up the stairs. He stopped at the top to listen for any suspicious sounds. He could only hear his loud breathing, though. Like a cop clearing out a drug house, he searched every room on the second floor. He started with the nursery. Since the toddler bed was on the floor, there was nowhere for an adult to hide. He investigated the furniture and her toys for any signs of tampering, though.

He moved on to the bathroom across the hall. He was nervous about checking behind the shower curtain. He raised the knife overhead, ready to turn any intruder into Marion Crane. After a deep breath, he pulled the shower curtain open. The bathtub was empty, so he lowered the knife. He checked the lock on the window. It was all clear.

He continued his search of the second floor—the storage closet, his office, the guest room. While searching his office, he grabbed his cell phone and put it in his pocket. The lack of evidence of an intruder so far dissuaded him from calling the police. He ended up in the master bedroom at the end of the hall.

He searched the bathroom and walk-in closet. He also peeked under the bed, like a kid scared of the boogeyman. He was home alone.

"I saw something," Nestor whispered, his palm against his forehead. "I swear I did."

The hairs at the nape of his neck prickled as he heard a creak in the hallway. He rushed to the door, knife raised over his shoulder. The hallway was empty. The door to his office caught his attention, though. It was the only closed door on the second floor, and he couldn't recall if he had closed it himself.

He stood in front of his office, looking the door up and down. He twirled the knife and held it in a regular hammer grip. Keeping an eye on the doorknob, he cautiously lowered himself to the floor while pointing the blade up. Face pressed against a floorboard, he peered through the half-inch gap at the bottom of the door.

He felt a draft. Sunshine spread across the room from the window above his desk. Specks of dust powdered the floorboards closest to the door. Every piece of furniture was in its rightful place.

He got up to his feet and stood quietly in the hall, running through all of the possibilities. He didn't see anything unusual in his office, but he feared an intruder could have been hiding in a corner of the room or standing on a piece of furniture. He gripped the doorknob while rotating the knife in his other hand back into the icepick grip.

He had never been in a knife fight—or any fight for that matter—before, but from all of the movies he had seen, the icepick grip seemed like the easiest way to stab someone.

Knife overhead, he turned the knob and shouldered the door in one swift move. He looked left, right, left, then right again, checking every corner twice. The room was empty.

"Fucking hell," he said, chuckling in relief.

He lowered the knife and put his hand over his chest. His heartbeat roared through his body—in his ears, in his fingertips, in his stomach. He took a seat in front of the desk and set the knife down next to his keyboard. His latest manuscript was open on his iMac. The cursor blinked at the end of an unfinished sentence. He wasn't sure if he was in the middle of writing it or deleting it.

He minimized the window, then opened a new Microsoft Word document. He saved it as: *Resort Slasher (First Draft).doc*. The title page read:

[Working Title]
Nestor Castle

On the next page, he dove straight into a new extreme horror story. It started with a couple enjoying a nighttime dip in a pool at a resort in Phuket, Thailand. He was planning to kill them off in their hotel room, then introducing the *real* main characters in the next chapter. In about twenty minutes, the word count read: 675 words.

Before he could get started disassembling bodies, however, he heard someone knocking on his front door. He checked his phone for any missed messages or calls since he wasn't expecting any visitors. With the knife in hand, he went downstairs. Looking through the sidelight, he could see there was no one there.

He checked the locks, then went back to his office. In a little less than fifteen minutes, 675 words turned into 900. With his period piece, he was lucky to cross

900 words after ten hours at his iMac. He was impressed by his progress. His fingers moved from muscle memory, typing without doubt.

Nestor stopped mid-sentence upon hearing more knocking coming from downstairs. Brow creased in a mix of befuddlement and concern, he grabbed the knife and exited his office. Halfway down the stairs, he heard more knocking, but he noticed it was coming from the back door in the living room.

He hurried to it and looked out the window next to it. The backyard was clear. A small boat drifted across the lake off in the distance.

Nestor made sure the doors on the first floor were locked before heading back up to the second floor. After taking a few steps up the stairs, he heard knocking on the front door.

"What the fuck!" he shouted as he barreled down the stairs.

He lost his footing towards the bottom but caught himself on the handrail. Legs moving faster than his mind, he couldn't stop himself from crashing into the front door. Fingers twitching with adrenaline, he fumbled around with the locks for fifteen seconds before he managed to open the door.

He stumbled onto the porch and swung his head around madly, looking every which way. His glare landed on Allen Peterson, his neighbor. The man was cruising by on a bicycle on the street. He looked over at

Nestor and waved, then did a very obvious double take. He saw the knife in his neighbor's hand.

Smiling awkwardly, Nestor hid the blade behind his back and returned the wave. Allen rode past the house without saying a word.

"Don't tell Mina, please don't tell Mina," Nestor murmured as he withdrew into the house.

He double-checked the locks on the door, then headed back up to his office. He set the knife down on the table next to his keyboard. He read the last paragraph, then continued working on his slasher.

A thousand words.

A thousand one hundred words.

A thousand two hundred words.

Type. Type. Type. Type.

Knock. Knock. Knock. Knock.

"Leave me alone!" he yelled.

He spun in his seat and hurled his thermal mug at the door. The lid popped off as it hit the wall. A wave of cold coffee burst out of the mug. Mina stood in the doorway with Melody in her arms. Their clothes were drenched in coffee. Drops landed on their faces, too. Although the mug didn't hit her, Melody cried because of the noise.

Eyes wide and mouth agape, Mina was speechless. She held her daughter closer to her chest and stepped back.

"Mi–Mi–Mina," Nestor stammered. "Wha–What are you... When did you..."

"Did you... just throw... your mug at us?"

"Not at you," Nestor said quickly, pointing two finger guns at them. He rose from his seat and said, "Someone's been knocking. Over and over and *over* and *over*. They've been trying to get under my skin. I–I thought you were someone else, I swear. I would *never* hurt you. You know that."

A flash of light on Nestor's desk grabbed Mina's attention. Her eyes wandered to the knife next to his keyboard, sunshine reflecting off the blade. Seeing the fear on her face, he looked at his desk, then back at her.

He said, "It's not what it looks like."

"Nes... Nestor, just wait there. Chelsea just dropped us off. Let me call her so she can come pick up Melody and take her someplace safe, then we can talk."

"I'm not going to hurt you or myself or anyone. I am damn sure I'm *not* going to hurt my own daughter. I'm telling you someone has been harassing me. They've been knocking on the doors downstairs. I've been going back and forth trying to catch them. That knife is for... for self-defense. I was scared, okay?"

"I'm hearing you, Nestor. But you're making Melody upset. You're upsetting me, too."

"That's because you're hearing me but you're not listening. I said someone's been–"

He was interrupted by the doorbell chime, followed by two knocks at the front door.

"You see!" he exclaimed, causing Melody to cry

louder. "I told you! This bastard's been playing this game with me all day!"

He grabbed the knife, then hurried out of the office. Mina cowered away from him in the hallway, shielding Melody's body with hers. Nestor went the opposite way and ran down the stairs. Mina reluctantly followed him. Nestor looked out the sidelight. He saw a deliveryman—a chubby guy with a patchy beard wearing a blue cap and matching polo shirt— standing on the porch. He was balancing a small box on one palm. A delivery truck was parked on the street.

Nestor didn't know every deliveryman in the city, but he knew for certain that he had never seen this man before. He didn't trust him. At the same time, he heard Melody crying at the other end of the room. He wasn't going to stab the man in front of his family. He put the knife down on the neighboring bench, then opened the door.

"What do you want?" Nestor asked.

The deliveryman cocked his head back, surprised by his hostility. He said, "Sorry to bother you, sir. You got a delivery."

He held the package out in front of him.

"What's your name?" Nestor asked.

"My name? It's Mark. It's right here on my name tag."

"Mark what?"

"Carrera. Right here on my name tag, sir. Now I

need you to sign for this package. I have other deliveries to get to."

Nestor took the small box, then signed for it on the deliveryman's tablet. He stayed in the doorway and watched the deliveryman walk up the driveway back to his truck. He didn't take his eyes off him until the truck disappeared behind some trees.

As Nestor closed the door, Mina said, "Let me take that."

"It's from John Doe. I guess he's in West Virginia now. Yeah, right."

"Nestor, let me take care of it."

The author ignored her. He used the knife to tear the box open. His heart dropped and his lungs froze. There was a pink thong inside of the box. It reminded him of Mina's underwear—her *missing* underwear. He dropped the box and teetered around. The room spun in one direction and his head in the other.

"It... It was him," he said. "He–He's threatening us. We have to call... the cops."

"Nestor, no."

"We have to. We have to."

"No. We shouldn't. Not now."

"He–He's gonna kill me," Nestor said, tears spilling down his cheeks.

"I'll call Candace."

Mina didn't want to involve the police because she didn't see an immediate threat. As a matter of fact, she was scared the police would see Nestor as a threat due to his unstable behavior. Beat cops weren't trained to deal with mental breakdowns. Some even shot first and asked questions later.

As Mina started to dial Candace's number on her phone, Nestor fainted. The side of his head hit the bench before his body dropped to the floor.

13

POLICE

NESTOR'S EYES FLUTTERED OPEN. HE SAW DOUBLE, triple, then double again. He was lying on the living room sofa. As he sat up, a bag of frozen chicken meatballs—one of Melody's favorite snacks—fell from his throbbing head and landed on his lap. He heard his daughter talking to herself to his left. She was playing in her playpen. A children's cartoon was playing on the television.

Mina stood on the other side of the living room, peeking out at the driveway through a window. Upon hearing her husband's groans of pain, she walked over to him.

"How do you feel?" she asked as she sat on the coffee table in front of him.

"What happened?"

"You fainted and hit your head. It looks bad. Do you feel nauseated? Disoriented? Confused?"

"The box. What happened to the box?"

"So, you remember what happened before you fainted. That's a good sign at least. How about everything else? Feeling nauseated? Disorient–"

"I'm not nauseous," Nestor interrupted. "My head hurts but it's not that bad. I don't think I have a concussion if that's what you're trying to get at. Where's the box?"

"We should probably go see a doctor just in case."

"Where's the box?" the author repeated.

There was a period of silence between them. Melody giggled. She was standing in her playpen now, eyes fixed on the TV.

Mina said, "It's on the counter. I saw what was inside. I understand why you had your... episode."

"Did you call the police?"

"I called Candace. An investigator is on his way."

"Like a private investigator?"

"A detective. I don't know all the specifics. You've been keeping me in the dark. Apparently, Candace has been speaking to the police on your behalf about a 'cyberstalking' case. She's been trying to contact you about it but she said you've been ignoring her calls. Damn it, Nestor, why didn't you tell me about this? About that story? That last email? Why'd I have to hear it from Candace?"

Nestor said, "I didn't want you to worry. I thought we could handle it. I didn't think it was going to end up like this. I messed up. I'm sorry. I'm sorry for everything."

Total disappointment stole Mina's voice. She couldn't look him in the eye anymore. She walked back to the other side of the living room. Nestor pressed the frozen meatballs against his face. He looked at the playpen. Hands on the playpen's mesh walls, his daughter was jumping in place and laughing. Her pure joy brought a small, short-lived smile to his face. Then his lips turned down in a pout of unhappiness as he dwelled on his mistakes.

Five minutes passed.

The doorbell rang.

Nestor tried to stand, but his legs were limp and his head was light like a balloon. The slightest movement aggravated his headache, too. Mina motioned for him to stay seated, so he did. Feeling useless and anxious, he watched her answer the door. She met a man in a tweed jacket with elbow patches. His graying hair was slicked back. His rugged face was clean shaven. After exchanging pleasantries, Mina welcomed him into the home.

"You must be Mr. Nestor Castle," the man said as he walked into the living room.

"Yes, sir," Nestor said.

The investigator pointed at the playpen for a second and said, "Cute kid."

Mina said, "Her name's Melody. I can take her out if she's too loud or just bothersome."

"No, no, let her enjoy her show."

"Well, I'll make sure she behaves herself. Please sit."

"Anywhere's fine?"

"Of course."

The investigator sat on the two-seat sofa across from Nestor. He pulled a notepad and a pen out of his breast pocket. Mina sat next to her husband and rubbed his back.

"My name is Dean Mueller," the investigator said. "I'm a detective in the Computer Crimes Unit. I've been working on your case with the assistance of a Ms. Candace Davis. I've actually been trying to get ahold of you for an interview for a while now but you haven't answered our calls. I stopped by here last weekend, too, but you weren't home."

"Last weekend?" Mina repeated. She looked at Nestor and said, "We were probably already at the hotel. We needed a break."

"Right. I must have missed you," Dean responded. "Now before we get started, Mr. Castle, I see you have a little bump on your head. Do you need a paramedic?"

Nestor said, "No, sir."

"Are you sure?"

"I'm fine, really. It was just a tap."

"If you say so. Why don't we start by confirming some facts then? You're an author, correct?"

Nestor nodded.

Dean asked, "What's your relationship like with your readers?"

"They've always been very supportive. They read and share my writing. I can't ask for anything else, but they're always willing to give more. I try to respond to their messages whenever I get the chance. Some of them are like, uh... pen pals, I guess. I wouldn't be here today if it wasn't for them."

"Any outliers?"

"Outliers?"

"Let me put it this way: Have you had any negative experiences with your readers?"

"Butterfly," Nestor answered.

Dean said, "And that's who we're trying to identify. I read through the emails you forwarded to Ms. Davis. This 'Butterfly' person mentions having chatted with you before reconnecting with you via this new email address." He flipped to a page in his notepad, then read a line aloud: "Admin@splattersociety.com."

"Well, did you trace the emails? The domain name? Anything like that?"

Dean snorted. Melody appeared to be laughing along with him. Nestor and Mina were stony-faced.

"I'm sorry," the detective said. "We get this all the time. 'Can you zoom in and enhance this poor-quality image to identify this person? Can't you just hack the server to erase the pictures? Can't you follow the email back to the sender?' Now, technology has improved over the years, but it's still a little more complicated than that. We were looking into the email address and the domain, but we hit a snag. The emails were sent through a proxy. The domain name is hosted offshore. And the owner may have used cryptocurrency as payment to keep his personal information from the registrar."

"So what? He's invisible?"

"For now."

Mina asked, "Then what's the plan?"

Dean said, "To be frank, there isn't much we can do because there isn't a whole lot of evidence. Your case will remain open, though, so we'll be ready to respond if the situation escalates. I can assure you: we will be keeping an eye out for the perp. In the meantime, I suggest you send me any suspicious material as soon as it reaches you. If you suspect this person is contacting you—through the internet, over the phone, or in person—contact us immediately. Do not communicate with this individual. If they pop up on social media, block them and report them."

"That's it?" Nestor responded, scowling as he leaned forward in his seat. "You're saying you want me to go into hiding?"

"Not exactly, sir. I'm advising you to–"

"You're advising me to 'block' this bastard, as if I didn't already do that. This is the same shit Candace suggested, and she's not even a cop. You couldn't come up with something better?"

"Honey, please watch your language in front of Melody," Mina said.

Paying her no mind, Nestor continued. "This is unbelievable. You really came here to tell me you've done nothing and you're not going to do a thing about it. You're useless."

"Nestor, *calm down*."

Dean pursed his lips and nodded, watching as they bickered amongst themselves. Giving Nestor a moment to cool down, he closed his notepad and crossed one leg over the other. He had been a part of law enforcement for over twenty-five years, so it wasn't his first time being berated. He understood his frustration, so he wasn't insulted by his tirade.

Once they quieted down, he said, "Mr. Castle, we're doing what we can with what we have. You give us more, we do more."

"I gave you everything," Nestor said.

"You gave us everything you are aware of *at the moment*. You use social media, correct?"

"Yeah. Facebook and Twitter. I usually only post updates about my writing or appearances."

"Look through your social media with a fine-tooth comb. See if you've been receiving other types of harassment—bullying, spam, theft of your intellectual property, fake profiles assuming your identity. You might even find someone following you and unfollowing you repeatedly. Take note of these accounts. Look for patterns in the usernames, their bios, their profile pictures, and the way they write. This 'Butterfly' person is most likely following you—*harassing you*—from multiple accounts. Sooner or later, he may unintentionally give us the information we need to identify him."

Mina asked, "I don't mean to tell you how to do your job, but isn't this something you should be doing?"

"We are. But we might overlook a small detail that might just *click* for your husband. We've never interacted with this Butterfly before but Mr. Castle apparently has, you see?"

"I guess that makes sense."

Nestor stood from his seat and hobbled over to the bench near the front door. He grabbed the package, then brought it over to the detective. He didn't take the pack of meatballs off his face for a second.

The author returned to his seat next to his wife and said, "His first letter was a short story. It came from Florida. I gave it to Candace. I'm sure she handed it over to you."

"She did," Dean said, staring down at the underwear in the box.

"He sent a second letter. I didn't open it or show it to Candace. I threw it away. But I think it was another short story from Butterfly. It came in the same type of envelope. I can't remember the exact address, but it was sent from Michigan. This package here is from West Virginia. I know this might sound stupid, but can't you track these return addresses? He's obviously using a fake name, but couldn't you find out where he sent these from and maybe find some surveillance footage of him? There has to be some sort of trail. He can be a ghost on the internet but not in person."

Dean sucked his teeth, then said, "We'll look into it, Mr. Castle. We already checked the first letter's return address. It led us to an abandoned building. A dead end."

"Shit. And what about the underwear? It's my wife's. He stole it from us and sent it back to us as a taunt. Hell, you could even consider it as a physical threat, right?"

"Nestor," Mina spoke up. "I was meaning to talk to you about that. I know what it looks like, but that's not mine. It's just a pink thong."

Dean lifted the underwear out of the box with his pen and said, "It still has a price tag on it."

"A price tag? Yeah, okay, fine. So, it's not her underwear," Nestor said. "But a pair just like that one went missing from our home recently. That can't be a coincidence. If he knew about the underwear, then it's safe to assume he's been lurking somewhere around here. And maybe he bought it somewhere nearby. That underwear, I mean. Can you track it? You know, find out where he purchased it?"

"Not with a barcode, no. It doesn't work that way."

"Then what *can* you do, goddamn it?"

Melody cried after hearing her father's angry voice.

Mina looked daggers at her husband. She picked up her daughter and took her to the kitchen, gently bouncing her in her arms to try to calm her. Dean tilted his pen, allowing the underwear to fall back into the box, then he put the package down on the seat next to him.

He said, "If you want to get a restraining order, you have to cooperate with us. Help us identify the suspect. Then we have to prove this person is dangerous. We're taking steps towards all that."

"Fucking baby steps, man," Nestor muttered.

"I have one more question for you before I go. Is your address public knowledge?"

"No."

"Yes," Mina said from the kitchen.

The investigator looked at her, then back at Nestor. He thrust his head forward and shrugged at him, as if to ask: '*Well, which is it?*'

Nestor sighed, then said, "It used to be public knowledge, I suppose. I have a newsletter, right? And to send a newsletter, you need to comply with the, uh... CAN-SPAM Act. Basically, your newsletters have to have a physical address on them. Earlier in my career, I was using my home address. I guess I didn't think it was a big deal. I switched it to a PO box a few years ago."

"Interesting," Dean responded, scribbling a few notes on his notepad. "You get any fan mail here? Hate mail?"

"Years ago, yeah. No one ever sent me any physical hate mail—I only get that on the internet—but I got a few letters and gifts from fans. Postcards. Homemade pens. Handbound notebooks. A couple readers sent me unsolicited books to sign. Overall, I'd guess less than ten people sent something. I don't have the original packages, though."

"Would it be possible for you to send me a list of your newsletter subscribers? Specifically, a list of those who were subscribed *before* you changed your address to that PO box?"

"Yeah... Yeah, I can do that. You think you can find him in there?"

"I'm being thorough, Mr. Castle."

Dean put his notepad and pen in his breast pocket. His hand came out with a metal case. He took two business cards out of the case and placed them on the coffee table. Then he grabbed the package and stood up.

He said, "Don't hesitate to call me. Keep me updated and I'll return the favor."

From the kitchen, Mina asked, "Are we in danger?"

"This Butterfly fella knows your address, but we don't know if he's even in the state. He might not even be in the country. I'm not saying these types of people are harmless, but these stalkers and 'trolls'—that's what they call assholes these days, pardon my language—are looking for reactions. They can be like stray animals. If you don't feed them, they usually go away."

Mina walked Dean to the front door. They said their goodbyes. Even Melody waved at the investigator. Nestor stayed in the living room, beads of condensation from the defrosting meatballs rolling down his cheek. His eyes were locked on the business cards. He didn't find any comfort in the detective's words.

"I have to do something," he whispered, his voice just loud enough for him to hear himself.

14

CORRESPONDENCE #5

DOM

@Dominik4779696

Anyone else hear @authornescastle was running like a little bitch at the Hidden Door? Heard he got busted trying to blow a guy in the bathroom lol

12:11 PM · Oct 20, 2022 · Twitter for iOS

Jake

@Jakey32424324

Everyone go ask @authornescastle about his book signing. They're saying he pissed his pants cuz he got scared of a black guy in the bathroom. I didn't know Nestor was racist! Should have seen it coming from a woke hypocrite hahaha

11:55 AM · Oct 20, 2022 · Twitter for iOS

N

@ NnnnMmmm8787

replying to @AuthorNesCastle

why'd you run from us at Hidden Door? Scared of your own fans? We waited around all day for you. That's the last time we support you. Don't let the door hit you on the way out, you fking tool

11:49 AM · Oct 20, 2022 · Twitter for iOS

Igor(e)

@ilovegoreandmore666

I heard @AuthorNesCastle only got his book deal because he's fucking his agent. He went soft after he met that bitch. Traitor.

12:25 PM · Oct 6, 2022 · Twitter for iOS

Kira

@HorrorLoverKira

replying to @AuthorNesCastle

Why is it so hard for you to just write HORROR? Stay in your damn lane. No one wants to read your 'take' on Nero. Period piece or not, I bet you're still going to try to shove your political beliefs down our throats.

9:36 PM · Oct 1, 2022 · Twitter for Android

Yuri

@YuriOfMayhem

Go watch the Worldwide Splatter Festival 2022 panel to see Nestor Castle STUTTERING through his speech. It looked like he was about to cry. I bet he'd hate it if we all shared it! #RTforRT

9:25 PM · Sep 24, 2022 · Twitter for iOS

Karina P.

@KarinaCaresAbout

replying to @ChildWelfareGov

I'm scared for a baby's life! Shaking right now! 'Extreme' horror author Nestor Castle could be torturing his daughter right now and CPS won't do anything to help. @POTUS please do something!

6:13 AM · May 15, 2022 · Twitter for Android

Karina P.

@KarinaCaresAbout

replying to @ChildWelfareGov

You have to check @authornescastle's attic and basement right away! His baby daughter could be in danger! He writes about TORTURING BABIES and KILLING CHILDREN!

6:25 AM · May 13, 2022 · Twitter for Android

Karina P.
@KarinaCaresAbout
replying to @ChildWelfareGov
You need to look into so-called author Nestor Castle
ASAP!! He shouldn't be in the same house as a baby!
Have you seen what he writes?? He's probably fanta-
sizing about hurting his own daughter if he's not
torturing her already!

1:35 AM · May 11, 2022 · Twitter for Android

Razberry
@Razberry1987
replying to @AuthorNesCastle
You can still write horror. You don't have to be a has-
been. Think about it before you make things worse for
yourself.

1:33 AM · Feb 27, 2022 · Twitter for iOS

Yuri
@YuriOfMayhem
The last Nestor Castle "book" was pure shit. I feel
ashamed even calling it a book. Too long. Too political.
I don't like long books and I don't need more politics in
my life! #amreading #DNF

6:30 PM · Feb 14, 2022 · Twitter for Android

Razberry

@Razberry1987

Don't be a sellout, man @AuthorNesCastle

2:00 AM · Jan 6, 2022 · Twitter for iOS

Kira

@HorrorLoverKira

replying to @AuthorNesCastle

I can't think of anything good to say about your latest. First of all, it's another thriller. (Ugh) Second, you had to bring politics into it?? I read fiction to get AWAY from the reality of the world. Stick with what made you, not this social justice political crap.

1:23 PM · Dec 24, 2021 · Twitter for Android

Razberry

@Razberry1987

Hey @AuthorNesCastle you done trying to get the mainstream to accept you yet? Still waiting for your next horror book.

1:14 AM · Nov 25, 2021 · Twitter for iOS

Andrey H

@AndreyH87

Look maybe it's just me but am I the only one who thinks that Nestor Castle shouldn't have gotten his book deal? The guy wrote an extreme horror book called HOOKS AND HOOKERS. Poor judgment from his publisher to sign this edgelord if you ask me.

6:27 AM · Oct 29, 2021 · Twitter for iOS

15

SECURITY

INDEX CARDS—EACH ONE WITH A DIFFERENT TWEET taped to it—were strewn across the floor in Nestor's home office. The tweets were organized in chronological order. Most of the accounts lacked profile pictures, represented by generic human silhouettes instead. Some of them used blurry images of characters from video games and anime. One of them—Karina P— used a Shiba Inu as their profile picture.

The accounts shared a number of similarities: they were all created after September of 2021; they had less than ten followers each, and their followers consisted of bots; they all focused on Nestor, sending negative tweets to and about the author.

Cell phone in hand, Nestor walked in circles around the index cards while staring down at them.

His review of his Twitter account had taken him

about eight hours. He searched his name and his user-name on Twitter, limiting himself to the past twelve months. He scoured through his list of followers for any suspicious accounts, too. He kept an eye out for any usernames or images related to butterflies but he found nothing of the sort.

Nestor had already emailed the collection of tweets to Dean. Still, he couldn't stop himself from conducting his own investigation. He sought a pattern, anything that could help him identify Butterfly.

So far, he could see the frequency of harassment increased after the announcement of his latest book. He got down on his hands and knees, sweeping his unblinking gaze over the tweets. He reorganized the cards, arranging them into columns separated by author. He noticed 'Razberry' and 'Karin P' tweeted about him the most, but they used different devices. He searched for them on his cell phone's Twitter app. 'Razberry' followed him but 'Karin P' did not.

He rearranged the cards again. This time, he placed all of the usernames with numbers in them in one column. He ran his eyes over the display names and usernames on those index cards. He started at the top of the column and made his way down, then vice versa. He slid two cards out.

He read the remaining usernames aloud: "N-n-n-n-M-m-m-m-87-87, AndreyH87, Razberry1987." He sat on his heels and juggled the numbers in his mind. He whispered, "You were born in 1987, weren't you? Just like me. You run all or most of these accounts, but your main profile is either... Razberry1987 or AndreyH87. Andrey... Andrey H. Andrey Hamilton? Andrey Harris? No, no. Andrey... What kind of name is that?"

"Sir?" a man's voice came from the door.

Nestor looked up. Tim Savage, a home security specialist, was standing there. He was wearing a blue windbreaker, dielectric safety glasses hanging from the collar, and holding a blue helmet in his hands.

"I'm sorry to bother you up here," Tim said. "I've been calling out to you for about ten minutes from downstairs. Even gave your phone a ring."

"That's fine. What can I do for you?"

"Well, the installation is finished. We can review the work together, then I'll need a signature from you before I'm on my way."

"Sure."

Nestor got to his feet. He followed Tim downstairs. The security specialist showed him the new alarm system. He helped him set up a password at the security keypad next to the front door, then taught him how to arm and disarm the alarm system. Outside, he showed him the new wireless doorbell camera. Then they walked around the property. Motion-sensing lights were installed at the front porch, the driveway, and over the side and back doors.

Brighter than headlights, the white LEDs turned the lake house into a lighthouse in the woods. The lights could detect activity from thirty feet away with 180-degree sensors.

Mina arrived at the house with Melody in their minivan just as Nestor was signing a form for Tim on the walkway. She had to lower her sun visor to block the bright light from blinding her. She parked behind their SUV in the driveway so as not to box in Tim's van. She climbed out of the van, opened the sliding door, then carried Melody and the diaper bag out.

"I'll be right there!" Nestor called out. He handed the pen and clipboard back to Tim and said, "Thank you. Have a good night."

"You too," Tim said. Walking over to his van, he waved the clipboard at Mina and said, "Have a good night, ma'am."

"Thank you," Mina replied, sounding confused but friendly.

Nestor kissed her and his daughter before taking the diaper bag. Mina caught a glimpse of the doorbell camera before heading into the house. Nestor locked the door and armed the alarm.

"What is all this?" Mina asked.

Nestor said, "It's a home security system. You always said we needed one, right?"

"I did. But you always said you didn't like doorbell cameras. You said you read somewhere that they were easy to hack and you didn't want hackers to get into our 'network' or something like that."

"Well, you could say I had an, uh... epiphany. I realized the good outweighs the bad. With those motion-detecting lights out there, we'll be able to see that stalker coming before he ever gets close to the house. And the doorbell camera? Say goodbye to mysterious mail, ding-dong ditching, and all that crap."

Mina side-eyed her daughter. She didn't want her growing vocabulary to be tainted by profanity. Melody was half asleep, spewing a string of baby talk and drool.

"Language, Nes," Mina said.

"Yeah. Sorry about that."

Nestor put the diaper bag down on the sofa in the living room.

Mina said, "I don't know if this Butterfly person has ever been here before. But *if* he has and *if* he comes again, what if he just goes to the back door?"

"Then I'll install some surveillance cameras."

"You don't know how to do that."

"You know what I mean. I'll *hire* someone. Wha–What's with this... this interrogation? We'll be safer now. I did this for us."

'*You didn't.*' Mina stopped herself from saying those words out loud. She knew he was only thinking about himself when she left in the morning with Melody for their daughter's checkup. Busy reviewing his Twitter account at the time, he didn't acknowledge them. His lack of questions—'*How was Melody's checkup?*' or '*How was your day?*'—confirmed her belief. She didn't want to argue with him in front of Melody, though.

"I'm just trying to see the big picture," she said. "What's your plan exactly, Nestor?"

"My plan? I'm, uh... Well, I'm trying to identify Butterfly before he takes this—whatever '*this*' is—too far. I think I've already found a couple of his profile accounts on Twitter. I'm starting to piece things together. With the doorbell camera, I'm going to record every single person who comes here. I'm going to try to make... profiles for them. You get what I'm saying? And when everything aligns, we'll have our Butterfly."

"We already spoke to the police about this. They're doing everything they can. We should be letting them do their job. And do you remember what Detective Mueller said? If you don't give this person a reaction, he might go away. Don't you think you might be giving Butterfly what he wants with all of this?"

"It's not like that. Installing lights and a camera, that's not what stalkers want. It's not the reaction they're looking for. They want us to *fear* them so they can strike when we're vulnerable. I'm letting him know that he can't mess with our family. And as far as the police go, I'm cooperating with them. That detective asked me to look through my social media, remember? I already sent them what I found."

"But he didn't ask you to create 'profiles' of our visitors," Mina said, voice laced with ever-increasing frustration. "Do you think Butterfly is a deliveryman? One of our neighbors? One of our friends? Or maybe

Candace? Because those are the only people who ever step onto our porch."

"It can be anyone," Nestor said with a shrug. "But thank you for reminding me about Candace. I have to give her a call."

"Nestor, I'm not done..."

Mid-sentence, Nestor dialed Candace's number on his cell phone and held an index finger up to his wife's face, as if to say: '*Hold that thought for a sec.*' Irritated, Mina shook her head and rolled her eyes. She sat on the sofa. Melody fell asleep with her face in her mother's bosom. Phone up to his ear, Nestor walked into the kitchen. He looked outside through the window over the sink. The dormant motion-sensing light gave him some peace of mind.

The call went to voicemail.

Nestor said, "Candace, it's Nestor. I'm just calling to update you on the new book. I know the deadline is still a few weeks away and I hate to say this, but... I'm going to need an extension." Eyebrows raised, Mina looked his way. Nestor continued, "I ran into some... roadblocks. I'm getting back on track, though, I promise. Give me a call whenever you get the chance and I'll explain everything. Thanks."

As soon as Nestor disconnected the call, Mina asked, "Why do you need an extension?"

Nestor returned to the living room. He stopped behind the sofa to Mina's right, hands on the backrest. He was getting tired of explaining himself. He wanted to say something along the lines of: '*What business is it of yours?*' But the sight of Melody sleeping relaxed him a little.

He said, "You already know the answer to that question. I've been distracted recently. But I'm going to finish the book as soon as I get this situation under control."

"And when will that be? When you've covered our home, inside and out, in surveillance cameras and motion-detecting lights? When they catch Butterfly? When they say he's no longer a threat? Or are we going to wait until *you* catch him? Is that what you're trying to do here?"

"You act like I want this. Like I'm trying to be a hero or something. Well, I'm not. I'm just trying to find this guy as soon as possible so our lives can go back to normal. People like Butterfly never give up. They have nothing better to do."

"But you do," Mina replied. "You can be using this time to finish your book. You could be spending time with us instead of wasting your time like this."

"Wasting my time? I'm making sure we're safe. Why can't you understand that? Look, if this is about money, don't worry about it. We're fine. You act like we're eating away at our savings."

"Oh my God, Nestor, I'm not worried about the money. I'm worried about you. You're changing. You haven't asked about Melody once since we got home. You haven't asked if I'm being harassed or if I've seen anything suspicious since this whole thing started. You didn't tell me about the lights or the new doorbell, either. That's not like you. Do you actually care about us or are you just doing this for yourself? You're becoming obsessed a–"

"I am not!" Nestor yelled. "I'm doing this for us!"

Melody awoke crying.

"Goddammit, Nestor," Mina muttered.

She hummed a lullaby and rocked Melody in her arms as she carried her up to the nursery.

Watching her go up the stairs, Nestor repeated, "I'm doing this for us."

Nestor lay on his back on the bed, fingers interlocked over his chest. Although the room was dark, he stared at the ceiling with a deep, contemplative gaze. He couldn't keep his eyes closed for longer than a blink, and as regular as clockwork, he only blinked once every thirty seconds. Stress, anxiety, and fear contributed generously to his insomnia.

He looked at Mina. She was laying with her back to him. They had hardly spoken since their argument about Nestor's behavior and their new security system during the previous day. He slid his legs off the mattress first, then sat up at the edge of the bed. He slunk over to the window, pushed the curtain aside, and peeked out at the backyard. The darkness was comforting.

He exited the room, lunging over the noisiest floorboards. He left the light in the hallway off. He could walk through the house with a blindfold anyway. He went to the bathroom to relieve his bladder. While peeing, he made sure the lock on the window was fastened. After washing his hands, he walked over to the nursery and checked on Melody. She was sound asleep.

Nestor returned to bed—same position, same gaze, same insomnia. He lay there for about ten minutes, battling with an intrusive thought: *You forgot to lock the doors. You forgot to lock the doors. You forgot to lock the doors.* He snuck out of the room and headed downstairs. He checked every lock on every door and window twice.

On his way back to bed, he stopped at the bottom of the stairs and stared up at the second floor. The intrusive thought grew louder: *You forgot to lock the doors!* He was convinced tonight was the night his stalker was going to pay him a visit. He rushed through the first floor, checking every lock and latch a third and fourth time.

Hands over his ears as if it would help him block out the voice in his head, he hurried back to the master bedroom. He climbed into bed and drew some deep breaths through his nose. Fingers entwined over his chest, he could feel his heart drumming against his sternum. He heard a sniffle in the room.

"Mina, are you awake?" he whispered.

She didn't answer. Tears oozed out from between her sealed eyelids. Her lips quivered as she held back a sob. She was saddened by her husband's downward spiral and her own inability to help him, so she didn't want to face him.

Nestor clenched his eyes shut as if in pain. In an attempt to stop his intrusive thoughts from hijacking his mind, he repeated one word in his head: *Sleep. Sleep. Sleep.* His eyelids felt heavy after five minutes. After ten minutes, he felt like his eyelashes were tied together.

Then a faint white light pierced his eyelids.

Nestor swung up to a sitting position, eyes wide open. Light—too white to be sunlight, too bright to be starlight—seeped past the window curtains. He jumped out of bed and reeled over to the window. The motion-sensing light in the backyard was on.

"He's here," he said.

He snatched his cell phone off his nightstand before jogging out of the room. Mina sat up in bed. Unable to keep her sadness bottled up, she whimpered as she watched her husband rush down the hall. While racing down the stairs, Nestor unlocked his cell phone and dialed 911 but he didn't tap the green CALL prompt.

He cracked the back door open and stuck his head

out. He heard leaves rustling with the breeze. He didn't see anyone in the backyard or on the deck or in the lake.

The motion-sensing light turned off.

Nestor's eyes remained wide open. He held his breath, thinking it would help his hearing. Twenty seconds passed.

Twenty-five.

Thirty.

A squirrel darted across the lawn, reactivating the motion-sensing light. The critter stopped, looked around, then scurried towards the trees.

"It's... not him?" Nestor whispered, voice tinged with confusion.

He closed the door and turned the deadbolt, then went back upstairs. He expected to find Mina waiting for him—scared or angry or both—but she was already lying in bed with her back to Nestor's side. She was awake, though. She was ready to jump out of bed and run over to Melody to protect her if Nestor was right.

But she didn't believe him. And she didn't want him to *think* she believed him out of fear reinforcing his paranoia.

Nestor went back to bed where he spent more time trying to sleep than actually sleeping. Intrusive thoughts kept him awake for the next five nights, too. He slept about three hours a night at most. The lack of sleep left him with dark circles under his bloodshot eyes. His stubble turned into an unkempt beard. Most of the time, he was irritable but quiet.

One morning, he awoke to a thunderous banging sound. He sat bolt upright in bed. The noise startled Mina as well.

"I told you he was coming," Nestor said as he ran out of the room in his underwear. "You believe me now?!"

Mina tossed on a robe over her nightgown before hurrying out of the room. She didn't follow her husband downstairs, though. She went straight into the nursery to check on Melody.

Nestor glanced around the first floor. All of the doors and windows were closed and locked. There was nothing out of the ordinary. He stepped out onto the front porch.

"Nestor!" Mina called out from the nursery. "Everything okay?"

"I... I think we're fine!" Nestor responded. While inspecting the porch, he said, "Someone must have thrown something at a window or a door. I don't see any..."

His voice petered out as he spotted the strip of tape covering his doorbell camera. And out of the corner of his eye, he noticed something hanging from his door. Face pale with dread, he moved closer. His breathing accelerated. A stack of Polaroid photographs was nailed to the door under the peephole.

"What did you say?" Mina asked, standing at the top of the stairs with Melody in her arms.

Ignoring her, Nestor squeezed the nail between his index and middle fingers. He pried it out with a tug while holding the Polaroids in his other hand. He dropped the nail. It bounced between his bare feet. He shuddered as he examined the photographs.

16

CORRESPONDENCE #6

ONE OF THE POLAROIDS DEPICTED NESTOR RUNNING down an aisle at the Hidden Door bookstore. The blurry photograph was taken from between two shelves on a bookcase in the neighboring aisle. From that angle, it showed the author's back with only part of his face visible.

In the second Polaroid, Nestor was standing in his kitchen, looking out the window over his sink. He seemed frightened but curious. It appeared to be taken from a shrub between the window and the side door.

The third Polaroid depicted Nestor's lake house between a cluster of trees. The photo was snapped from across the street. It was an elevated shot. The edge of a roof—a gutter and some shingles—lined the bottom of the photograph. It looked like it was taken from the second floor of his neighbor's house.

17

CONFRONTATION

"Nestor, what is it?" Mina asked.

She stood at the bottom of the stairs, still holding their daughter in her arms. Although the front door was only halfway open, she could see the anger on her husband's face and the Polaroids in his shaky hands.

Imitating her mother but speaking slowly, Melody said, "What is it?"

Nestor didn't hear them. Barefooted and in his underwear, he stomped off up the driveway. Mina's eyes widened in surprise. She ran to the porch. She watched him cross the street without looking both ways. She lost sight of him behind a hedge.

"Daddy?" Melody said.

Mina stuttered, "Eh–Everything's okay, honey. Daddy's just... He's going over to say good morning to our friends."

Nestor walked onto his neighbor's porch, banged

on the front door with his palm, and barked, "Allen! Get out here, you fucking asshole! Open up! Come out!"

He stepped over to the window next to the door. He struck it twice with his palm, then tried to pull it open. It didn't budge.

He hit the window again, glass rattling and frame groaning, and he shouted, "You think this is funny, you sick bastard?! You think you can just fuck with me— with my *family*—and get away with it?! Get out here and face me! Don't make me come in there, you coward!"

He stumbled off the porch. Crushing the Polaroids in his hand, he grabbed a handful of small stones from the walkway's rock edging. He hurled one at the door, another at the window next to it, then one at a second-floor window, then he threw the last four at the porch in one volley.

From across the road, Mina yelled, "Nestor, stop! Stop it!"

The front door swung open.

Allen Peterson stepped out. He was an old but athletic guy. He was already dressed for a day at the lake. Panicky, muffled voices escaped the house through the open door behind him.

The man said, "I don't know what the hell has gotten into you, Nestor, but Ann is calling the police right now. I will–"

"I should be calling the police on you!"

"–press charges on you if you don't stop this."

Nestor marched up to the porch. Allen took a step back. He stopped in the doorway, using himself as a barrier. He could have slammed the door in Nestor's face but he wanted to send him a message: '*You'll have to get through me if you want to get to my family.*' He wasn't the type to back down from a conflict.

"Who do you think you are?" Nestor said. "You've been harassing me and my family for weeks, and now you want to pretend like *I'm* the bad guy? Like–Like... Like *you're* going to call the cops on *me*?"

"Harassing you? Nestor, I haven't spoken to you in weeks, and now I find you screaming and hollering out here in your underwear. What are you going on about?"

Nestor said, "The emails. The tweets. The letters. The stories. *These photos.*" He showed him the Polaroids, then continued, "And you stole my wife's underwear, you sick motherfucker. I should have known it was you. You're probably wearing them right now."

Allen stood there in stupefied silence, mouth ajar and eyes narrowed. He had no idea what he was talking about. Over Nestor's shoulder, he saw Mina making her way across the road.

"Nestor, pal," he said in a quiet voice. "Are you... on something?"

"Don't try to turn this on me. It's... It's not me. I'm

not crazy. Tell me it was you. Tell me you're Butterfly. Admit it."

"Butterfly?"

"Stop acting stupid, you old bastard! I caught you! I have photographic evidence! I have your story with your damn car in it! It all leads back to you!"

"Nestor!" Mina cried out as she walked up the driveway.

Allen said, "You need help, pal. You're hurting your family. Think about your daughter. Do you want her to see you like this?"

"I know you've been thinking about my daughter," Nestor responded, nodding rapidly.

"Excuse me?"

"Yeah, I remember what you wrote in that story you sent me. Is that what you want to do to my baby girl? You wanna smash her face with a hammer, huh?"

"Jesus Christ," Allen muttered with a sneer. "You're a psychopath."

"I won't let you touch her. I'll *beat* those sick thoughts out of your head–"

"I'm done talking to you."

"–before you cross that street again."

"Tell it to the police."

Allen stepped back into his home and went to close the door when Nestor lunged at him. The author threw a punch at him. But he had no experience, no training, no hand-eye coordination. Allen dodged the punch with ease. He pushed Nestor back while he was off-balance. The author lost his footing and spilled down the porch steps. His knee hit the walkway hard.

Retreating into his home, Allen yelled, "The cops are on the way!"

He slammed the door and fastened the locks. Nestor jumped up to his feet. A throbbing pain radiated from his injured knee with his first step up the porch stairs. He fought through it, though. He turned the doorknob and slammed his shoulder against the door—once, twice, *thrice*. His shoulder hurt as much as his knee.

In a frenzy, he limped over to the porch chair to his left. He picked it up and held it by two of its legs. He swung it to his left, getting ready to throw it through the window to his right. But then he heard sobbing. It was the type of crying that sounded like it hurt— harsh, raspy, breathless. He looked over at the walkway.

Mina and Melody were crying hysterically. They had both been calling out to him since he fell from the porch but he hadn't heard them until that very moment. Although he hadn't touched them, they were traumatized and pained by his violent behavior. He could see Mina had given up on reaching him, too.

He was familiar with their pain. They were silent victims of second-hand abuse. He refused to continue harming them.

He dropped the chair and, as he limped off the

porch, he said, "This isn't over, Allen. You're going to jail. I swear you'll pay for what you've done to us."

———————

Patrol cars lined the road between the lake houses. Beat cops interviewed Allen about the incident and inspected his home for damage. Nestor sat on the bench on his porch, holding a pack of frozen broccoli against his injured knee. He was now wearing a robe. Within earshot with the front door wide open, Mina sat on the bench at the foyer of the home. She let Melody toddle around in front of her. The little girl was playing with a toy police cruiser one of the cops had given to her, moving it through the air as if it were a flying car.

"I hear... lil' birdies," she said as she looked at the door.

Birds were chirping from the trees outside.

Teary-eyed, Mina smiled and said, "Yes, honey, those are birdies."

"I like birdies," Melody said, giggling.

Nestor and Mina had already been interviewed by the police as well. Nestor told the beat cops about his suspicions, but he sounded like a madman rambling about short stories, photographs, and butterflies. The police couldn't connect the pieces. With Mina and Melody on his mind, Allen had decided against pressing charges as long as Nestor agreed to stay off his property. But Nestor refused to agree to the terms until he could speak to Detective Dean Mueller about his case. They were all playing the waiting game now.

Dean pulled into the driveway in an unmarked sedan. He climbed out, took a few minutes to speak to one of the beat cops and look over Allen's written statement, then he moseyed over to the porch.

"Morning, ma'am," he said to Mina as he walked past the front door.

Mina answered with a tight-lipped smile and a nod.

"Good morning," Melody said.

"Good morning to you, too," Dean said.

The little girl had already forgotten about the dispute at their neighbor's house. The detective brought his attention to Nestor.

He asked, "Your leg okay?"

"I'm fine," Nestor said.

"First your head. Now your knee. I'm not going to find you with a new injury every time I come out here, am I?"

"*I'm fine.*"

"All right, all right. Then let's get down to business," Dean said as he leaned back against the guardrail across from Nestor. "Let me start by explaining something to you, Mr. Castle. Your neighbor, Allen Peterson, says he doesn't want to press charges on you. That does *not* mean we cannot arrest you. You could be charged with trespassing. Disorderly conduct. Assault."

"I didn't touch him."

"You don't have to touch someone to assault them. An attempt or a threat is enough to get you charged with simple assault. So, if you want to stay out of jail, I suggest you cooperate."

"I can't believe you're actually considering arresting me. *Me*. I'm the victim here. This guy's been stalking my family. Knocking on our doors at random times of the day, sending harassing emails and threats, stealing my wife's underwear, and who knows what else. He's Butterfly. He needs to be locked up. Have you even questioned him about any of this?"

"We have."

"*You,* detective. Have *you* questioned him? Because these other cops... I don't think they know what they're doing. They're just eating up whatever bullshit he's feeding them."

Dean glanced over at the beat cops standing on the walkway. They could hear Nestor clearly. Mina felt a stab of embarrassment for her husband.

The detective said, "I read his signed statement. You showed up at his doorstep in your underwear, claiming he's been stalking you. You threw rocks at his door and windows—one of which you damaged, by the way—then attempted to strike him after he came out to confront you. He says he has no idea what you're talking about. I believe him."

"You... You what?"

"I don't believe he's Butterfly."

"So, you read a couple of his words on a sheet of paper and you decided it's not him? You don't even bother to ask me for my side of the story?"

"That's what I'm here–"

"I have photographic evidence!"

Nestor held the Polaroid photographs out. They were bent and dirty. He had shown them to the other cops but he refused to let them take them. He feared they were going to dispose of them in order to protect Allen. He wasn't sure if he trusted Dean with them, either. His paranoia had reached new heights.

Dean put on a pair of gloves, then took the photos from him. He examined each one, tilting and turning them as if it would help him see more.

He said, "Yes, these are very suspicious, but they don't prove that Mr. Peterson took these pictures or delivered them to you. This one here." He showed the author the elevated shot of his house. He said, "This could have been taken by a drone from outside the second floor of Mr. Peterson's house."

"Oh c'mon, you can't seriously believe that? Look at it. I mean, really look at it. It looks like it was taken from *inside* his house."

"We'll look into that, sure, and I'll take these in as evidence. Don't expect us to get any fingerprints off of these with the way you handled them, though."

"What about the story?" Nestor asked. "You read the story, right? The one I gave to Candace?"

"The Castillo Family Murder. Yes, I've read it."

"It mentions a Tesla. The same exact model that Allen owns."

"All that proves is that this stalker has been in the area. He may be a serial prowler. It's not like your neighbor's hiding his vehicle. It's parked in plain sight. I saw it as I was turning into your driveway. So, when you think about it, anyone could have written that story. You, your wife, me, Mr. Peterson, or possibly— but not likely—another neighbor."

Disgruntled, Nestor huffed and shook his head. He felt like his concerns were being carelessly dismissed. Mina hoped he would take it all as a wake-up call for him to seek help.

"He asked me for an autograph once," Nestor said.

Dean smiled and said, "If I wasn't focused on finding your stalker, *I* would have asked you for an autograph, Mr. Castle."

"Okay, fine. So, what's next? Hmm? You're not going to do anything about him. These other cops aren't going to help me. What am I supposed to do now?"

"Well, I need you to agree not to bother your neighbor again. That includes staying off his property —unless there's a serious emergency, of course—and refraining from menacing behavior."

"Menacing behavior?"

"Mr. Peterson mentioned seeing you standing on your porch with a knife a few weeks ago."

"God," Mina gasped.

She put her hand over her mouth and cried.

Melody dropped the toy car, then toddled over to her mother. She placed her tiny hands on her mom's knee and looked up at her questioningly. Nestor leaned forward and glanced over at the doorway. He couldn't see her but he could hear his wife's stifled cries.

"It's not what it looks like," he said to her. He looked at the detective and repeated, "It's not what it looks like."

"I need you to agree not to bother Mr. Peterson again," Dean said.

"I was on my property. I had a knife because someone was knocking on my door over and over and over. I wasn't 'menacing.' I was defending myself."

"I don't need to hear any excuses. Do you agree to stay away from Mr. Peterson?"

For a brief moment, Nestor considered rejecting the offer again. He reckoned he would be safer in a jail cell after all. But he feared Butterfly would simply start targeting his family with him out of the picture.

He said, "I agree."

Dean gave a thumbs-up to the beat cops in the driveway. They went over to the Peterson house to update Allen on the situation.

The detective said, "Mr. Peterson has a doorbell camera. Even if he's not home and you step on his property, he's going to call the cops and you're going to be arrested. No second chances."

"The doorbell," Nestor said.

"Did you hear me?"

Nestor took his cell phone out of his robe pocket and opened his doorbell security app. Before the tape was slapped over the lens, the camera caught a frame of a gloved hand and the sleeve of a jacket. The mysterious visitor had climbed onto the porch from the side to avoid the camera prior to nailing the Polaroids to the door.

"Shit," he muttered. He showed the image to the detective and said, "I almost had him."

"That's from your doorbell?"

"Yeah."

"Email it to me. We'll look into it."

"How did he know I installed that camera? Was he watching me when we set it all up? Is he watching me right now?"

"We're going to have our officers increase patrols in the area. I'll also be talking to some of your neighbors. If they have doorbell cameras or other surveillance equipment, hopefully they'll be willing to share some of it with us. Maybe we can catch him making his way to your place. In the meantime, I hate to say this but there's not much else we can do. I need you to stay calm until we catch this 'Butterfly' person. If someone's knocking on your doors in an unusual manner, if you find more photographs or suspicious packages, don't take matters into your own hands and start assaulting your neighbors. Call me right away. I'll either give you some advice or I'll come over here myself. How does that sound?"

Staring fixedly at the trees beyond the lawn to his right, Nestor said, "I understand."

"Good. I'll get out of your hair, and we'll clear out."

"Thank you, detective."

Dean walked away. He stopped at the door and looked into the house but he didn't say anything. He placed the photographs in an evidence bag in his car, then reversed out of the driveway. Nestor sat on the porch and inspected his surroundings. The beat cops piled into their patrol cars on the road. They left the area one by one. The last cop stayed for about ten minutes, writing a report while speaking to his supervisor. Five minutes after he departed, another neighbor cruised past the lake house in his pickup truck. The atmosphere of tranquility returned to the neighborhood.

To Nestor, it felt like the calm before the storm.

He limped into the house, beads of cold water running down his injured leg from the defrosted broccoli. The first floor was empty.

"Mina?" he called out.

She didn't answer. Gripping the handrail to steady himself, he hobbled up the stairs. He heard footsteps in the master bedroom.

"I have an idea," he said as he walked ploddingly towards the room. "I can call someone to come and cut those trees and hedges and bushes down. There won't be anywhere to hide. I can probably pay some of the neighbors to do the same. You know what? Since the police won't do a thing about this, we can start our own neighborhood watch. What do you..."

He stopped mid-sentence as he reached the doorway to the master bedroom. Melody was sitting on the bed. Mina was packing a duffel bag on the floor. She changed from her nightgown to a pair of sweatpants and a zip-up hoodie.

"What are you doing?" Nestor asked.

"We're going to go away for a while."

"Oh... Where are we going?"

"Just me and Melody."

"I, uh... I see. And where are you going?"

"I haven't decided yet, but I'll let you know when we get there."

Nestor blew an exasperated breath, then asked, "You're just going to drive around and hope you find a hotel? You know how dangerous that is?"

Mina zipped up the duffel bag, then said, "We have family. I have friends, Nestor. I'm not cooped up at home all day fighting imaginary monsters."

"What, you think I'm lying about everything? You think I'm making all of this up? The photos are proof that I'm right. Mina, you were in bed with me when that psycho nailed them to our door. You think I snuck down there, hammered them into our door, then came back up here and jumped into bed before you could notice?"

"That's not what I'm saying."

"You can't seriously tell me that you think my mind

is playing tricks on me or that I'm doing all of this myself."

"That's *not* what I'm saying!" Mina repeated, raising her voice.

"Then what is this about? Why are you trying to get away from me all of a sudden?"

The room went quiet. Mouth hanging open with a drop of drool hanging from her bottom lip, Melody shifted her gaze back and forth between her parents.

Mina said, "I know you're not making all of this up. I know someone is harassing you. I know this person is dangerous. I'm scared. I'm... I'm terrified. Because you're right, Nestor. You're absolutely right. He could be out there watching us right now. He's getting bolder and bolder. He could hurt us. But that doesn't mean I'm not afraid of you, too."

"What are you saying?"

"You're not yourself. You went out there and *assaulted* our neighbor. What were you going to do to him if he didn't stop you? Huh? And what if he was the stalker? What if he hurt you? What if he *killed* you right there and then? You think he would have stopped with you? Or would he have come after us next?"

Tears stood in Nestor's eyes. He didn't have any answers. The truth was, he didn't go to Allen's house with a plan. He hadn't considered the possible consequences of his actions.

Mina continued, "You put Melody's safety in jeopardy. That's not how you handle things. You should have called the police. You should have stayed with us. But... you're not you now. We can't..." She paused as her voice started to break. She choked down the lump in her throat, took a deep breath, then said, "We can't be around you until you're ready to help yourself. I can't let you traumatize Melody. She may not know it and we may not see it now, but you could be scarring her mentally. You know, toddlers can... They can get PTSD, too. We can't do this to her."

With a blink, tears cascaded down Nestor's cheeks. Mina slung the duffel bag over her shoulder, lifted Melody from the bed, then squeezed past Nestor. She stopped by the nursery to grab her diaper bag.

"Are you leaving for good?" Nestor asked.

Dumbfounded, he hadn't moved from the master bedroom's doorway. Mina stopped at the top of the stairs, sniffling. Melody wiped her mother's tears off her cheeks. Although she didn't understand every-thing, she was getting to the age where she was capable of empathizing with people.

Without looking back at him, Mina said, "This isn't easy for me. I love you so much and I know you need help... but I need to put Melody's wellbeing first. She can't be here with a psycho out there and a... a..."

"A psycho in here?"

"A... An unstable father at home. I can't force you to do anything you don't want to do. Only you can decide if you want to get help. For now... we need a break from each other."

"Mina, I'm *not* sick anymore."

Mina walked down the stairs. Nestor leaned forward, as if he were going to run after them, but his legs were frozen. He heard the door slam downstairs.

Then silence.

18

HOME ALONE

Every exterior door was replaced with a reinforced door. Security bars were installed over every window on the first floor. Additional motion-sensing lights were set up along the walkways in the front and back of the lake house as well as along the driveway. In the corner above the front door, a new security camera recorded the porch.

Nestor had purchased more surveillance cameras to cover the other areas surrounding the lake house. He had been preparing to install them all by himself since there were no appointments available for a week, but he became distracted by a *cracking* noise in the woods next to his home. He stood between trees and shrubs, head swiveling as he scanned the area.

Holding his cell phone up to his ear, he listened to the ringback tone. He had dialed Mina's number on his cell phone prior to investigating the noise.

The call went to voicemail.

Nestor said, "Mina, hey... It's been a few days since I've heard from you. I get it. You're afraid you'll have second thoughts about this, uh... temporary 'split up' if we talk. I don't expect you to tell me where you are. Maybe it's better if I don't know anyway. As far as we know, Butterfly could be listening to our calls."

His eyes rose to the branches above him upon hearing a *creaking* noise. A part of him was hoping to find his stalker sitting on one of those trees. Passing between the leaves, shafts of dark orange sunlight beamed down on him. It was getting late.

He continued, "I just want to know that you're both okay. Send me a sign if you can. Call me back and hang up. Send me a text. Anything. I know you're still angry at me. I'm angry at myself. I let this go too far. I admit that I've been having trouble... processing everything. But it'll be over soon. I'm going to get proof, and I'm going to send it straight to the police. I'll do it the right way this time."

He didn't have enough light to properly set up the rest of the surveillance cameras. So, he walked back to the house, unlocked the back door with his new key, then went inside. He secured every lock and checked them twice.

Peeking out the rear window, he said, "I just need you to trust me. I hope you're far away from here. I want you two to be safe until this is over. That's all I've ever wanted. I've been doing this for us. Sorry if I sound like I'm rambling. I'm okay, so please don't worry about me. And yeah, that's... that's it, I guess. Call me when you get the chance. I love you two more than anything else in the world."

Nestor lowered the phone and stared down at it. The call continued for another five seconds before he ended it. From the outer edge of his vision, he saw something move. He snapped his head up. It was getting darker. There was no one outside.

A floater in my eye? he wondered.

His eyes whirled as he searched for a squiggly line or a dark speck in his vision. He spotted a few floaters but he wasn't a hundred percent sure it was the same movement he had seen at the corner of his eye.

"The lights would have turned on if someone was out there," he said to himself.

He went to the kitchen, still walking with a slight limp from his fall at his neighbor's house. He served himself a glass of tap water. As he chugged it, he heard a faint *rustling* sound outside and at the lowest periphery of his vision, he saw the bushes swaying under the window.

Some water went down the wrong pipe, leading to a coughing fit. He slammed the cup down on the counter, cracking the bottom of the glass. He leaned over the sink and peered out the window, spraying water and spittle onto the glass with each cough.

Yet again, there was no one outside.

"Fuck!" he shouted. Fingers deep in his thick, messy hair, he turned his back to the sink and mumbled, "No light, no movement. No light, no movement. No light, no... no movement?"

Doubt invaded his mind, filling his head with terrifying alternate scenarios: *I could have installed the lights incorrectly. Butterfly could have already hacked into my security system. Or I could be imagining everything.*

He hurried over to the front door. Out of habit, he made sure the locks were secured. Then he peeked out the sidelight. It was nighttime now. The porch and driveway lights were on while all of the new motion-sensing lights were off. Transparent, shadowy blotches, specks, threads, and squiggly lines dirtied his vision.

He felt a sudden sense of pressure in his right eye, as if it were growing in its socket. The sensation was accompanied by a stabbing pain. He shut his right eye and cupped his palm over it as he staggered away from the door. The pain spread across the right side of his head in waves, reaching a crescendo at the back of his skull each time.

"Oh God," he groaned through his clenched teeth. "Not again."

Then a surge of giddiness—mixed with a touch of nausea—hit him. Along with the debilitating pain, the sense of pressure in his eye intensified. He felt like his eyeball was going to *pop* and the side of his head was going to burst open. He dug his fingernails into his sealed eyelids, tempted by the idea of gouging his own eye out.

He wobbled over to the cardboard boxes in the corner of the room. He fell to his knees in front of them. They were filled with supplies he had ordered for his home improvement project.

Voice broken by his agony, he stammered, "If–If–If I can–can't see you... you–you can't see me. You can't... You can't fuck with me anymore!"

Keeping his right eye closed, he retrieved a roll of duct tape from the box. The box tipped over as he struggled to his feet. Two more rolls of tape bounced out of it. Stumbling from window to window, he covered every glass pane with strips of duct tape. None of the light outside—artificial or natural—could enter the first floor.

But he couldn't quit there.

He ran clumsily up the stairs, his body bouncing between the guardrail and wall like a Ping-Pong ball every step of the way. He went into the nursery and covered every inch of the window in duct tape. Then he zigzagged between the other rooms—the bathroom, his office, the guest room—duct-taping every single window.

Although it didn't have a window, he even barged into the storage closet with a strip of tape ready in his hand.

He ended up in the master bedroom where he taped up the last window. With the lights off and the windows completely covered, he fell into the bed and curled up into a ball with his hands over his face. His bellows echoed through the house. Seeping past one of his hands, a mix of saliva, tears, and mucus soaked the bedsheet.

In total darkness, he wept until his throat was raw, his facial muscles cramped, and his eyes dried up. His screams faded to whimpers. He lost track of time. He could have checked his cell phone but he was trying to stop the world from entering his domain. He wanted to be alone—*utterly alone.*

Staying in the fetal position, he popped the lid off his phone and removed the battery. He continued whining until his headache subsided. Then he lay there with his eyes closed. He wanted to sleep so he could escape from his living nightmare. The darkness wasn't enough. He wanted his mind to go blank.

Light couldn't pierce the taped windows but an unintelligible voice managed to penetrate the walls.

"Mina?" Nestor whispered.

He sat up and turned on the nightstand light. He looked at the taped window to his left. It sounded like the voice was coming from somewhere in the backyard or the lake. He got out of bed and headed downstairs. As he reached the back door, the voice got clearer. It was a woman's. He couldn't look out the windows, so he planted his ear on the door to hear better.

The speaker's voice had an unusual rhythm, words delivered with different tones and unnatural pauses.

He heard his name.

"Nestor."

After turning all of the locks, he cracked the door open and looked outside. The voice was now clear. From the grainy quality, he could tell it was coming from a cheap device. The recording was just loud enough to reach the lake house but not loud enough for the neighbors to hear it. It sounded familiar.

"You're... so... handsome," the woman's voice said. "Nestor... I... love... you. Do you... love... me?"

From the same device, Nestor's voice came out: "Yeah."

With no emotion in his response, it sounded like he was answering a different question.

"What the hell?" Nestor muttered as he pulled the back door all the way open.

The woman's voice continued, "Do you... love... me... more... than... your... loving family."

It didn't sound like a question.

"Yeah," Nestor's voice followed.

It was the same 'yeah' as before.

The woman asked, "Would you... *kill*... your... loving family... for... me?"

"Yeah," Nestor's voice repeated.

Same pitch. Same tone. Same everything.

"Not Mina," the author said as he squinted into the darkness. "Can... Candace?"

He swung his arm out in front of him to activate the motion-sensing light. He cocked his head back in surprise as the light washed over the yard. There was a small white box tied with a red ribbon. A digital voice recorder lay next to the bow on top of the box. The audio clip kept playing. In the recording, voice choppy and abnormal, Candace continued showering him with compliments.

Her voice stopped, then there was a series of sexual noises: moans and groans, panting and grunting, slapping and squelching. The sounds didn't come from Nestor or Candace, though. They were taken from a pornographic movie and spliced into the clip.

Nestor's eyes blazed with anger as he pieced it all together. He slammed the door and fastened the deadbolt, then ran into the kitchen and snatched a paring knife from the knife block on the counter.

"It was you," he said as he rushed back to the door. "I should have known it was you, you bitch!"

He stormed out of the house, leaving the door swinging behind him. While walking over to the box, he did a slow spin with the knife raised over his shoulder in the icepick grip. He didn't see anyone in the area. He stopped in front of the box but he continued spinning. He was surrounded by silence and darkness.

His spinning came to a halt with him facing the box. He stared down at it, wondering what was inside.

Another voice recorder?

More Polaroids?

His wife's head?

Melody's body?

A bomb?

He gave it a little kick. The box was light. He heard something sliding inside of it. He dug his fingers under it, counted to three in his head, then picked it up. He kept staring at it, expecting it to explode, but nothing happened. He carried it in the crook of his arm and glanced around again.

"Candace!" he yelled. "You think you can blackmail me?! Huh? Or what? Hmm? You trying to drive me crazy? Trying to get me locked up so you can... take over my work?! So you can *fuck me over* and take my money?! That's what it's always been about, hasn't it?"

There was no response.

Huffing and puffing, he walked back into the house. He made sure to lock the door behind him. He placed the box down on the kitchen bar and cut the ribbon with the paring knife.

"What else do you have for me, you bitch?" he muttered as he took the lid off the box.

His angry expression was replaced by a curious one. Inside of the box, there was a USB thumb drive and a sticky note. Handwritten in black marker, the note read: *PLAY ME.*

He had a powerful urge to pay Candace a visit and confront her about the recording, but he figured it wouldn't hurt him to check the thumb drive before departing. He was better off with the full picture after all. He went up to his office and plugged the thumb drive into his iMac. He found one file.

It was a video titled: *Inspired by Nestor Castle*.

Nestor moved the cursor to the file and double-clicked it. The video started playing.

19

CORRESPONDENCE #7

THE ACTION CAMERA MOUNTED ON THE LURKER'S CHEST recorded a white two-story house across the street. The sun fell behind it, the sky a canvas of orange and black. Brick partitions lined with hedges separated the property from the neighboring homes. The camera caught the sound of the Lurker's heavy breathing.

There was a jump cut in the footage.

It was nighttime. The Lurker crouched in a hedge at the side of the house. His camera recorded the window in front of him, an orange glow shining through the glass. He shuffled towards it. The curtains and blinds were open. Inside the house, there was a console table with a vase of flowers under the window. There were doors to the left and right, then the short hallway opened up to the living room.

Candace entered the picture through an archway to the right. Dressed in her silk pajamas, she was holding an iPad in her hand and speaking out loud. It looked like she was talking to herself. Her cell phone was on a table in the living room with her current call on speakerphone. The Lurker reached out and caressed the window with his gloved hand. His fingers slid down to the windowsill. He drummed his fingers against the frame, tempted to pry the window open so he could leap through.

Candace turned to face the window but her eyes were fixed on her iPad and her mind was focused on the call, so she didn't notice the shadowy figure standing outside her window. The Lurker stumbled back and fell into the hedge. He held his breath for twenty seconds and, when Candace didn't appear at the window, he exhaled with a nervous giggle. His laughter sounded like it was suppressed by a mask.

There was another jump cut.

Hunched over, the Lurker used a lockpick on the back door's deadbolt, thrusting a rake in and out of it while delicately rotating a tension wrench. It unlocked with a *click*. He repeated the process on the other lock. In what felt like slow motion, he turned the doorknob, then pushed the door open. He sighed with relief upon realizing the house wasn't equipped with a security system.

Inside, he took off his shoes and set a duffel bag down next to the door. The first floor was dark, but he could see he was in the kitchen. He opened the refrigerator and browsed the shelves. He took a carton of orange juice out. The camera caught the sound of him chugging the juice noisily—gulp, gulp, *gulp*. He put it back inside.

As he walked away, a fruit basket on the kitchen island caught the Lurker's attention. He peeled two oranges and left them on the counter. The living room didn't interest him, so he crept up the stairs near the foyer of the home. Just three steps away from the top, he heard the sound of a toilet flushing, then running water.

He took two steps back and crouched, the stairs creaking under his weight. The noise stopped as he steadied himself, standing as still as possible. From his position, he could see most of the dark hallway. Light came out of the gaps under two parallel doors. The sound of running water stopped.

The door to his right swung open.

Candace turned off the light in the bathroom as she stepped out into the hall. She entered the room across the hall—the one with the light—and shut the door behind her. After about three minutes, the light in the room went out.

The footage sped up. Since the camera moved with the Lurker's every breath, the video became jittery with the edit. But he didn't move an inch or make a sound for what looked like over thirty minutes.

The video returned to its normal speed.

The Lurker walked up the steps. He stopped at the top of the stairs and listened. The silence was comfort-

ing. Feet gliding across the floor, he shuffled down the
hall. He stopped outside of the room Candace had
entered, cracked the door open, and peeked inside.

With a queen-sized bed all for herself and a sleep
mask covering her eyes, Candace slept like a log. The
pitter-patter of rain played from a speaker on a nightstand at a low volume. A glass of water stood next to it.

The Lurker crept down to the back door and
grabbed his duffel bag. On his way back up to the
second floor, he unzipped the bag to prepare for the
next step. He tiptoed into Candace's bedroom.
Standing next to the bed, he pulled a bottle filled with
a colorless liquid and a white rag out of his bag. He
soaked the rag in the liquid, then he gently placed it
over Candace's mouth and nose.

She twitched and groaned as it tickled her face.
Her head moved slightly from side to side, too. But she
didn't awaken.

The footage sped up again while the Lurker stood
there and watched his victim. Candace was fidgety,
head shaking, limbs spasming, lips fluttering under
the rag. Shorter than the previous sped up segment of
the video, the footage returned to its normal speed
after a few seconds.

The Lurker took the rag off her face and tossed it
onto her nightstand. He gave her cheek a soft slap. She
didn't react. He slapped her a little harder. She stayed
unconscious. Laughing with a sense of pride, he
turned on the lamp on the nightstand. He threw the

blanket off her, then removed her pajama pants and underwear at the same time.

He stroked her pubic stubble with the back of his fingers. The camera recorded the sound of his lips smacking. He took a pink thong out of his duffel bag and put it on her. Then he rolled her onto her stomach. Using zip ties from his bag, he bound her arms at the wrists behind her back and her legs at the ankles.

He flipped her over onto her back. With two fingers on her chin, he pulled her mouth open. He forced a black ball gag between her teeth. He latched the straps together at the back of her head. Then he slapped a strip of duct tape over her lips for good measure. The tape wrinkled as she tried to breathe through her mouth. She began to snort. Her eyelids moved under her sleep mask.

She was awakening, but the Lurker didn't seem bothered by that fact. He retrieved a claw hammer from his bag. He tapped the tip of her nose with it.

Speaking in a quiet, hoarse voice, he said, "Wakey, wakey. Hey. *Hey*, can you hear me? It's me Nes... Nes..." He tittered, fighting to contain his excitement. He took a few shuddery breaths, then said, "It's me... Nestor. It's time to wake up. You don't want to keep me waiting, do you? C'mon, you know what happens when I get impatient."

Candace could only groan. The Lurker unbuttoned her top, revealing her breasts. He rubbed the cold face of the hammer against one of her nipples, making it hard and erect. A slurping noise came out of his mouth, followed by a sensual moan. He slid the hammer across her chest, stopping at her other nipple. He circled the areola. She shivered.

In a daze, Candace tried to speak but couldn't. The camera caught some syllables but they were all slurred together.

As she babbled, the Lurker raised the hammer overhead, then swung it down at her breast. Her body jerked violently. An intelligible syllable seeped past her gags: *Ow!* The pain jolted her fully awake. The Lurker struck her other breast with the hammer. He cycled between them—left tit, right tit, *left tit, right tit*— putting all of his weight behind each swing.

Although she was conscious now, Candace wasn't totally aware of her surroundings or the ongoing attack. She couldn't remember falling asleep. She hadn't seen the intruder or heard his voice, either. All she knew was that she was in tremendous pain and she couldn't move her limbs. And the pain was so severe that she couldn't think straight.

After the eighth blow to her chest, she rolled onto her side. The hammer collided with her shoulder. Something *popped* and *crunched* inside. The Lurker rolled her back. Gripping her busted shoulder to stop her from rolling over again, he continued pounding away at her breasts with the hammer.

She rocked wildly from side to side. She swung her head around, too, as if she were trying to get the sleep mask off her face without using her hands. Her cries intensified as her suffering worsened. She couldn't breathe without igniting flares of pain in her lungs due to her broken ribs. A layer of cold sweat coated her body, droplets jiggling on her skin as she shook.

The Lurker stopped beating her after the thirtieth blow. Her breasts, swollen a size larger, were bruised blue and purple. Patches of petechiae—tiny, bloody spots under the skin—spread across her tits. Segments of the blue veins running across her breasts turned red. In circular red marks, the face of the hammer was stamped on her chest nine times.

Candace breathed in short, infrequent gasps. She stopped resisting her captor, too, because the smallest movements sent twinges of pain rocketing through her. It was the kind of pain that echoed. Her sleep mask was soaked in tears and the tape over her mouth absorbed her saliva.

"Nestor's hungry," the Lurker said as he leered at her battered chest. "Nestor wants strawberry milk."

He grabbed her breast and squeezed it hard, digging his fingers into her bruised flesh. Candace bit down into the ball gag in her mouth and held her breath, trying to stop herself from screaming. The pain was worse this time, though. A series of strong tremors raced through her body. She whined as the Lurker relaxed his grip.

Then he grabbed both of her breasts and squeezed,

relaxed his grip, squeezed, relaxed, and squeezed again.

"I think you're ready," he said on the verge of laughter.

He reached up to his face for a few seconds, then he bent over his victim. The camera recorded her abdomen. He made cliché baby noises—'*Goo goo, ga ga, goo*'—then some suckling noises. He let out a moan of pleasure while his victim howled. There was a wet *crinkling* noise. The camera moved as Candace struggled under him.

The intruder slurped something, then gulped it down. From above, a drop of blood rolled into the video's frame. The Lurker stood straight. A little more than half of Candace's left nipple had been removed, leaving a mushy, bloody crater behind. Teeth marks bordered the wound. The severed nipple was nowhere to be found. The Lurker swallowed something with another loud gulp.

"I'm full," he said. "Now let me fill you up."

He walked over to the other nightstand and raised the volume on the Bluetooth speaker, then returned to his duffel bag. He pulled a cordless power drill out of it. It had a large flat wood drill bit. Pointing it at her face, he cackled and squeezed the trigger. The drill bit spun rapidly. The power tool's buzzing was louder than Candace's stifled screaming.

The Lurker released the trigger but continued chuckling. With the tape and ball gag loosening due to her saliva, Candace was able to say one word: "No!"

"Yes!" the intruder responded mockingly.

"No!"

"Yes!" he laughed.

He squeezed the trigger in front of her face, the loud buzzing drowning out her next shout. She couldn't see the drill through the sleep mask, but she could tell it was a power tool from the noise. Fearing it was close to tearing her nose off, she turned away. The intruder released the trigger. She flinched as he touched the blood on her abdomen with his gloved fingers.

"Calm down, darling," he said. "I'm just lubing it up. I know you get dry down there."

He rubbed the blood on the drill bit's head. He rolled her onto her stomach and pressed his knee into the small of her back right between her restrained wrists. Candace hadn't noticed her underwear had been changed, but she felt the thong rise from between her ass cheeks. The intruder pushed the string aside, exposing her anus and pussy.

She convulsed under him, but she couldn't knock him off of her. A blob of saliva fell from his mouth. It hit her ass cheek with a splat. He dug his knee deeper into her, pushing the air out of her and limiting her movements. He adjusted his aim, then let another cord of drool fall from his lips. It hit her anus, and the tail of it landed on her ass cheek.

"Bullseye," he whispered.

He pressed the drill bit against her asshole. As soon as she felt it, she instinctively clenched her ass cheeks, unintentionally trapping the drill bit. She wiggled her hips and wailed. The Lurker rammed the drill into her ass. Her screams reduced to whimpers in an instant, Candace's body locked up as an unusual sense of pressure filled her rectum and a searing bolt of pain shot up her spine. She held her breath, as if that were going to lessen the pain, but it only increased the tension in her body.

The drill bit's sharp, hard edges nicked her rectal walls. A droplet of blood seeped past the drill bit's shank. It dripped down and lined her labia like lipstick.

The Lurker pulled the drill bit out an inch, then thrust it back in. He continued sodomizing her with the power tool, driving it deeper each time. The burning pain drained her energy, so she couldn't fight back. But the intruder still met some resistance because her anal sphincter tightened around the drill bit with each thrust. It ended up five inches deep in her rectum. Hands clenched and toes curled, she felt like her pelvic cavity was a sparking transformer and her spine was a downed power line, sending flashes of electrifying pain through her body.

"You stopped moaning?" the intruder said wonderingly. "Not big enough for you? You like my cock more, huh? Don't worry, I can make this feel better for you."

He squeezed the power drill's trigger. Candace shrieked as the drill bit spun in her rectum. She felt her rectal walls tearing and twisting. Blood sprayed out of her anus in thick hazes, splattering on the Lurker's arm and the bedsheet. It shot up into her large intestine, too. The Lurker felt the vibrations from the power drill on his knee. The mattress vibrated as well. Out of breath and in a state of shock, Candace fell unconscious. Her head fell into her pillow face-first.

The Lurker released the trigger. The drill bit stopped with a grinding noise. Candace's gaping asshole spewed out another thread of gooey blood mixed with semi-liquid feces. He pulled on the drill but it was jammed. It took a few tugs before it plopped out. Strings of her butchered rectal muscles were tangled around the drill bit. In a bloody prolapse, a piece of her rectum slid out of her anus like a turtle peeking out of its shell.

He put the power drill back in his bag, then he bent over Candace. He moved her head to the side so she wouldn't suffocate herself with the pillow. She was still breathing.

He stroked her hair and said, "Snack break."

There was another jump cut in the footage.

The Lurker stood in front of the open refrigerator, drinking from a two-liter bottle of diet soda. Torture was a tiring activity. He chugged a little less than a liter of the drink without ever taking his mouth off the bottle. He put the bottle back in the fridge, kicked the door closed, then took the peeled oranges off the counter.

Another jump cut.

The intruder was back in the bedroom, sitting on top of Candace's lower legs. She was still unconscious. He pressed one of the oranges against her prolapsing rectum. He pushed her prolapse back in, then the fruit slid into her anal opening. Half of it stuck out like an orange prolapse. Applying gentle pressure, he pushed it in deeper using the other orange.

A dark orange liquid—orange juice blended with blood—squirted out of her asshole like explosive diarrhea. Her anal sphincter had squeezed one of the oranges.

The video skipped again.

The camera was close to Candace's crying face. She was awake now. Mucus frothed out of her nostrils with each panicked breath. The tape over her mouth was loosening, the edges peeling away from her cheeks. The intruder put the camera down on the nightstand with the lens facing the bed. He adjusted the camera a little, then a little more.

He was wearing a black balaclava. It was folded up to his nose, revealing his defined jaw and bloodstained lips.

As he sat at the edge of the bed, he said, "I think our fruit is ripe for the picking."

He reached into her asshole, pinched one of the oranges, then plucked it out. It had been dyed red by her blood. He stuffed his fingers into her rectum once more. She sobbed as she felt his fingers wiggling around in her mutilated innards, aggravating the cuts and gashes and abrasions. He rolled the other orange out. It was partially crushed but red like the other one.

He bit into one. Bloody orange juice streamed into his mouth and dribbled down his chin. He slurped and chewed loudly, ensuring every sound was caught on the video.

One cheek inflated with the fruit, he held the other orange out to his victim's face and asked, "Want a bite?"

She didn't know what he was offering, but she knew it came out of her asshole. She could smell the scent of the orange, tainted by the stench of her blood and feces. She shook her head and cried.

"No?" the Lurker said. He took a bite of the second orange, then shrugged and said, "More for me then."

He devoured the oranges, then sucked the juice off his gloved fingers. He crawled over Candace and grabbed the glass of water from the nightstand. He drank it all in one swig. A satisfied gasp escaped his mouth, followed by some snickering. But, as he sat on her lower legs and stared at the back of her head, his lips drooped into a neutral expression.

Deadpan, he looked directly at the camera. He sat motionless for about thirty seconds. Then he brought his gaze back to his victim.

Voice shifting from raspy to smooth, he said, "I

recognize you. I've been in this room before. I remember how this ends."

He looked and sounded like he had awakened from a trance. He swung the glass at the back of her head. Upon impact, it shattered and sliced her scalp open. Drops of blood splashed on the headboard. She groaned helplessly. The Lurker flipped her onto her back, then shuffled up on his knees until he was straddling her waist. He grabbed a shard of glass—the largest one he could find—from the pillow underneath her.

He shanked the side of her neck with it, severing her jugulars. He sawed into her throat as blood squirted out of her neck. The glass cut through his glove and sliced his fingers, too, but he didn't feel any pain. The shard's jagged teeth ate away at her thyroid cartilage and windpipe. It wasn't long enough to reach her esophagus. Before he could reach her other jugulars, the glass broke into three pieces—one stayed in his hand, another fell to the mattress, and the third was stuck in her neck.

As his victim thrashed about under him, the Lurker grabbed onto the headboard to stop himself from falling off her. He kept staring at her face, though. It was as if he were afraid she was going to change into another person if he blinked. She tilted her head back and arched her neck. A geyser of blood jumped out of her throat, missing the Lurker's face by a foot. She stopped moving after a minute.

She had choked to death on her own blood.

The Lurker staggered off the bed, blood dripping from his sliced fingers. He waved his hand and hissed after finally feeling the sting from the cuts.

As he reached for the camera, he muttered, "Why does it always end like–"

The video ended mid-sentence.

20

PERSONAL DELIVERY

IN FULL SCREEN, THE VIDEO PLAYER ON NESTOR'S monitor had stopped on the last frame of the snuff film. It showed the Lurker grabbing the camera as well as the bottom half of his face. Behind the intruder's arm, Candace's dead body—her slit neck painted red with blood—lay in the background.

Nestor sat in stunned silence with his hand over his mouth. His keyboard was dappled with wet spots. He was flicking tears off his eyelashes with each blink. Fighting a bout of nausea, he retched and burped. He had seen graphic videos of real murders and deadly accidents throughout his life while conducting research for his extreme horror books.

A group of cartel members forcing a dog to eat a rival's genitals.

A trio of terrorists beheading a pair of young backpackers in a wooded area.

A teenager with her mangled, unrecognizable face split open like a flower's blossoming petals after a car accident.

Nestor had learned to desensitize himself to the violence, but it didn't make him emotionless. And it was different when the victim was a person he had known for years.

"N–No," he stuttered in a meek, scared voice. "No way, no... It–It can't be real. It can't be..."

With some reluctance, he leaned closer to the monitor and examined the image. He searched for any clues that could disprove its authenticity. He wanted to believe it was a movie. He remembered Candace talking about optioning one of his horror novels to a movie producer, so he knew she had connections in the industry.

It's all special effects, he told himself.

But he didn't believe himself.

The video was recorded in high definition, so every detail was clear. The carnage looked real. The sounds of suffering sounded real. It all felt *real.* The video reminded him of the snuff films he had seen in the past—the amateur camerawork, the gruesome imagery, *the raw emotion.* He didn't think Candace was capable of pulling off such a convincing performance.

Yet, rocking back and forth in his seat, he kept trying to talk himself into believing it was all a ruse.

"It's part of her trick, her–her... her mind game," he said, his hands clasped over his mouth. "That's what this is. It has to be. She was... going to blackmail me, right? Or maybe she wants me to overreact. She's trying to drive me crazy so she can get me committed to a mental hospital. Then she'll steal the rights to all of my work. Something like that. Right? *Right?*"

He refused to believe his agent was slaughtered by his stalker. He rifled through the drawers in his desk, searching for his old contracts. He assumed he missed some fine print that Candace was looking to exploit. He didn't find anything useful, though. His breathing sped up. He felt another migraine coming on.

He grabbed the mouse and moved the cursor to the top of the video player. He tried to close it, but his hand was shaking so badly that he kept missing the prompt. So, he pressed the Control, Shift, and Eject keys on his keyboard simultaneously to turn off the display instead. He went rigid before he could breathe out in relief.

The only light in the room came from the hallway. On the reflection of his monitor, he saw someone standing behind him.

A blow to the back of the head knocked him unconscious.

Nestor awoke to a nasty, pounding headache drumming through his skull like a jackhammer. His eyes cracked open. The amber light in the room was blinding. He felt like he was staring directly at the sun. The light exacerbated his headache, so he closed his eyes. He attempted to speak but could only utter a sluggish groan.

He tried to reach for his face, wanting to rub his eyes and massage his temples, but he couldn't lift his arms. He could wriggle, shake his head, swing his hips, lift his shoulders, but he couldn't move his legs. As he jerked his limbs, he heard wood creaking and something squeaking under him.

He opened his eyes again. They still stung, and the right one still felt like it was going to pop at any second. Although his vision blurred, he could see he was laying spread-eagle on his bed. His head was propped up on two pillows. The bedsheet remained but the comforter was gone. His limbs were tethered to the bedposts with handcuffs at the wrists and ankles. Countless questions swirled through his mind, but three demanded immediate answers.

Why am I naked?

Why can't I speak?

Who is this man in my room?

An intruder sat on the dresser across from the bed. He was wearing all black—a t-shirt, jeans, socks. His shoes were nowhere to be found. A black jacket, a pair of gloves, and a balaclava were on the dresser next to him. And on the floor next to the dresser, there was a duffel bag. It was the same one from the snuff video. Except for his thumb, the fingers on his right hand were bandaged. The dried bloodstains on the gauze roll looked black.

He was a tall man with strong arms, wide shoulders, and a thick neck. His brown hair was buzz cut. His eyes shone a brilliant blue. The jagged atrophic scar on his left temple was visible from across the room.

"Welcome back," he said in an unsettlingly calm tone. "Allow me to introduce myself."

Nestor's eyes bugged out. It only took those seven words for him to recognize his voice from the snuff film. He twisted and turned on the bed, handcuffs rattling and bedposts groaning. He shouted something, not realizing his mouth had been taped shut.

The intruder continued, "My name is Harrison Hammer. You won't recognize me because we've never met in person. We've only communicated through email and private messages and comments on Facebook and Instagram and whatnot. I've sent letters in the mail, too—*snail* mail, y'know?—but who knows if you ever got them. I guess you might know... or you might not. I bet you get a lot of mail. Anyway, my point is, you've never seen my face or heard my voice before. Well, before tonight, I should say. You saw me co-starring with your agent in that little 'indie' movie of ours, didn't you?"

The guy snickered—proud, *devious*. During his speech, Nestor had given up on trying to break free from the handcuffs. *Did you really kill her?* he had tried to say but it sounded like he was humming. He followed with another muffled question: *Did you hurt my family?*

As he strolled over to the side of the bed, Harrison said, "You have a lot to say, don't you? You are a writer after all. A storyteller. A man of many words. Don't fret, Nestor. You—a man of many *words*—and I—a man of many *murders*—will have plenty of time to chat." He took a seat at the foot of the bed and smiled at his prisoner. He said, "You'll know everything about me and I'll know everything about you by the time we're finished here. Oh, wait. What am I saying? I already know everything about you."

Nestor got a better look at him. Like a drug, a huge dose of fear brought changes to his body. His pupils expanded, a tingling sensation spread through him, his jaw muscles cramped, and his skin became hotter. He noticed the scar on Harrison's temple was shaped like a butterfly.

"Did you like the movie?" Harrison asked. "Be honest, okay? It was my directorial debut after all. I wouldn't call it my first 'performance,' though. Before that movie, I guess you could have thought of me as a... 'stage actor' per se. I didn't record the first few. I broke into the homes and *slaughtered* those families. Then, on a–a... a 'high'—a *rush*, y'know?—I sat my ass down at my computer and typed out my actions in short story form. My fingers were working faster than my mind. I mean, I was putting words together in ways I never really thought of before. I guess you probably experienced something like that when you first started writing, huh?"

Nestor was quiet, eyes fixed on his captor's scar. Although he had spent weeks searching for him, it was hard for him to believe his stalker was sitting before him. People caught butterflies every day, but this 'butterfly' had caught him. He thought about the short story he had received in the mail: *The Castillo Family Murder*. When he had first read it, he believed it was a work of fiction. Now, he wondered if Harrison had actually committed those violent murders. He feared he was in the presence of a sadistic serial killer.

"Oh, c'mon," Harrison said. "I know you can't speak with that tape over your mouth and I can't take it off —*yet*—but you could at least nod or shake your head."

Nestor wasn't in a position to argue, so he nodded.

"That's it. That's what I like to see," the captor said. "So, let me keep it simple for now. Yes or no questions only. About my little movie, did you recognize the scene? Did it look familiar?"

Nestor shook his head.

Harrison blew out a frustrated sigh, then said, "You can't expect anyone else to respect you if you don't respect yourself. The power drill, the hammer to the tits, the throat slitting, I took it all from your old books. The good ones. Sure, I took some artistic liberties with the oranges and the rectal drilling—I know your version was in the vagina—but everything else was accurate. The 'blood' oranges weren't bad, by the way. I recreated those scenes because I wanted to... to reach you. That's all I've been trying to do this whole time. Since you threw away my last story without reading it—I saw it in your trash in case you're wondering how I knew that—I had to do something drastic to get your attention. I had to get to *my* point before you got to *your* point of no return. You get what I'm saying?"

Again, Nestor shook his head, aghast and confused. A lance of guilt spiked his gut. He felt responsible for Candace's death. He had written so many murders and devised so many torture methods for his books that he couldn't remember if his writing had inspired the slaughter of the Castillo family as well. *Did a baby die because of me?* he asked himself. Tears welled in his eyes as images of his daughter flashed in his mind.

Harrison continued, "I guess I shouldn't be expecting you to understand all of this so soon. It's *a lot* to take in, right? You have a lot of questions. I have a lot of answers. You probably noticed my scar. I don't think I need to explain this to you, but just in case your brain's not functioning at a hundred percent because of that nasty blow to your head—sorry about that, by the way—this is why I call myself 'Butterfly.' It looks just like one, huh? And I'm sure you know this already as well, but I'm your biggest fan. Seriously, Nestor, if anyone else says otherwise, it would be blasphemy. And the punishment for blasphemy is... death. So, I'll kill 'em for... blaspheming? Is that a word? Whatever. The point is, I won't hesitate to kill 'em if they do it."

Nestor could tell Harrison liked the sound of his own voice by the way he spoke. He imagined he had been practicing his speeches in front of a mirror. *A stage actor,* he thought. He had a hard time focusing on his rambling considering the circumstances. He was still struggling to accept the fact that he was being held hostage by a psychotic, murderous fan.

He was aware of the true horrors of the world. Someone, somewhere, was being murdered or tortured every minute of the day. Although he had been preparing for the worst, he felt like this wasn't supposed to happen to people like him. It happened to strangers. It happened to neighbors. It happened to friends of friends.

But not him.

Harrison said, "You probably think I'm here because I want you to write me a story. I wouldn't blame you if you did. I was kinda harsh towards your books in my emails. You wanna know why I'm *really* here? Why this was so important to me?"

Nestor didn't respond in any way. The killer interpreted his silence as a yes. He got comfortable, turning his upper body to face his prisoner, bringing his right leg up onto the bed, then tucking his right foot under his other thigh.

He said, "We have a connection. You can't see it. Others definitely can't see it. But we can *feel* it. At the

beginning of your career, you published a book titled
'The Demons We Inherit.' I don't need to tell you what
it's about. You wrote that *masterpiece* after all. But I'm
here because of a scene in that book. The main character, a kid named Cameron, experiences something
horrific in the opening chapter. His alcoholic father
had killed and cooked his dog—his *best* friend in the
whole wide world—because Cameron had forgotten to
do his chores for the hundredth time. Terrible, right?
But it gets worse. It always does in your books, huh?
Dad orders the boy to *eat* his dog. Cameron reluctantly
tries because he wants to protect his siblings from his
father's wrath. But he struggles with it. One thing leads
to another and, next thing you know, a big fight erupts
in the house. Dad breaks a whiskey bottle against his
son's face, then murders Cameron's bedridden mother
in front of him. It's such a *vicious* opening. I've read the
reviews for that book. People called it 'trauma porn.'
They said it was far-fetched. Said it was unrealistic and
gratuitous. Said no one ever suffered from abuse like
that. But they were wrong."

He took a break to let his words sink in. The smile
had left his face and the excitement in his eyes had
fizzled out. He was deep in thought, ruminating. He
was making direct eye contact with his prisoner, but it
looked like he was staring straight through him.

He said, "They don't understand that life itself is
gratuitous. In the grander scheme of things, our lives
are meaningless. No one asks to be born, right?

Therefore, gratuitousness is ingrained in human nature. And they don't see the true *suffering* people experience every day. The type of suffering that's too morbid even for the mainstream media and their sensational ways. That chapter, Nestor... It is a near-exact reflection of my childhood. The names are different, the house is different, but everything else is identical. It was like I was reading my memoirs. At first, I was... *baffled.* I wondered if you were my long-lost brother or one of the responding officers from that fateful night or a journalist or something like that. But the more I looked into you and the more I read your books, the harder it was for me to reject the truth."

Nestor said something unintelligible.

"You're asking: *What truth?*" Harrison said.

He was right, and that made Nestor's skin crawl. After five seconds of silence, the author nodded.

Harrison said, "The truth is... Our souls are intertwined." Nestor narrowed his eyes and cocked his head to the side. The killer continued, "And it's not just about 'The Demons We Inherit.' You've been writing about me—*to me*—for years. There's a part of my life in *every... single... horror book...* you've ever written. In 'Red Light,' the main character, Taylor, gets into a fight with a pimp at a brothel. He gets stabbed twice in the lower abdomen. The same thing happened to me in my early twenties. It was on the local news in Elko, Nevada. You can look it up yourself. Not now, obviously, but whenever you get the chance. Hell, I even have the scars to prove it."

The killer lifted his t-shirt, revealing the two straight one-and-a-half-inch-long scars just above his left hip. Nestor studied the marks with an expression that said: *What the fuck?*

"Still don't believe me?" Harrison asked. "All right. Okay. I've got another good one for you. This one goes beyond your books. Guess what day I was born."

Nestor didn't know why, but a date immediately popped into his mind. He sniffled. A blink sent warm tears rolling down his cheeks. Again, he spoke unintelligibly.

"November 10, 1987," Harrison said. "It's right around the corner. That was your guess, wasn't it?"

The author nodded.

"Then you were right," Harrison said. "Your birthday is *our birthday*. I bet we were born at the exact same minute, too. Maybe even the same second. Morning, right? *Early* morning, hmm?"

Yet again, the killer was correct. Nestor found himself questioning everything. His birthdate was public knowledge, but he couldn't remember mentioning his time of birth to anyone other than Mina once early in their relationship during a casual conversation. He thought back to his writing. He ended every book with a letter to his readers. In those letters, he discussed his writing process and upcoming projects as well as his personal life. But he had written so many books—so many letters—that he couldn't recall all of the information he had shared.

Harrison stood up. He rotated his shoulders and stretched his legs, then walked to the foot of the bed. He looked down at his captor.

"I understand we're different people with different families and different backgrounds," he said. "But I feel like we share the same mind—the same *soul*. I believe our connection has given you... visions of my life. Visions that you used to create your books. You've never seen me or heard my voice before. We've already been through that. But maybe—*maybe*, Nestor—you've walked in my shoes and seen through my eyes in your dreams. Well, nightmares, I suppose. That's what my life has been since I was born after all. You know that already, though. I need to get to the point, don't I?"

He started pacing up and down at the foot of the bed. Nestor followed him with his eyes without moving his head.

The killer said, "I believe our connection weakened when you moved away from the extreme horror genre —from my reality. I tried contacting you several times so we could rebuild our connection and get to the bottom of this... phenomenon, but my correspondences went unanswered. I share some of the blame. I had to switch emails because I was 'put away' for a short while and I lost access to the old address. The one I used to contact you for the first time, remember? It was something about, uh... two-factor authentication. Lost my old phone number, forgot the answer to my security question, so I gave up on the account. But now I'm just giving you excuses. How about this?" He stopped pacing and pivoted on his heels to face him. Holding an index finger up, he said, "We're both at fault. Sound good?"

Nestor just stared at him. A fresh flood of tears filled his eyes, making his vision hazy. He welcomed his distorted sight, though, because it turned his captor into a featureless human-shaped figure. He felt better facing a boogeyman than a human monster.

"Good," Harrison said, taking his silence as acceptance. "Anyway... *the point*. I realized you couldn't 'feel' me anymore. That's why you stopped responding to my messages and quit writing extreme horror books. I was the muse you never knew you had and, for some reason, you either couldn't hear me or you decided to ignore me. Our connection got weaker and weaker and weaker. So, I had to speak louder, make more noise, so that we could hear each other again. And you know what they say, actions speak louder than words. Tonight, we're going to reconnect. But, before we do that, we need to take some precautionary measures. Safety first, right?"

Throat clogged up with sputum, Nestor finally let out a choked sob.

21

FOR BOTH OUR SAKES

"I LEARNED THIS FROM YOU, Y'KNOW?" HARRISON SAID AS he dug through the duffel bag next to the dresser, crouched with his back to the bed. "You ever notice how many of your books end with the same, uh... cliché? 'Trope' might be the word I'm looking for, I'm not sure, but you get what I'm saying anyway, don't you? Someone always ends up restrained and tortured at the end of your novels. Tied to a bed. Tied to a chair in the kitchen. Tied to a pillar. Is that why you quit? Couldn't think of anything new?"

He paused, as if giving his gagged prisoner a moment to answer. Nestor wasn't interested in an analytical discussion about his books, though. The nightmare unfolding before his very eyes gripped him. He still couldn't believe it was real. He watched Harrison from the bed, whimpering and jerking his limbs helplessly. He saw him pull a claw hammer and a box of common nails out. The intruder placed them on the floor next to him, then plunged his hands back into the bag.

Harrison said, "It didn't bother me. Not really. Even if I did start to notice it, I was okay with it. I understood what you were going for. I was entertained. I just wanted to read more of your stories. I wanted to hear your voice like you were hearing mine. That was all." He took a bottle of rubbing alcohol out of the bag before continuing. "But some of the reviews were kinda harsh, weren't they? No, that would be putting it lightly. They were *brutal.* Some people take things too literal, right? They'll be like... like... 'Hair can't lick your shoulders' or... or 'Voices can't wade.' Or how about those readers who can't put themselves in other people's shoes?"

His hand came out of the bag with a pair of kitchen shears. He stood up and walked over to the side of the bed.

Wagging the shears, he continued, "If something doesn't align perfectly with *their* experience, then they can't believe it. They think it's impossible that someone would go out and do something as simple as getting revenge. Either way, at the end of the day, it's fiction. Sure, you based some scenes on my life and other true crimes but it's still a novel. What *they* would have done in these situations doesn't matter because *they* are not the characters in your stories. I never understood why they didn't get that."

He took a seat at the foot of the bed. Nestor couldn't break free from the handcuffs but he managed to slide his torso to the other side of the mattress. He lifted his head from the pillows and screamed. Despite the tape over his mouth, his cry was clear.

'*Stop!*'

Staying on topic, Harrison said, "I want you to know that I don't share their opinions, regardless of what I may have said in my messages to you. I was only copying what they were saying because I was angry, and angry people do irrational things. You understand that, right? No hard feelings?" Nestor sobbed and shook his head frantically. The intruder smiled and said, "Wow. I wasn't expecting you to be so forgiving. Well, I appreciate it. It'll be a while until you earn my forgiveness, though. We have a lot to talk about. But before we get to that, to make sure you don't try anything stupid for both our sakes, I'm going to hobble you. Just like in your books."

'*Stop!*' the author tried to scream again.

Harrison climbed onto the bed and pressed his knee into Nestor's right thigh, pinning down his leg. He opened the shears, then slid one of the blades under the crook of his knee. He tilted the shears upward. A sharp pain rippled across Nestor's leg as a blade cut into his popliteal fossa—the 'kneepit.' Although the shears were cool, it felt like a heated rod of stainless steel—so hot that he imagined it had turned blue—was wiggling around *in* his knee. The blade scraped away at his femur and tibia bones. Blood dripped out of the cut, hitting the bedsheet in a rapid succession of *plops*.

Harrison squeezed the shears' handles. The blades cut through the bony hamstring tendon at the back of Nestor's knee with a *crunch*. Nestor shut his eyes, arched his back, and moved his shoulders like a seesaw. He ground his teeth and groaned loudly. Having lost his bearings, he didn't notice Harrison adjusting himself on top of his leg. The intruder slid a blade under the other side of his knee, then twisted the shears and tilted them up. He closed them, slicing the side of his knee, tearing through his kneepit, and severing his other tendon with one snip.

Out of breath, Nestor could only whine. His leg trembled uncontrollably, blood streaking the bedsheet in crimson dotted lines. He could barely manage to crack his eyes open—partially because his heart was poisoned with fear, partially because his brain was overloaded with pain. He saw Harrison situating himself on top of his left leg. He knew what was coming next, so he closed his eyes, held his breath, and gritted his teeth with dread.

One by one, Harrison cut the tendons at the back of his other knee. Nestor felt them *snap* and heard them *pop*. His legs, covered in sweat and blood, were blazing with pain.

Harrison got off the bed and said, "Don't worry, pal. I'm going to patch you up when we're done... but we're not done yet. You might not be able to run comfortably, but if you somehow broke free from those handcuffs and distracted me or knocked me out or *killed me*, you'd be able to limp out of here. We don't want that. That's why we need these precautionary measures. You know all of this already, right? You came up with them after all."

He tucked the bloody shears in his pocket, careful not to cut through the thin fabric. He gathered the rest of his supplies—the hammer, the bottle of rubbing alcohol, the box of nails—carrying them in his arms like a bundle of twigs for a campfire.

He said, "I know it's not exactly like what you wrote in your books. You always go for their Achilles tendons. But I thought it would be more interesting this way. I figured we could subvert expectations. How do you think this is going to end? You get away with some life-altering injuries, inspired to write again? Or maybe there's a plot twist, hmm? Like, uh... you find out your wife and daughter have been in the other room the whole time?"

Nestor's eyes flew open upon hearing the suggestion. Despite the tape over his lips, he yelled out two clear words over and over: '*Mina! Melody! Mina! Melody!*'

Over his screaming, Harrison asked, "You like that one? No? Well, the cops could come in here and shoot me. Or—*or*—maybe we get the 'good' ending: You and I become best friends. We'll see. We'll see." He walked to the door, then stopped and looked at his prisoner. He said, "I'll be back. Even if you see an opportunity, don't you get off that bed. I have a gun on me. If you fight me, I'll kill you. I *really* don't want to do that. I don't know how our 'soul connection' works after all. If I kill you, I might end up killing myself, too, and I don't want that. Not yet at least."

Harrison exited the room, leaving the door wide open behind him. The hallway was pitch black. His footsteps wandered away, dying out halfway down the stairs. Nestor kept screaming for his wife and daughter, tears running down his face. He wondered if Harrison was toying with him or if his family was actually in another room. He pictured them, bound and gagged in his office, then in the nursery, then in the storage closet. He was worried his daughter would suffocate if she had a strip of tape over her mouth.

'*Take it off! She'll die! Don't let her die! Take it off!*' he tried to yell but every word came out as a blurt of nonsense.

Lightheaded from the lack of oxygen, he stopped screaming and started panting through his nose. He whined as he stared at the door and listened for a response. The silence in the other rooms provided him with a pinch of relief. He only heard the sound of his breathing and the handcuffs rattling as his legs trembled.

They're not here, he told himself.

He looked at his kneecaps. A cold, concerning

tingly sensation spread around the wounds while hot blood tickled his skin. He glanced around in search of an escape route. Breaking the bedposts was his best bet. He tried to pull his limbs inward towards his torso, but as soon as he lifted his knees an inch, fiery pain pulsed through his legs.

The mattress vibrated as he let his knees drop. Fresh blood streamed out of his mutilated kneepits. He roared in pain, then went back to panting.

Staring at the ceiling, he thought about Harrison's words. *Are we really connected?* he wondered. The idea of having a mysterious muse watching over him had never crossed his mind. Some of the scenes in his books were, in fact, inspired by his nightmares, though. The coincidences were uncanny, too.

But coincidences could be fabricated.

He's lying, Nestor told himself. *He has to be lying. He's just copying my books. He's creating the 'connection' himself.*

He controlled his breathing and steadied his legs to minimize the pain. He glanced around the room. He had slept in that room nearly every day for several years, but now it felt unfamiliar and filthy and dangerous. He saw himself as a human experiment in a spaceship about to get probed by an alien—as a victim in a serial killer's dungeon about to get tortured repeatedly.

He looked to his right—to his wife's side of the bed. He wished Mina was there, lying next to him, telling him everything was going to be okay.

'It's good that you're not here,' he tried to say out loud, as if he were speaking to someone.

He turned his attention to the window to his left. It was covered in tape, so he couldn't see anything outside. He couldn't remember when he was rendered unconscious and he had no idea how long he had been out. He figured he was knocked out for at least twenty minutes, though; enough time for Harrison to heave him into the bedroom, disrobe him, and handcuff him.

He was hoping someone—his wife, a neighbor, a mailman, anyone—would show up at his door, notice the tape over the windows, and notify the police of suspicious activity.

The sound of unhurried footsteps at the stairs interrupted his thoughts. They grew louder in the hallway.

Harrison emerged in the doorway. Wearing gloves now, he was holding the hammer in one hand and a ceramic bowl in the other. The box of nails and bottle of rubbing alcohol were gone. He walked up to his prisoner and checked the bedposts.

"You didn't do anything stupid," he said. "Good. I appreciate that. I'm sorry about the wait. Had to make sure these were nice and hot. Heard it makes the penetration easier."

'Penetration.' Nestor's heart skipped a beat upon hearing that word. He lifted his head from the pillow, shook his head, and babbled incoherently.

Harrison chuckled, then said, "Sorry, not *that* kind

of penetration. This is not a... a 'sexual' thing. I'm sure you understand that. Anyway, let me get to the point before these things cool down. I'm going to continue hobbling you. These nails..." He shook the bowl, making the nails clatter inside, before continuing, "They've been sterilized with rubbing alcohol, then I heated them up on your stove. It should be a clean job as long as you don't fight me. Once we're done with this, I'll clean and bandage your wounds. Then we can take that tape off your mouth and get to business. Got it?"

Nestor wagged his head quicker and, although he didn't make a lick of sense, he spoke faster.

"Great," Harrison said with a grin. "Let's get to work."

He placed the bowl on the foot of the bed between Nestor's legs. Then he knelt on the author's right shin, holding the leg down while aggravating the wounds at the back of his knee. The author slammed the back of his head against the pillow and bawled. Harrison held one of the nails up to the front of Nestor's ankle and swung his hammer at it. The hot nail sank *into* his ankle. A big drop of blood dribbled out.

Nestor squinched his face up in agony. Traces of rubbing alcohol on the nail sent throbs of stinging pain up his leg. It amplified the agony in his knee, too.

Harrison struck the nail's head again, driving it deeper into his ankle joint. It stopped with a crack upon breaking his talus bone, right under his tibia.

The killer took another nail out of the bowl. He pressed the sharp tip against Nestor's sole at the hind-foot and hit it. The nail entered his heel from below, cracking the calcaneus bone. He gave it another tap to make sure it wouldn't fall out.

Nestor's body tightened up, jaw and fists clenched. He wanted to fall unconscious, but his body—his survival instincts—forced him to draw shallow breaths.

Another nail.

This one Harrison hammered into the center of Nestor's sole. A splash of blood leapt out of the wound as the nail skewered a muscle. It ended up wedged between a pair of metatarsal bones. He took a fourth nail out of the bowl. Although Nestor was shaking like a mechanical bull, he used the hammer to drive the nail through the ball of his foot.

He wasn't done, though.

The fifth and sixth nails pierced the arch at the inner side of his foot. The seventh one went through the top of his foot, stuck between a *different* pair of metatarsal bones. Then the eighth nail impaled his Achilles tendon horizontally. With each *thud* from the hammer, wet crackling and crunching and crinkling noises came from his foot.

"One down, one to go," Harrison said as he climbed onto the bed.

Although parts of his foot had gone numb during the torture, Nestor was in a pain-induced stupor. There was nothing on his mind. He only wanted the suffering to end. Harrison knelt on Nestor's left shin. He scooped another nail out of the bowl, held it up against the front of his victim's ankle, then struck it with the hammer.

He repeated the torture, following the playbook in his head to a T. He hammered the nails into Nestor's foot in all the same places as the other one. He missed a few swings, beating his foot and hitting the mattress a couple of times. Circular patches of blood stained the bedsheet under the prisoner's feet, growing with each hit.

Nestor felt fresh surges of pain blasting through his left leg. The nails had cooled down but the coats of rubbing alcohol lingered. His skin went numb quickly but he felt like the insides of his feet—the muscles, the tendons, the veins—were on fire. He didn't have the energy to continue fighting, hanging onto consciousness by a thread.

Once he was finished with his left foot, Harrison got off the bed and examined his work. He had turned Nestor's feet into two bloody maces of flesh. He dragged his gaze to his prisoner's face. Nestor's eyes, empty and glazed over, were half-lidded and fixed on the ceiling. The color faded from his cheeks. He had gotten a grip on his breathing, though.

"Oh, don't be so melodramatic," Harrison said. "It wasn't *that* bad. In fact, I tried to make it as easy as possible for you. I could have waited minutes between each nail, could have toyed with you, could have covered your legs in nails from your toes to your hips. But no. I worked *fast* and *clean*. I stuck to the plan and got the job done. Just look at yourself."

He walked to the foot of the bed and bent over, giving himself a closer look at Nestor's nailed feet. The skin around the nails was swelling, red and bruised.

He said, "Listen, I know what you're thinking. It would have been easier for the both of us if I had just stuck to your script and severed your Achilles tendons. I considered it. I really did. But I don't know. I guess I wanted to impress you. I bet you weren't expecting it to go down like this. No. No way. I subverted your expectations, didn't I? Mission accomplished?"

Nestor didn't answer. His torso only moved when he breathed. Harrison stood straight and looked back at his prisoner's face, disappointed by his lack of response. He grumbled indistinctly and went to his duffel bag, then returned to the foot of the bed moments later with a pack of gauze pads in one hand and a gauze roll in the other.

He said, "Well, you'd be proud of me if you weren't the victim. Anyway, I promised I'd patch you up when we were done and... we're done... for now. And I like to keep my promises." He walked to the side of the bed before saying, "Remember, I sterilized everything, so the chances of you dying from an infection should be slim to none. Still, I'll clean and bandage you up to control the bleeding. You know, I actually didn't want to do this to..."

Nestor's ears rang as Harrison pressed a gauze pad against the back of his mangled knee, reigniting the pain. His head spun on the pillow, the walls and ceiling revolving and swirling around him. An avalanche of pain left him disoriented. He couldn't tell up from down or left from right. He caught glimpses of Harrison. He saw his mouth moving but he couldn't hear his voice. His eyes rolled up, then he passed out.

22

CHATTING

Eyes heavy with sleep, Nestor awoke to Harrison humming the tune of *Here's to You* by Joan Baez and Ennio Morricone. He lifted his head slightly from the pillow and looked down at himself. His knees and feet were swathed in bloodstained gauze rolls. Nails stuck out from between the bandages around his feet. His legs were propped up on two throw pillows under his calves.

The humming stopped.

Nestor looked to his right. Next to the bed, Harrison sat on a dining chair he had brought from downstairs.

"Hey," he said. "Thought I lost you. I knew you weren't dead, but I don't know so much about comas. I wasn't keeping track of time, but I'd say you were at least out for forty-five minutes. Maybe an hour. I hope those pillows weren't important to you. I took them from the sofas in your living room. I just wanted to make you comfortable. That okay with you?"

Nestor was anything but comfortable. Echoes of pain lingered in his aching legs, reminding him of the torture. It wasn't as bad thanks to the numbness around the wounds, though. Yet, he didn't dare move a muscle below his hips out of fear of restarting his suffering. Nevertheless, he nodded at Harrison. He was hoping appeasement would open the door to mercy.

"Good," Harrison said with a little smile. "I've had a lot of time to think about my actions and our future. We're not going to make any progress unless we communicate. You've been listening to me all night, but it's not a conversation if I'm the only one speaking, right? So, can I take that tape off your mouth?"

Nestor nodded again, this time with more enthusiasm. With his nose clogged up, he just wanted to breathe through his mouth.

"We have a lot to talk about, huh?" Harrison said. "But you have to promise we're going to talk in peace. No screaming. No spitting. No biting. Just *talking*. If you do anything stupid, I'm going to put that tape back over your mouth, then I'm going to give you a prostate exam with my hammer. Might even use the claw to tear that little 'walnut' out through your asshole. Are we clear?"

Nestor was scared shitless by the threat. Although he hadn't planned on fighting him, he was reluctant to accept the terms. At the same time, he assumed

Harrison was going to continue torturing him if he didn't play along anyway. He responded with another nod. The room went quiet for a few seconds.

"Good," the killer said.

He leaned closer to the bed, his ass barely rising from the chair. He peeled the tape off Nestor's mouth, tearing some of his beard hair with it. He left the strip dangling from one cheek. Mouth wide open, Nestor fought for breath. The oxygen cleared his mind and soothed his lungs. He cried feebly as he stared down at his brutalized feet.

"Well?" Harrison asked.

They locked eyes. There was awe and disbelief in Nestor's and curiosity in Harrison's.

Voice raspy from all his crying, Nestor asked, "Are you real?"

"Am I... real? Do you think I'm a figment of your imagination? You believe I'm... I'm your alter ego set free and gone wild? Or maybe I'm a character from one of your books that has somehow come to life?"

Harrison stared at him with a straight face for a few seconds before laughing. The ideas were absurd, but Nestor had been humoring them. He sought an explanation for all of the coincidences. A part of him wanted it all to be a fantasy he had unwittingly concocted in his head. He didn't want to face reality.

"Is my family okay?" he asked.

"I didn't hurt them."

"Are they here?"

"I can't show my hand or you won't cooperate. Let's focus on us."

"But... But they're okay?'

"I did *not* hurt them."

"I–I'll do whatever you say. You can do whatever you want to me. Just please don't... don't hurt them. Don't drag them into this. I'm the..."

He coughed harshly, then his breathing was wet and gurgly. His throat was sore and tight. He felt like he was choking.

"Can I... have... water?" he asked, voice softer than before.

Harrison came prepared. He went to his duffel bag and took a water bottle out. He unscrewed the cap, then bent over the bed and poured some water into Nestor's mouth little by little. He helped him drink half the bottle, then placed it on the nightstand.

"I've got something else for you," the killer said. He went to the duffel bag, then came back with a half-full bottle of whiskey. He said, "Dad's favorite. He once told me it helps with all sorts of pain. He also taught me this bottle can give one hell of a concussion—and leave one hell of a scar. You should take a swig. It'll help you relax."

"I want more water. Please."

"You've had enough water. Take a swig, Nestor. Don't make me do it the hard way."

Nestor was in no position to argue, so he tilted his head back and opened his mouth with his lips quivering. Harrison poured the whiskey slowly into his mouth, trying to eyeball a shot glass' worth of the liquid. Nestor ended up with a little less than two ounces in his mouth. He swallowed it in two gulps. It stung going down.

"Feel better?" Harrison asked as he set the bottle down on the nightstand.

"No–Not really. I need an ambulance. My head hurts. It feels like it's going to explode. I'm lightheaded and I feel like I'm going to throw up. My chest aches, too. I–I could have a heart attack. And my feet are... *fucked*, man. They–They're going to have to... Oh fuck, they're going to amputate them. Shit, I could even bleed out."

"You won't bleed out."

"I don't wanna die like that," Nestor whined, tears racing down his cheeks. "Don't let me bleed out. Please don't. I don't wanna die. Don't let me die."

"Calm down."

"I–I'm sorry if I did anything to offend you. I swear, I'm so sorry. If you let me live, I'll... I'll do whatever you–"

"*Calm. Down,*" Harrison interrupted, raising his voice. Nestor closed his mouth but kept crying. The intruder said, "You're not going to die. Not from this. I bandaged your injuries so you wouldn't bleed out. I'm not a doctor or a nurse, but I know what I'm doing. Besides, your books taught me that humans are capable of amazing feats of survival."

Nestor whimpered louder. From his research into grisly accidents, true crimes, and real snuff videos, he knew some people died easily and others were like cockroaches. He had seen people survive for several minutes after being dismembered and even bisected during car wrecks, having their torsos skinned and dissected, and getting their heads scalped and set aflame.

But it wasn't really survival because all of those cases ended with death. It was more like the human body's natural resilience—and a whole lot of bad luck for the victim.

"What do you want from me?" Nestor asked.

"I told you already," Harrison responded as he sat on the dining chair.

"The... connection?"

"Our connection, yes."

"Even if you were right about... about all of that, what can I do about it? What do you... God, just tell me what you want me to do. I–I'll do it. I'll do anything. Then you can... you can let me go, right? If–If I cooperate, you'll let me go, right?"

"It's not about letting go, Nestor. It's about coming together. In order to do that, I suppose we have to find out why our connection weakened in the first place. So, let me ask you something. Why did you stop writing extreme horror? Why did you stop writing to me?"

Nestor hesitated to respond. One wrong word

could have led to another session of torture. But only the truth came to mind.

"I'm sorry, but I was never writing to you," he said. "I didn't know about you before tonight. If there was a connection... I never felt it. I don't know what the hell is going on with my books and your life. I just know that I need a doctor. Can you please let me go?"

Disregarding his request, Harrison responded, "It's only the two of us in here. There's no need to lie anymore. You don't have to worry about your wife thinking you're going crazy. You don't have to worry about your publisher, either. It's not like I'm accusing you of plagiarism. I'm not trying to extort you. I'm not going to sue you. You're safe with me. I promise."

"I *wasn't* writing about you or to you. I'm telling you, I–I've never had any dreams or–or visions about your life. It–It's a misunderstanding. I know it's hard to believe—even I'm struggling to understand this—but they're all coincidences. Please believe me. Don't do this. Don't hurt me anymore. I'm begging you. I'm begging you. I'm begging you."

"Coincidences? A coincidence is a fan meeting his favorite author on a train or a plane. A coincidence is–"

"Oh fuck, my feet hurt so much."

"–meeting someone with your exact same name. We're talking about something beyond coincidences. I've given you so much evidence to prove our lives are intertwined."

"You haven't given me anything!" Nestor snapped, losing his temper.

Harrison was taken aback by the roar. Like a boy scolded by his parents in public, tears stung his eyes and his cheeks turned red.

Nestor yelled, "A coincidence is sharing a fucking birthday with someone! A coincidence is seeing... seeing resemblances to your life in books and movies, man! They're coincidences! And I don't even know if you're telling the truth about them. Your birthday could be some other day. You could have given yourself those scars, you psycho!"

Rocking to and fro in his seat, Harrison's face alternated between a grimace of embarrassment and a scowl of rage. Nestor felt a pang of regret in his stomach. He could tell he had pushed him too far.

He said, "I'm sorry, but this is all wrong. You've been seeing things that aren't there. If you help me, I can help you, but you have to let me go. Please stop this. I... I have a family."

"*Fuck you,*" Harrison hissed through his gritted teeth.

"Please."

"We are one!" the killer growled as he jumped from his seat. "One soul shared by two bodies! One sickness shared by two minds! We must come together! That is our destiny!"

Nestor was shocked by his deep, gravelly voice. Moving his head from side to side, he followed the intruder as he paced around the bed, floorboards howling with each step.

Harrison continued, "And you can't run from destiny. But *someone* tried to stop it. You're protecting them. I know it. I felt it before. Your agent? I know she was part of the reason you abandoned us. She wanted you to switch to a more popular genre so you could sell more books and she could make more money. I know that already. But it's not her. It can't be her. She's already out of the picture."

"Don't do this."

"Was it because of the critics? No, not personal enough, huh? Was it your wife? Mina? No, no. You were still writing to me when she came around. It was the baby, wasn't it? Yes... *Yes.*"

"No! Leave them out of this!"

The sound of the creaking floorboards came to an end as Harrison stopped at the foot of the bed.

He pointed at Nestor with both index fingers and said, "You haven't been the same ever since she was born. You went soft. You used to write that–"

"Stop it!"

"–hardcore shit and now you write fantasies about queens and princesses and social justice and all that bullshit. You turned your back on us!"

"I didn't owe you shit!"

"You turned your back on yourself! You betrayed *yourself,* Nestor! I see it now! I get it now! We made you who you were, then you threw it all away because you had a baby. You subconsciously talked yourself into... into self-destruction. It's like that saying, 'You are your own worst enemy.' You sabotaged yourself, and in the process, you sabotaged our connection. Maybe you didn't know it, maybe you didn't do it on purpose, but you're the reason our 'link' weakened."

Nestor shook his head and said, "You're out of your mind."

"And you wanna know something else?" Harrison prattled on. "We have, in fact, been living vicariously through each other. It's like I theorized earlier: If I kill you, I die. You self-destructed mentally with the birth of Melody–"

"Don't say her name, you son of a bitch."

"–and so did I. That's why I'm here now. I lost control of myself because *you* lost control of yourself. You were scared of being a dad, scared of your daughter finding all of the horrors you wrote, so you started spiraling."

"Wha–What?"

Nestor was dumbstruck. Although his claims could apply to most parents—prenatal anxiety wasn't rare after all, especially among first-time parents—Harrison was right. Before Melody's birth, Nestor had struggled with the fear of becoming a father. Considering he frequently depicted taboo themes and hyper-violence in his books, including violence committed against children, he no longer felt comfortable writing extreme horror with a daughter on the way, either, so he switched genres.

How does he know this? he wondered. *It's impossible. He's guessing. But how is he always guessing correctly? Coincidences? Or is it destiny? Is he...*

A bank of brain fog gassed his mind, derailing his train of thoughts. He squeezed his eyes shut as the first dull thud of a migraine pounded the right side of his skull.

Harrison stepped to the side of the bed and said, "You always used to say you were nothing without your readers. Well, I think I speak for all of us when I say we're nothing without you. We need to re-establish our connection. We need to come together to bring balance to the universe."

"No," Nestor cried. "You're wrong. You have to be wrong. This is crazy. What is happening?"

Harrison gave him a death stare and asked, "After everything I said, you're still rejecting me? Still rejecting the truth?"

"You need to stop this, man. Sooner or later, someone's going to show up and notice something's wrong. My neighbors are going to wake up soon if they're not awake already. They'll go jogging or biking like they always do and they're going to hear me scream. They used to hear Melody cry, so they can hear me. I know they can. Let me go, call an ambulance, then leave. I won't tell anyone anything about you, I swear."

"You really haven't been listening to me, have you?

You say you're willing to give me what I want, but you're still trying to get away from me. I guess I have to teach you a lesson."

"No, God..."

"And don't worry about the noise. No one is coming to save you."

Nestor looked at the window to his right and shouted, "Help! Help! He's killing me! Somebody help me! Somebody–"

He shrieked and convulsed as his foot burned. During his panic, he hadn't noticed Harrison had taken the bottle of whiskey from the nightstand. He was pouring the alcohol on Nestor's feet. It came out with a glugging sound. The handcuffs clinked and clanked while the bed frame groaned and thudded against the wall. The ruckus reached the street in front of the house and the lake in the back but no one was around to hear it.

"You see?!" Harrison shouted as the last drop left the bottle. "No one is coming to save you!"

Nestor entered a cycle of gasping for air, screaming, gasping, screaming, and gasping. The gauze rolls were doused in alcohol. The whiskey ran down the nails' shanks and seeped into the wounds, flowing deep into his feet. The hot pain rose through his body, colliding with the throbs from his migraine.

Holding the bottle by its neck, Harrison swung it at Nestor's head. It exploded against the left side of his face, shards flying in every direction. There was a deep slash above his eyebrow. Smaller cuts were scattered across his forehead, nose, and cheek. The glass opened a nasty, circular gash on his left temple, too.

It reminded Harrison of the butterfly-shaped scar on his own forehead.

Nestor was knocked unconscious by the blow. A strip of blood covered his eyes like a domino mask. After five seconds of snoring, he began twitching and screaming with his eyes closed, as if he were experiencing a night terror. Harrison held the broken bottle up to his neck. The shards dimpled his skin, so close to piercing it.

Harrison said, "I should cut your throat open just like my father did to my mother. It would be so damn easy... but I'm not ready to give up yet. I have hope. I believe in us." He threw the broken bottle aside. He stroked Nestor's forehead and said, "You don't get what I'm saying to you. You're not seeing straight. It's time to open your eyes."

He elbowed his face, sending him back into the abyss of unconsciousness.

23

AN EYE-OPENING EXPERIENCE

THE RIGHT SIDE OF NESTOR'S VISION FADED IN AND flickered, like an old lightbulb turning on. He saw a blur of red and orange. He tasted blood in his mouth. The elbow to the face had left him with a busted nose. The sting from the cuts on his face couldn't compete with the stabbing pain in his right eye socket. It was worse—*sharper*—than his regular migraines, though. When he tried to move, he found his head was taped down to the mattress at the jaw and forehead.

He groaned as the pain in his right eye socket increased. He felt something pinching and tugging on his upper eyelid. He felt something else—something cold and hard—grazing the top of his eyeball, too. His other eye fluttered open. Everything was blurred, although he could see the ceiling and the headboard.

From the side of the bed, Harrison leaned into his

eyesight. He gripped Nestor's jaw tightly to stop his head from moving.

"Careful," he said softly. "You don't want to panic. No, no, don't panic or it'll get worse for you."

"My–My eye hurts," Nestor stuttered. "I–I can't blink."

"And you don't *want* to blink. Not with what I've done to you."

"Wha–What? Why? What... What did you do to me?"

"I put a fishhook through your upper eyelid. The fishing line–"

"God," Nestor sobbed.

"–is tied around the headboard. It's wound tight. If you blink, your eyelid will be torn off like a Band-Aid."

"God," the author repeated, his voice cracking.

He had gone to church a few times when he was a child, but he wasn't a religious person. He couldn't remember the last time he prayed. Yet, racked by pain and abandoned by the world, 'God' was the only word that came to mind. Out of options and facing unending torment, he unthinkingly placed his hopes on a divine intervention to save his life.

Harrison said, "But blinking is only a reflex, Nestor. We do it to keep our eyes moisturized. You won't have to blink because your blood and tears will work as a lubricant. You might be feeling a strong urge right now, but after a few minutes, you'll be fine. And this isn't going to take very long anyway."

"God..."

Harrison moved away from Nestor's line of sight. Nestor could hear him moving things around on the nightstand. He had control of his eyes, but he was too scared to move. He kept his eyes stuck on the ceiling. He felt a warm liquid trickling down the side of his face. He wasn't sure if it was a tear or a drop of blood.

Don't blink, don't blink, don't blink, he repeated to himself quietly.

"You're not seeing the big picture, Nestor," Harrison said. "We need to open your eyes before it's too late. If we don't fix our connection, if we don't come together as *one*, we will... *perish*. That's the correct word, isn't it? I'm saying we need each other to survive in this world. Does that make sense to you?"

Don't blink, don't blink, don't blink.

Harrison reappeared in Nestor's vision and said, "I read your memoirs, *Violent, Cruel, Disturbing and Unusual*. I bought a signed copy from you, actually. You wanna know some other so-called 'coincidences' I learned? We were both bullied in elementary school. You said you were a loner. So was I. You said you were jumped in a bathroom in fifth grade. So was I."

"I–I'm going to... to blink. I need to... blink."

"We both had abusive parents," Harrison said. "My dad—my *real* dad—beat me and my siblings every day. He beat us real bad until he got locked up. Then, after we were all separated, my adoptive father molested me for years. Your mother liked to lock you in the basement for weeks—windows covered, no lights, no sound, no company."

"I'm gonna blink, I'm gonna blink," Nestor blurted out. "I can't hold it."

His pierced eyelid was twitching erratically. With each twitch, the hole in the thin flap of skin expanded with a soft crackling sound. A fresh layer of blood coated his eye, blending with his tears. It lubricated it but it also stung. His lower eyelid was twitching, too, rising towards the center of his eye.

"And it wasn't to punish you," Harrison went on, dismissing Nestor's concerns. "You didn't do anything to deserve that. She just hated you and your existence. She hated you so much that she couldn't stand to see you. And when she really wanted to hurt you, she locked you in the closet or stuffed you in the drier. Somewhere cramped. My dad—my *real* dad—liked to do that to my little brother. Anyway, you, uh... you blamed your mother for your... your, um... I'm sorry, what was it called again?"

"My eyelid's ripping!" Nestor screamed, teeth clenched.

"Your condition, Nestor, what was it called? When you were in college, you said a psychiatrist suggested you may have been living with... schizo? No, I don't mean schizophrenia. I mean–"

"Schizoid! It's schizoid! Now get this fucking hook out of my eye!"

Over Nestor's crying, Harrison said, "Yes. Schizoid personality disorder. That's it. But you left before you could get any treatment. Actually, you left even before you were officially diagnosed with anything. But you felt like the diagnosis didn't matter. You said you knew it was something you can't easily recover from anyway, right? No cure? And that's why you put the tape over your windows, too, huh? You wanna say it was because of me, but it was because of your mother—because of something she put inside of *you*. Right?"

"Yes! Yes!"

Nestor wasn't just telling him what he wanted to hear. Deep down, he agreed with Harrison's assessment. The stalker acted as a catalyst to his mental breakdown, opening up his emotional scars.

"So, do you understand what I've been trying to tell you now?" Harrison asked.

"Yes!"

"Really?"

"Yes, damn it! Yes!"

"Then tell me."

"Tell you what?!"

"Tell me what you understand," Harrison said as he sat on the edge of the bed. "Tell me and I'll take that fishhook out."

Nestor's upper eyelid was close to tearing in half vertically, the fishhook holding on by a string of bloody skin. It wasn't what Harrison had imagined—he

wanted to see the eyelid tear off and fly off his face—
but it had the same effect.

Fighting to keep his eye open, Nestor stammered,
"We–We–We... have a... a connection. We... We are one.
We're like... one soul separated at birth. The same
mind born into different bodies. I–I get it. I get you."

Harrison was quiet. Despite the tape over his forehead and jaw, Nestor managed to shake his head as the
pain from his eye buzzed through him like a cold chill.
The bloody tears—more blood than tears—spilled out
of his eye socket. One stream went up to the tape on
his forehead. Another drop lined the side of his nose.
The third one tickled his cheek.

"Can you see anything from your right eye?"
Harrison asked.

"N–No."

"It's better that way."

"What... What are you saying? What are you going
to do?"

"I'm going to get that fishhook out. I hope you don't
mind. I borrowed some stuff from your bathroom."

Harrison grabbed a four-blade shaving razor from
the nightstand. He straddled Nestor's chest, his knees
under his armpits, then he thrust the razor's head into
his right eye. Nestor bellowed and instinctively tried to
shut his eye. The fishhook ripped his upper eyelid in
half vertically. A chunk of the thin skin, eyelashes
sticking out of it, was severed. It landed in Nestor's
hair.

Harrison rubbed the razor against his eyeball. The blades shredded the outermost layer of his eye—the cornea. Bloodied collagen smudged over his pupil, Nestor felt like he was looking through a glass lens smeared with red Vaseline. The white of his eye, which had been covered in blood, was now completely red with hemorrhages.

He thrashed under his captor. He even moved his legs, despite the nails in his feet and the severed tendons in his knees. The tape around his head loosened.

Harrison slapped his hand over his forehead and pressed down, stopping him from moving his head. He continued grinding the razor *into* his eye. He whittled down the iris and sclera. The mutilated tissue was swept under his lower eyelid. Then the blades cut into the choroid—the thin layer of tissue located under the sclera. More blood was leaking from his eyeball than his sliced eyelid now.

The shaving razor snapped. The detached razor cartridge sank *into* his eye, sending blood erupting out of it in geysers. The right side of Nestor's vision blackened instantly. Bloody vitreous fluid dripped from the corners of his eye. A wave of dizziness overtook him while his ears rang. He stopped thrashing but continued whimpering. The pain was unreal, overwhelming his other senses.

Harrison threw the broken handle aside and shouted, "You lied to me! You don't understand a thing, you... you... you goddamn parrot! Repetition is *not* the same as understanding! It's not!" He hopped off the bed. He muttered, "I knew you were going to lie to me. I knew it. You wouldn't give in so quickly. No way. You wouldn't ignore me for months just to understand me in a matter of minutes. You snake."

Nestor could hardly hear him over the thrumming and buzzing in his ears. He couldn't see him at all. He heard more objects moving to his right, though. For a short period, he remembered Mina waking him up every once in a while as she blindly reached for the bottle of water she kept on her bedside table during her sleep. A shaky smile tugged on his lips. The memories melted away as the bed shook.

Nestor felt one of Harrison's knees against his rib cage. He still couldn't see him, though.

The intruder said, "You need to understand that I know when you lie to me because a part of you is in me. It's like a... a beacon inside of me. It sends... signals. I knew when you were happy, sad, angry, suicidal. I knew when you were writing when I felt my fingertips tingle. I knew you were fucking your wife—*our* wife—when I was *hard* for no reason." His voice high and quavering, he said, "I can feel your pain now, and it's killing me inside. I don't want to do this to you... I don't! But I can't stop until we... we're on the same page in the same book. You get me?"

Tears glistening in his eyes, he stared down at his

prisoner. He shook his head with self-disgust. He had pared a fifth of Nestor's eyeball away. A corner of the razor cartridge stuck out of his eye.

Harrison sniffled, then said, "You need to find—*feel* —the part of me that's in you. We can't fix our connection without all of the pieces after all. Until then, I have to punish you or you won't learn."

He was holding a bottle of alcohol-based mouthwash in his hand. He tilted it and let the liquid spill onto Nestor's face. It irritated the cuts on his nose and cheek before splashing in his eyes. Some of the mouthwash flowed *into* his shaved eye, filling up its vitreous chamber. Nestor screamed for three seconds before passing out. His mind just turned off mid-scream, unable to withstand the pain. His body continued shuddering and twitching.

When he regained consciousness, his face was still burning. Due to the mouthwash swirling around in his eye, he felt a stinging sensation *in* his skull. With the buzzing in his ears and the heat in his head, he wondered if his brain was frying. He saw Harrison leaning over him through his blurred, partial vision.

"No," he whined.

Harrison shushed him, then said, "Calm down. I'm trying to help you right now. Don't fight me."

"Plee–Please don't do this."

"Calm. Down."

Nestor felt him pressing down on his right eyebrow,

then on the rim of his eye socket. Although he was gentle, Harrison's touch aggravated his butchered eye.

"It's only an eye patch," the intruder explained. "It's a sterile bandage. A good brand, I promise. It'll protect your eye—what's left of it—and stop the bleeding. Take it as a gesture of goodwill."

Nestor wanted to argue with him. '*A gesture of goodwill.*' It sounded absurd under those circumstances. It was equivalent to a man shooting a driver's tires out, causing a violent accident, then offering to change his victim's tires as a 'gesture of goodwill' during the aftermath of the wreck.

But Nestor was more scared than mad. The eye patch told him that Harrison had come prepared—that it was all premeditated. It was all part of a plan.

And it wasn't over yet.

"Are you going to kill me?" Nestor asked.

As he removed the tape from his forehead, Harrison said, "I will if I have to, but that's not why I'm here."

"I... I think I'm dying."

"You're not dying. There's still plenty of blood in you. Your pulse is irregular, but it's not alarming. You can handle another round before we take a break."

"No, no, no. Please, I–I'll do whatever you say."

"All I want you to do is think about our connection. Find the beacon inside you. Once you do, we can find a way to sync our signals."

"You don't have to do it like this! We can work together! Please!"

Peeling the tape off Nestor's jaw, Harrison said, "I'm sorry, but I have to break you to fix you. It's the only way."

"No! I'm begging you!"

"It's the only way..."

24

WRITER'S CHOICE

"If you don't call an ambulance soon, I'm going to die here," Nestor said.

Harrison was walking back and forth at the foot of the bed, talking to himself inaudibly. He seemed troubled, like he didn't want to continue the torture—or he didn't know what torture method to use next. Nestor couldn't read him. He wasn't sure if he was dealing with a remorseful person or a serial killing perfectionist.

He said, "If I die... there won't be a connection. You'll go to prison and you'll be alone."

Speaking up, Harrison responded, "You're not going to die. We're not going to die."

Then he went back to mumbling to himself.

"I know you're having second thoughts," Nestor said. "I can, um... Ow, shit, it hurts. Fucking hell, it hurts..."

With each word out of his mouth, he felt a shooting pain in his right eye. He was reluctant to move his jaw. The sense of pressure in his eye from his migraines lingered, too, mingling with the burning pain.

Barely opening his mouth, he said, "I can feel... your reluctance. We can talk about this. I can give you money."

"Money?"

"I can pay you. I have... savings. I'll transfer it all to you. You can run and–"

"You think this is about money?" Harrison interrupted, stopping dead in his tracks.

"I know it's not. It's about our connection. But you can... Ow... take the money and run. Find somewhere to lay low and maybe—I don't know—do some research on our 'phenomenon.' There has to be other cases like ours, right? And I won't tell the cops you were here. I swear I won't. When I recover, I'll contact you and... we can start again. I'll work with you. We can talk through this without the handcuffs... or nails... or any of this. Because this—*this*—isn't working. I'm going to die here. You said it yourself: You're not a doctor."

"I've been keeping track of your vitals."

"But you're *not* a doctor. You–You can't... *eyeball* how much blood I've lost. You can't tell me what I'm feeling or how much more I can tolerate. I feel... anemic. Do you know what that means?"

"*Yes,* I know what that means," Harrison said,

sneering and waving a hand at him before going back to his pacing. "I'm telling you, you're fine. I know what I'm doing. You're just trying to play me."

"I'm not, I swear. I–I can feel our conne–"

"You're lying to me! Again! You wanna 'talk' through this? You wanna 'work' together all of a sudden? I gave you that opportunity time and time again when I sent you those emails and letters. You put yourself in this position."

"I'm sorry. I'm so sorry. Give me another chance. I'm begging you."

"A chance? How about I give you a choice instead?"

Harrison stopped pacing again.

"What?" Nestor asked.

"I told you we were going for another round. I was thinking about giving you a break, but you keep pushing me. Now, do you want to keep writing with your hands or would you like to dictate all of your future books?"

Nestor's face twisted into a hideous wad of wrinkles and fleshy trenches. He asked, "Is that what this is all about? You want me to write another book? A–Another extreme horror book, right?"

"Now? No. I'm just giving you the opportunity to continue telling stories in the future. I'm sure when our connection is re-established, you'll be inspired again. Remember, I'm not here to hurt you. This isn't fun for me. I'm only trying to save us."

"Yeah right. Yeah *fucking* right. If you want me to

write, I'll write! I'll write whatever you want! Sequels, prequels, spin-offs, a whole new damn series with you as the main character. I'll do it. Just let me go."

"You see that? You hear yourself?" Harrison said, jabbing a finger at him. "This proves you still don't understand a thing. I don't want you to write a book for me, Nestor. I'm trying to re-establish our connection. I'm trying–"

"Mission accomplished!"

"–to get my message through to you."

"We're connected again! I feel you! I feel everything!" Nestor cried.

"Liar! I don't want to hurt you, but I don't know what else to do! You have to see what we are! You have to believe!"

"Let me go! Let me go! Let me... Let me..."

Nestor dissolved into a blubbering mess. Harrison retrieved a knife from his duffel bag. It had a short, curved blade, honed like a scalpel.

"I guess I'll be making the choice for you," he said.

"No! No! No!"

Harrison knelt on Nestor's right arm, digging his knee into the crook of his elbow. With his free hand, he grabbed his forearm and pushed it down to the mattress. The handcuffs clattered. Then he pressed the blade against his inner wrist, right above the cuff. It tore his skin with the utmost ease. He sawed into his wrist carefully. He wasn't trying to amputate his hand after all. He stopped sawing upon hitting some resistance. The blade rested against Nestor's carpal bones.

Harrison pushed the knife forward, sliding the blade towards the edge of his wrist. The blade *clanged* against the handcuff repeatedly while drops of blood *plopped* on the bedsheet. He dragged the blade to the other side of his wrist. Nestor moved his hand as if he were trying to swat it away. He couldn't reach the knife, though. He could only feel it as the blade circled back to the initial incision. The intruder had carved a jagged ring around his wrist.

With the blade buried in his wrist, Harrison turned the knife so the tip was pointing at the ball of Nestor's thumb, tilted the handle up, then thrust it forward. Traveling under his skin, the blade sank into his palm. Pins and needles coursed through Nestor's hand. Harrison wiggled the knife around, separating the skin from the muscle. The tip of the blade poked through the skin a few times. Nestor's fingers wriggled involuntarily in a gory jazz hand.

Blood rushed out of the massive wound. It pattered on the corner of the bed, splashed on the headboard, and raced down his forearm. A few drops landed on Mina's nightstand.

"Stop!" Nestor roared. "You fucking bastard! Stop! Oh God, it burns! What are you doing to me! God, stop it!"

Harrison was in Nestor's blind spot, so he couldn't grasp what was happening to him. He reckoned the killer was trying to amputate his hand. Parts of his arm had gone numb because of the weight on his elbow. Yet, the pain in his hand was fierce—and it was getting worse and worse. He felt the blade slide around his thumb, then grind up against his bones at the back of his hand. His skin was pushed up, away from his wrist, crumpling like paper.

Harrison could see a rainbow of colors in the enormous wound—shades of blue, green, purple, white, and a lot of red. As his hand swayed uncontrollably, Nestor felt the cold handcuff riding up against the hot, skinless base of his hand, amplifying the pain. He knew he could have reduced the pain if he stopped resisting, but he couldn't control his body's natural reaction to the torture. He felt a hint of relief as Harrison pushed the cuff back down to his wrist.

The killer did this for two reasons: He was afraid of Nestor's hand slipping free, and he needed some space to work.

He dug his fingers *under* the skin, gripped it firmly, then started peeling it away while continuing to saw into the muscle. Short of breath, Nestor unleashed a ghastly croak. He heard his skin tearing, like a sheet of paper being ripped to pieces. Torn away from the muscles and bones, the detached skin of his palm folded up to his knuckles.

Harrison ran into some trouble while trying to flay Nestor's fingers. Keeping the blade under the skin, he thrust the tip at his knuckles. He avoided the webbing between his fingers, though. He was meticulous, breathing easy, eyes unblinking, hands steady. He had a plan, and he was going to stick to it.

He kept thrusting the knife while tugging at the mass of bloody skin bundled up at his knuckles. After a few minutes, the skin on his fingers tore as well. Nestor's hand was degloved. Some skin remained on his fingers, mostly on the sides. His hand was a wet slab of meat and bones, shiny with blood.

The detached skin landed on the corner of the bed.

A strong cramp seized Nestor's stomach. He held his breath and shimmied. Veins stood out on his neck and cold sweat shimmered across his body. He retched but there was nothing in his stomach to vomit. Saliva foamed out of his mouth instead. Harrison got off the bed but Nestor didn't feel or see him.

He was in a haze of pain, conscious but unaware of his surroundings. He was thinking about his hand. He realized he had experienced a horrific degloving injury. He was now wishing Harrison had amputated his hand instead. Then thoughts of death crept into his mind. He was ready to give up.

What's the point of living after something like this? he pondered.

He was broken.

Harrison appeared at the other side of the bed. Nestor turned his head to get a better look at him. The killer was holding a hammer in one hand and a long seven-inch iron nail in the other.

"Ki–Kill me," Nestor stuttered.

"I think I know what we have to do now, but I can't stop here," Harrison said. "I'm not doing this to punish you. I don't *want* to hurt you anymore. No, really."

"Kill... me."

"I'm doing this so you won't be tempted to interfere. So you can focus on... well, the matter at hand. Sorry about the play on words. I just want you to know that this is for your own good."

Harrison knelt on Nestor's left arm. He pushed the tip of the nail down against the center of his palm. Nestor was too weak to make a fist. Harrison struck the nail's head with the hammer. The nail skewered his hand, tearing through the muscle between two metacarpal bones. The tip of the nail cut through the bedsheet and pierced the mattress, too. Blood bubbled out of the wound on his palm and dripped from the back of his hand.

Harrison struck the nail again and again—*and again*. He hit it until only an inch of the shank stuck out from Nestor's palm.

During the torture, Nestor drifted in and out of consciousness—blacking out for a minute, waking for a few seconds, blacking out, waking, blacking out. In this inconsistent state, he lost track of time and reality. There were moments when he wasn't sure if he was dreaming or if he was awake or if he was in the process of dying. Like the flash from a camera, he saw flares of white light, then he saw stars sparkling in a void of darkness, then images of his family shuffled through his mind.

When he regained consciousness, his vision was cloudy. He saw Harrison sitting next to him on the bed, stroking his face with the back of his fingers. He felt hot and feverish all over. The beads of cold sweat had turned warm. His hands burned with a ceaseless stinging sensation—the right hotter than the left, but *both* hotter than the rest of his body. He glanced at his right hand, then at the left. Despite his damaged, blurred vision, he could see his hands had been bandaged. The large nail, buried in the mattress, still stuck out of his left hand, though.

"It's over," Harrison said. "I'm not going to hurt you... right now. I've seen the errors of my ways, Nestor. During your... 'punishment,' I had an epiphany. And I realized you were right."

Nestor let out a little huff, like an angry dog. *Now you believe me?!* he was screaming in his head. *Now?! Now?!* He wanted to bite Harrison's hand but he didn't have the energy to attack.

"I mean, we were both right about our connection, but I just like the way you put it," the intruder continued, pulling his hand away from his victim's face. "I said 'one soul shared by two bodies,' and you said 'one soul separated at birth.' Yeah, I like yours more. It encompasses everything I've been saying while also acknowledging our shared birthdate. I thought you were just copying me, but... you were understanding me. I was wrong for doubting you. *But,* there is a silver lining. If we hadn't gone through this experience, I wouldn't have had my epiphany."

Nestor was scowling at him but he looked like he was grimacing in pain because of the cuts, bruises, and lumps on his face. The bandage over his mangled eye didn't help his appearance.

Harrison said, "When I was hurting your body—sorry about that, by the way—I felt our beacons sync up. That was when it came to me. Our solution. If it hadn't, I would have degloved your other hand and shaved your voice box down with a potato peeler. Seriously, that was my *original* plan. But no. I know what we have to do now." He reached over and caressed Nestor's cheek. He said, "But before we get back to business, you've earned a break."

As his vision cleared up, Nestor noticed Harrison's hand was abnormal. In a split second, his rage turned to gut-wrenching fear. He once again found himself questioning whether he was awake or asleep. He was seeing things he had imagined were only possible in nightmares and in hell. Harrison was wearing Nestor's skinned hand like a glove over his own. His own fingers were visible in the gashes on the skin. It was the perfect fit, though.

Harrison said, "We're finally on the same page, but I can understand why you'd want to get away from me. I fucked up. I acted too soon and I took things too far. But don't bother trying to escape. With those nails in your feet and that other nail in your hand, you won't be able to get off this bed without alerting me. You'd only be wasting your energy and hurting yourself. Please don't do that. When you hurt, I hurt. Focus on your breathing and remain calm. It's time for us to heal our soul and come together. I'll be back soon."

He exited the room, leaving Nestor to wallow in his misery.

25

RECONCILIATION

CAN I KILL MYSELF BY HOLDING MY BREATH? NESTOR thought.

He had spent his time alone thinking about ways to commit suicide without getting off the bed or using his hands. He contemplated moving his hands and feet to widen and deepen his wounds. He figured it would either accelerate his bleeding and cause him to bleed out or the pain would send him into neurogenic shock. But if it didn't work, it would have only led to more suffering. He was surprised he was still alive. He remembered what Harrison had said earlier in the night: '*Humans are capable of amazing feats of survival.*'

"I'm a cockroach," he whispered, voice barely audible. "A human cockroach."

He heard the stairs creaking down the hall. The slow, heavy footsteps approached the bedroom. Harrison stopped in the doorway. He held a tray table with the legs already unfolded. On the tray, there was a glass of water, a bowl of plain yogurt, a bowl of chicken noodle soup, and two spoons. Careful not to spill anything, he walked up to the bed and placed the tray table over Nestor's abdomen.

"I made this for you," he said. "Well, I didn't cook it from scratch, but I mean I heated it up and served it and, uh... You know what I mean. I'm just telling you this because I want you to eat comfortably. This is fresh from a can of soup and a carton of yogurt. The water's from the tap. I still have that other bottle from earlier, but that water was getting warm. I didn't touch anything else or help myself to your food or anything like that, I promise. So, what do you want to eat first?"

Nestor gave him a one-eyed glare. He considered spitting in his face, hoping to antagonize him enough to force him to kill him. *Like suicide by cop*, he thought. *Suicide by... serial killer?* His mouth and throat were so dry it hurt to breathe, though. He hated the idea of cooperating with his torturer, but with death out of the question, he didn't have many options on the table.

"Water," he croaked out.

"Oh yeah, of course. You must be parched after all that."

Harrison grabbed the glass. Holding it with both hands, he tilted it and poured the cool water into Nestor's mouth little by little. Nestor guzzled it, his Adam's apple bobbing with each gulp. While drinking, he noticed Harrison hadn't removed the human glove. It sickened and jarred him to see his skin on another person's body. Yet, he couldn't stop drinking.

"More," he demanded as Harrison pulled the glass away.

"You need to pace yourself. Drinking too fast will either give you a stomachache–"

"More."

"–or lead to water intoxication."

"Please."

"Do you know what happens with water intoxication? Your kidneys fail and your brain swells. You know what they say, too much of a good thing can kill you. We don't want that, do we? I'll give you some more after you eat something, okay?"

Water intoxication didn't sound so bad to Nestor. Although it sounded painful, he believed it could work as a hands-free suicide method. Harrison set the glass down on the tray table.

"Don't worry, I don't have any more whiskey," he said with an innocent laugh.

He grabbed the bowl of soup and blew on the hot liquid to cool it down. He fed him a spoonful at a time. Nestor didn't realize how hungry he was until he smelled the soup. He sipped it up, taste buds buzzing with delight. The food and water revitalized him. He didn't have the energy to break free but he had enough to speak and think clearly.

"I really am sorry about all of this," Harrison said

as he spooned some more broth into his victim's mouth.

There were tears in his eyes. He put the bowl and spoon down on the tray table, then folded his hands over his lap and hung his head as if in shame. Nestor watched him with a glint of skepticism in his eye. He sensed sincerity in his captor's voice and body language. But Harrison was unpredictable.

"Maybe you don't believe me anymore," the killer said. "I wouldn't blame you if you didn't. But I want you to know that it really does hurt me when I have to hurt you. I said before that I could feel when you were writing and even when you were, um... having sexual intercourse with your wife. I was a little crasser about that second point, though. I'm sorry about that, too. I know those were private, intimate moments between you and her. In the heat of the moment, I said too much. But you get my point."

Nestor looked at the right side of the bed and thought about Mina. Seeing the huge bloodstain at the corner of the mattress made him shiver.

Harrison continued, "I used to feel your emotional pain, too. Remember 'Predators and Prey?' You published it a few years ago. It was one of your first books to, y'know, really blow up. It got your name out there. But it wasn't all, um... 'peaches and cream,' as they say, was it? People were offended—*outraged*. You wanted to show the world the truth about child preda-tors and the true extent of the horrors their victims were experiencing under them. But instead of these readers getting angry at those predators, they got angry at *you* for making them think about *them*—for putting those gruesome but true-to-life images in their heads and ruining their days."

Nestor recalled the harassment he had faced after publishing his book. Most of the personal insults and threats had come from readers who were not part of his intended audience. He had never expected his extreme horror story to reach so many people from so many different walks of life.

"I was always there to defend you," Harrison said. "Every time the mobs came out, I was there to fight them back with the truth. They'd call you a psychopath. They'd say you were writing out your own fantasies. And when you announced you were having a daughter—you know this already—when you made that announcement, they were saying you weren't fit to be a father. They said your girl was in danger. There was an organized effort to get CPS to investigate you. And I was there telling them you were one of the nicest guys I had ever met... even if we hadn't met in person. I told them how kind and friendly and approachable you were. I tried to explain to them that, although your stories are inspired by real events, you write fiction and you are not the characters in your books. But they never listened. Those types of people never do."

Nestor opened his mouth to speak but he stopped himself before he could make a sound. *Thank you,* he almost said. It didn't feel right, though. He always appreciated it when his readers defended him and his work. He was always there to support his readers' tastes as well. Glancing around the room, the killer started drumming his fingertips against each other while bouncing a knee. He had a lot on his mind.

Harrison looked Nestor in the eye and said, "I want to make amends. I want to reconcile. I believe it'll make this process easier. Can you forgive me?"

"I can."

"Really?" Harrison said with a big, surprised smile. "Oh my God, I can't tell you how re–"

"But first," Nestor interrupted. "You have to tell me the truth. Did you hurt my family?"

The killer's smile vanished. He scooted over to the head of the bed, then leaned in closer to Nestor, giving him a close-up of his face.

He said, "I told you the truth the first time: I did *not* hurt your family."

"Where are they?"

"A friend's house."

"If you're not specific, I'm going to assume you're lying."

"They're at the Griffins' house. Chelsea Griffin is one of Mina's long-time friends. Chelsea is married to a man named Marcus. He owns a hardware store. Well, he inherited it from his father. Lucky son of a bitch. Anyway, they have a five-year-old son named Asher and a daughter named Kaylee. Melody and Kaylee are about the same age, so they've had a few playdates. Now, is that specific enough for you?"

Nestor believed him. Overwhelmed with relief, tears sprang to his left eye. He felt a burning sensation in his right eye socket, too. His tear gland was functioning, despite the damage to his eyeball. The pain couldn't spoil his temporary happiness. He was busy picturing his daughter playing with Kaylee in a yard, smiling and giggling while tottering about.

Interrupting his daydream, Harrison said, "If you think they're interfering with your beacon, I can kill them for you."

"*What?*" Nestor hissed.

"The Griffins. Your family. If you wish, I can take them out of the–"

"Watch your fucking mouth."

"Okay, okay," Harrison responded, leaning away from him with his hands raised in a gesture of peace.

Nestor said, "Stay away from them—from all of them. This is between you and me. This... This stays here. It doesn't leave this house. It will never leave this house because... because you know what's going to happen to us, right? You're going to get gunned down by the police, and I'm going to... to succumb to my injuries. We're going to die here."

A brooding silence befell the room. Harrison stood up, took two steps forward, then turned to face the bed. A smirk broke on his face.

"I like the way you're talking now," he said. "You're

starting to look at us—you and I—as a single entity. *We* are going to die here. That's what you said."

"What? That's not what I meant."

"You did. Maybe it was subconscious, but it *was* what you meant, Nestor. Your beacon is coming back online. Our connection is getting stronger."

"N–No, you–you're twisting my words," Nestor stuttered, appearing hurt and discombobulated.

"I said exactly what you said."

"You know what I mean, damn it."

"You don't even know what you mean," Harrison replied. He began walking around the bed with his hands clasped behind his back, moving from nightstand to nightstand. He said, "You remember when we spoke about subverting expectations? I suppose I never really gave you the opportunity to respond. And I guess I have your answer now. You know, about how you think this is going to end. You believe we're going to die here."

"Yes," Nestor said, voice laced with defeat. "Even if you called an ambulance now, I'd be... dead by the time they got me off this bed. As soon as they take these nails out, I'm either going to bleed to death or die from shock. I know this already. I–I can't believe I'm still breathing. And you? You're stubborn... like me. When you believe something, *you believe it*. You're not going to go out without a fight."

"Yup, I'm a lot like you and you're a lot like me. I get what you're saying. Your prediction—I think that's a good word for it—is bleak. It's depressing. It's just like the ending to one of your books. You know, none of them have happy endings. That's one of the many things I liked about them. They felt real. The only happy ending I ever had was in a massage parlor. And I wasn't really 'happy' when all was said and done. I felt filthier and lonelier than ever. That's what life's all about: Filthiness and loneliness."

"I guess so."

"But it's all subjective, right? Our filth and our loneliness might be someone else's dream. Some people like getting handjobs at massage parlors. Some people like being alone."

He stopped to Nestor's right. He knelt next to the bed, folded his arms on the edge of the mattress, then rested his chin on one of his wrists and gazed at his prisoner.

He said, "What's our true happy ending? To some people, it would be... Let's see... I die but you survive. You recover and you go on to write—maybe 'dictate' is more accurate considering what happened to your hands—a bestselling horror novel based on this experience. Not bad, huh? To others, they might see both of our deaths as a happy ending. Think about it. From the outside looking in, they might see us as sick, lonely, suffering souls. Might think it's better to, y'know, put us out of our misery. There are people who think death is a cure."

"Death stops the pain."

"Are you one of those people? 'Aunt Jane has schizophrenia. Better take her out back and put a bullet in her head. Oh, Grandma busted her hip, I guess we'll have to euthanize her.'"

"You're twisting my words again," Nestor snarled.

"I'm kidding—kinda. But, anyway, there is another happy ending. Picture this: You finally come to understand me. I mean, you *fully* understand me and you *fully* believe in what I'm saying. I'm not talking about becoming best friends or whatnot but imagine us putting our *minor* differences aside to focus on our *substantial* similarities. Imagine you realize our purpose and we come together to become *one*. That's what this is all about. That's our destiny. We can survive this together."

"What are you going to do to me?"

Harrison pushed himself up to his feet, then said, "I'm going to do everything in my power to ensure we have our happy ending. I think you're starting to get the picture. You understand what we are, but you can't see what we're supposed to become. But don't worry, I'm not angry about that. In fact, I'm... I'm ecstatic. We're *finally* making progress. I think you just need a little bit more to... become enlightened. I'm not going to hurt you as punishment anymore."

"I can't... understand you," Nestor said weakly. "I don't feel so good."

"It's okay. You just need some more food and liquids. Save your energy."

The killer sat next to him. He fed him the rest of the soup and some more water. Then he grabbed the bowl of yogurt and the other spoon.

As he stirred the yogurt, he said, "I'm going to give you something from me and, in return, you're going to give me a piece of you. That's how we become one."

Before Nestor could say a word, he shoved a spoonful of yogurt into his mouth. It tasted tangy with an unusually bitter aftertaste.

"There you go," Harrison said before spooning some more yogurt into his mouth. "Eat up. It'll make you feel better."

26

TWINS

"Did you know twins can have two different biological fathers?" Harrison asked. With his back to the bed, he was crouching near the dresser and rummaging through his duffel bag. He said, "It's called superfecundation. Have you heard of it?"

Nestor could barely see the back of Harrison's head from his position on the bed. He had a bad case of the shivers, his handcuffs rattling nonstop. Most of the blood on his skin had crusted over and yogurt stained the corners of his mouth.

"No," he said.

"Well, it's when two eggs from the same mother are fertilized by two different men in separate sexual encounters. Of course, those sexual encounters have to occur during the same cycle. Could be on the same day. Could be a few days later."

Nestor gave a feeble one-syllable laugh, then asked, "Are you suggesting we're twins?"

"My father frequently cheated on my mother. I heard it from her all the time, and I saw his infidelity with my own eyes after she got ill. And like you said in your memoirs, your mother was a whore."

"I never used that word."

"It's possible that my dad and your mom ran into each other and had a fling directly before or directly after *your* father planted his seed in that woman. Then when we were born, your mother gave me to *my* father and kept you. So, maybe—*maybe*—we are brothers."

"You seriously believe our parents could have kept a secret like that for so long?"

"Why not? No one really knows what their parents were like before they were born. And we don't really know if we were born naturally or via C-section, or alone or with a sibling or two. We just kinda... fade into existence and believe what we're told. And it's not like your mother is going to tell you she had sex with two different men on the week of your conception, right? It's not something we're going to ask about, either. I didn't know about superfecundation until a few years ago. By then, both of my parents were dead. Like yours."

Nestor caught himself nodding. He shut his good eye and shook his head, as if arguing with himself. *Why is he suddenly making sense to me?* he wondered.

"Where did I put those?" Harrison muttered as he stood up.

Hands on his hips, he walked in circles and inspected the floor. He stopped next to the bed and looked at Nestor.

He said, "I know it's a lot to digest. A few hours ago, I would have told you that it's a crazy idea. But now that our connection is getting stronger? I can believe it. I'm starting to see the resemblance, too."

"We don't look alike. You can't... trick me into believing that. I know what I look like."

"What about the scar on your temple? It looks a lot like mine."

"Scar? It's a gash. *You* cut my face up."

"I struck you with a bottle, Nestor. What are the chances that a hit like that would create an identical scar? Oh, sorry, a soon-to-be scar."

"I haven't even seen the cut. How do I know you're not lying?"

"I can go look for a mirror and show you. But then I would have to take off those bandages. I don't think that's a good idea. I especially don't think it's a good idea for you to see yourself like this. It might cause your heart rate to spike. I know CPR—I mean, I've watched some YouTube videos before—but I don't know if I'd be able to restart your heart. And, unfortunately for us, I forgot my handy defibrillator at home."

He chuckled playfully. Nestor stayed quiet. He

racked his brain, trying to think of a way to refute Harrison's claims.

"Our eyes aren't the same color," he said.

"Siblings can have different eye colors. Hell, every single member of a family could have different eye colors. It's not impossible."

"Our–Our facial structures are different. Our hair is different. You're shorter than me, too, right? Yeah, you look shorter. And–And... And there has to be more."

"Those differences are negligible."

"There has to be more," Nestor repeated with doubt.

Squinting his good eye, he looked back and forth between himself and Harrison. He had trouble remembering his own appearance. Harrison's eyes surveyed him in a similar manner.

The killer sighed, then said, "There is something that's been bothering me. Something that's different about us. I think it's unfair that you got to keep yours but I didn't."

"Keep mine?"

"If I can correct this anomaly—this *injustice*—then we'd really be like twins. Maybe it would even help our connection."

"What are you talking about?"

"I'll show you."

Harrison hooked his thumbs over the waistbands of his underwear and jeans. He pulled them down all together, revealing his bare crotch.

"Ow," he complained as something scratched his thigh.

He looked down at the inside of his jeans and found the kitchen shears had cut through his pocket. Holding his pants up with one hand, he took the shears out.

"There you are," he said to the inanimate object. "I've been looking all over the place for you."

Meanwhile, Nestor's good eye had grown huge in his bloodied, pallid face. The pieces had fallen into place in his head. He had identified the difference between them: *Foreskin*. Harrison was circumcised but Nestor wasn't.

"No, no, no, no, no," he said, words shooting out of his mouth like bullets from an automatic rifle. "Please, please, please don't do this."

"If I couldn't keep mine," he paused and pointed at himself with the shears before aiming the blades at his prisoner and saying, "you shouldn't keep yours."

"No, God, no."

"Fair is fair, Nestor. Besides, for all we know, that little bit of skin might be what's interfering with our signal. And don't worry, I'll make it quick, I promise. You know I keep my promises. Don't think of it like torture, okay? It's just a little... trimming and tidying up. Like a haircut."

"Don't do it. Please don't do it. Harrison, listen to me. Please listen. You said we're... we could be twins, right? You said we could be brothers. Brothers don't do this to each other. No, man, no. We're supposed to take care of each other."

Harrison pulled his pants up and said, "That's what I'm trying to do. If you can't think of it as a haircut, think of it as tough love."

Nestor screamed and swung his hips to the left, trying to put some distance between himself and the attacker. The handcuff around his right wrist slid up and hit his skinned hand, reigniting the pain. It was so bad that he didn't notice Harrison had grabbed his flaccid penis. The killer pinched his foreskin between his thumb and index finger with his right hand. He pulled it upward, stretching it like soft dough as far as possible. He could see the outline of the corona of the glans through the foreskin.

"Don't shake so much," Harrison said. "Hey, I'm serious. I could end up cutting the tip if you keep moving like that."

Nestor was moving his hips like a belly dancer. Harrison opened the shears, then held the foreskin between the blades. He bent over and gazed at the penis, marveling at it as if it were a piece of art.

"On three, okay?" he said, eyes locked on the penis. "One."

"No! Ow, fuck, my hand! No! Stop!"

"Two."

"Please, Harrison, don't fucking–"

"Three."

The killer squeezed the shears' handles. The

blades cut through the layers of his foreskin without any trouble. His right hand flew up with the severed foreskin between his fingers.

Nestor's screech was cut off by a throaty gasp. He tried to pull his knees closer together as he writhed. His dick—mutilated, *desecrated*—burned. Hot inside and out, he felt like his cock was melting. In what felt like endless tsunamis of lava, the immense pain radiated into his testicles, then into his pelvis, then up into his abdomen. His balls felt like they were going to burst while his organs twisted and turned.

"Breathe, brother," Harrison said.

He dropped the foreskin on the mattress, then leaned over the bed to examine Nestor's penis. Only some outer foreskin remained. There was a bright red ring of skinless, wrinkly flesh around the shaft, directly under the glans. Purple veins squiggled down the skinned patch of the shaft. Although it was unscathed, blood was smeared on the glans.

He said, "Shit, I missed this little piece. I'm going to cut it, okay? It'll be quick."

He was talking about the frenulum—the small band of elastic tissue under the glans. Nestor couldn't hear him over his wheezing, though. Harrison jabbed one of the shears' blades into Nestor's urethra. He wiggled it a little, widening the opening, then he snipped, snipped, *snipped* until he tore the frenulum. In the process, he sliced into the glans a few times and cut the urethra open. Blood dribbled out of the opening, like semen during a ruined orgasm. It ran down the shaft, then rode the grooves of his scrotum.

Nestor's head swung frenziedly. A spray of projectile vomit launched out of his mouth. The slimy, yellowish puke splashed on his nose and cheek as well as the pillow and headboard. Harrison rushed to the head of the bed and placed the shears on the nightstand. He grabbed Nestor's jaw in one hand and the top of his head with the other. Fearing he was going to choke on his vomit, he turned the victim's head to the side. Nestor kept trying to move, though. Foamy puke flowed out of the side of his mouth, traveling through his beard.

"There you go, get it all out," Harrison said in a soothing, caring voice. "It's okay, it's okay. I'll feed you more later. You're fine now. It's finished. Faster than a haircut, huh?"

"It... It hurts... so... so bad," Nestor rasped.

"I know, I know. But the pain is only temporary. It'll go away soon, I promise. And don't even worry about infections or anything like that. I'm going to wrap it up for you."

Nestor could only sob. Harrison went to his bag, took a gauze pad and a gauze roll out, then returned to the bed. He was about to wipe Nestor's penis with the gauze pad when a thought stopped him.

He said, "Did you know some doctors actually use their mouths to suck the blood off the penis after circumcisions? I've never done it before, it's never even crossed my mind, but..." He paused for a long time, deliberating with himself. He said, "If you think it'll help with the pain, I can do that for you. It's not a big deal. It's a medical thing, like sucking poison out of a snake bite. So, what do you think?"

Nestor wasn't thinking about anything in particular. Agony had addled his brain. Harrison took his weeping and gasping as a no.

He said, "Okay, okay. I get it."

He wiped Nestor's penis with the gauze pad, soaking up the blood. Nestor winced with every touch. After cleaning it up, Harrison wrapped the gauze roll around the penis. He collected the shears and the severed foreskin.

"I'll be back in a few," he said. "Remember what I told you: focus on your breathing and everything will be fine. Call my name if you need me."

Nestor didn't hear him or see him leave the room. Eye closed, head swaying, dick burning, he thought he was still being tortured. Minutes felt like hours. By the time his mind started to clear up, Harrison was back in the bedroom, holding a plate and a glass of water. He set the plate down on the nightstand, then sat next to Nestor and poured some water into his mouth. He splashed a little on his face, too.

He put the glass down on the nightstand, then grabbed the plate and said, "Nestor, hey. Can you open your eye? I want you to look at me. Hey, I need you to see this."

Nestor's eye flickered open. Harrison held the plate over the author's chest, tilting it downward so he could see what was on it. Surrounded by red smudges, there was a small black chunk of *something* at the center of the plate. Nestor was seeing triple, so it was hard for him to identify it. It looked like a charred piece of fried chicken skin. A burning smell and thin plumes of smoke rose from it.

Harrison picked it up with his gloved fingers and said, "It's your foreskin. It got a little burnt, but it shouldn't be a problem. Looks good, doesn't it?"

"Don't," Nestor whispered.

He was convinced he was going to force him to cannibalize himself. He was starving but he wasn't *that* hungry.

He stuttered, "I–I can't... do this... a–any..."

His mouth flew open and he drew a sharp breath. Like a potato chip, Harrison tossed the burnt foreskin into his own mouth. He was beaming from ear to ear as he gnawed on the skin. It was crispy but chewy. He swished it around in his mouth like a piece of flavorful bubble gum, then choked it down. He let out a satisfied sigh.

"A piece of you inside of me," he said.

Nestor was thoroughly freaked out. His foreskin— severed and cooked—was *in* another man's stomach. Due to all of the violence, his memories were getting foggier and the truth blurrier. He knew Harrison had tortured him, but he couldn't remember why they were there in that bedroom or how their night had started. He was beginning to believe Harrison was actually his brother.

And the only question in his mind now was: *Why did my brother eat my foreskin?*

Harrison said, "And there's already a piece of me inside of you."

"Wha–What?"

"I'm sorry for tricking you, but I... Well, I ejaculated into your yogurt."

Nestor dry-heaved.

"Hey, don't be like that," Harrison said.

Nestor dry-heaved again.

The killer said, "It had to be a fair trade. You give me something of yours, I give you something of mine. At least it wasn't painful, right? You wouldn't have even noticed if I didn't tell you."

Nestor gagged, then burped, then puked out some water. Everything hurt—his hands, his feet, his crotch, his stomach, *his brain, his heart.* He grew sick and dizzy. He felt like he was strapped to a bed that was free-falling through the sky.

Harrison leaned over him and, while pouring more water into his mouth, he said, "Breathe. Breathe. You're okay. Everything's..."

Nestor fell unconscious.

27

SHARING IS CARING

NESTOR'S EYE CRACKED OPEN. HE SAW A SHADOWY figure standing at the foot of the bed. It got clear after he blinked. The outline of the figure looked like a woman holding a baby in her arms—like Mina holding Melody. Despite all of his gruesome injuries and disfigurements, he felt at peace for the first time in months.

He heard his wife's voice say: "You're okay."

"Yes," he responded.

"Good. I was worried about you."

"I'm sorry."

"Don't apologize. I took things too far again."

Nestor closed his eye, shook his head, and said, "What? No, this is my fault. What are you saying?"

"I appreciate that. Maybe we both share the blame, too."

"N–No," Nestor said brokenly as the realization set in.

He opened his eye and saw Harrison standing at the foot of the bed. And just like that, peace was replaced with sorrow and fear. He sobbed despairingly.

Harrison sucked his teeth, then said, "Don't be so hard on yourself. We've made so much progress. We're almost finished, too. In fact, I feel like we're closer than ever already."

Nestor continued whimpering. Harrison sat next to him and stroked his beard tenderly. The hair was crusty with dried blood and vomit. He shushed him, as if he were trying to put a baby to sleep. He gave him all the time he needed to cry it out. After a few minutes, Nestor calmed himself. He was still shaking all over and taking trembly breaths, though.

"I only wanted to live in peace," he said, staring at his captor's face. "I don't care about the money. I need it, everyone needs it, but I never wanted to be rich. I... I don't want fame, either. I was happy hiding at home and writing in my room. And I don't care what anyone thinks anymore. I like being home and alone. I don't need friends. I only need my wife and my baby. God, I... I need them."

"They're safe, Nestor."

"I wanna see them. I wanna hold them. They're the only people I love. I feel different with them—and *only* them. I feel comfortable. I feel like myself. I felt...

hollow when I had to do those conventions and book signings. But with them, with Mina and Melody, I felt full and alive. I felt comfortable. It took so long to find someone I could truly bond with. I can't lose them like this."

"You won't."

"You–You have to promise me we'll see them again. Promise me, Harrison."

"We... Yes, *we* will see them again. You have my word."

Lips cycling between an unsteady smile and a pout, Nestor said, "Thank you. Thank you so much."

Harrison let him cry for a few more minutes, shushing him and patting his chest gently. He pitied him. He didn't enjoy seeing him that way—hurt, puzzled, *miserable*. Yet, he felt some happiness, too. He felt like they were getting closer and closer. He believed Nestor wanted to introduce him to his family.

"I understand you," Harrison said. "I mean, I understand your ailment. I know you don't like talking about it because you weren't 'officially' diagnosed, but I get your pain. I know what it's like to be a recluse."

"Do you?"

"Your parents abused you. Your mother locked you in bedrooms and closets and even the trunk of your family car. Sometimes it was for a few hours. Sometimes it was for a few days. There were months when you wouldn't be allowed to leave your home. It must have been hard to sit in your bedroom—*your prison*—

as a young boy, watching your classmates play outside during summer vacation."

"It was."

"And your father neglected you. He was so, *so* cold. In your memoirs, you said he barely spoke to you and you couldn't remember if he ever said 'I love you' to you."

"I don't want to talk about them anymore," Nestor said, sniffling. "Please stop. Please."

"Okay, okay. But I want you to know that I understand you. Your pain started during your childhood and it stayed in your heart. You've tried to keep it locked away, but... you know it doesn't work that way. You can't bury anguish. You were scared to find love because you didn't want to *lose* love. You didn't want friends because you didn't want to *lose* friends. You've always wanted to be alone because you felt *safer* by yourself."

Although he knew it was going to hurt, Nestor couldn't help but cry and nod in agreement. He had flashbacks to his conversations with a psychiatrist at his college's counseling office. But, instead of seeing the psychiatrist—a young blonde woman—he saw himself sitting in that office with Harrison. The blonde woman couldn't help him because he wouldn't let her help. He found some comfort with Harrison, though.

"You don't have to be scared anymore," the intruder said as he caressed Nestor's cheek. "You have me and

Mina and Melody. We're not going anywhere. We'll be here to support you, to listen to you, to love you."

"Thank you," Nestor responded. "You don't know how much that means to me. All my life... *All my life* people have been telling me they get me, but they never did. They were always trying to push me into the public eye because they thought the experience would help. They'd tell me to 'loosen up' and 'stop stressing' and–and... 'just don't feel so anxious,' as if it were something I could just turn off. They told me to imagine people in their fucking underwear during my appearances as if I were a kid in elementary school. But I could only imagine myself hiding from them— from everyone—trying to pretend like there was no one in the audience. If they're not there, they can't hurt me. If they're not there, they can't hurt me... they can't hurt me."

Harrison leaned over him and went in for a hug. He slipped an arm under his body and rested his chin on his shoulder. Nestor's back was sore since he hadn't moved from the bed in so long, but he welcomed the hug.

"It's okay," Harrison whispered into his ear. "No one can hurt you now. We won't let them."

Nestor felt the peace return to his aching body. They embraced for another minute, then Harrison stood from the bed. He wiped the tears from his face before turning around to face his prisoner.

He said, "I'm going to move forward with the plan.

It's going to hurt, but in the long run, it'll be for the best. I'm going to ensure we never lose our connection again. I'm going to make it so that we're always together. I know you forgave me already, but I think this is how I truly atone for what I've done to you. It'll be easier if you trust me, okay? You trust me, right?"

"I do."

"Good," Harrison said as he pulled his knife out of his pocket.

Nestor closed his good eye and took a big breath, bracing for the pain. But it didn't come. He wondered if every inch of his body had gone numb. When he opened his eye, he saw Harrison holding his knife up to his own right eye. His palm on his scalp, he was holding his upper eyelid open with his free hand. He pointed the curved blade at the top of his peeper.

"I'll go first," he said.

He thrust the knife into his eye socket. The blade slid over his eye. Blood gushed out, cascading over his eyeball. The right side of his vision blurred and reddened instantly. His legs wobbled, close to buckling, but he stayed on his feet. Panting, he sawed around his eyeball with the knife, severing the muscles attached to it. The blood in his socket overflowed, running down the right side of his face in multiple streams.

He staggered this way and that way. He was about to fall, but the wall next to the nightstand stopped him. He hit it hard with his shoulder. He stopped cutting with the blade under his eyeball. He had unknowingly cut through half of his lower eyelid as well. Although his bloodied, sweaty red face was screwed into a grimace of agony, he gave a nervous laugh that sounded like '*hee-hee.*'

"What are you doing?" Nestor asked, voice filled with horror.

Speaking quickly, Harrison said, "I'm okay, I'm okay, I'm okay."

He continued cutting around his eye, severing the muscles one after another. By the time the blade reached the initial incision, his eyeball was jutting out of the socket, attached only by the optic nerve. He grabbed his eyeball and gave it a tug. The pain made him stumble forward. He caught himself on the night-stand. His knees against the furniture and his shoulder against the wall, he slid up to a half crouch.

He slipped the curved blade behind his eye, then he swiped it against the optic nerve. A spurt of blood flew out but he failed to sever it. He growled while trying to bear the pain. He swiped at it again and pulled on his eyeball simultaneously. He heard the optic nerve *snap*. He dropped to his knees with his severed eyeball in his hand. It was red all over, covered in nicks, and lubricated with blood. He was queasy and woozy.

"What have you done to yourself?" Nestor asked.

Harrison needed a few minutes to compose himself, sitting on his knees while leaning against the wall. Adrenaline helped him fight through the pain, but it also brought a wave of nausea with it. His cheeks inflated as he threw up in his mouth. It was chunky and sour, and for some reason—a reason unknown even to himself—he swallowed it. Nestor could barely see him over the nightstand. All of the noise from his stomach and throat concerned him.

Harrison set his eye down on the table, then pushed himself up to his feet. He lumbered over to the bed.

"Halfway done," he said. "Still trust me?"

"I... I do."

"Good."

Harrison peeled the bandage off Nestor's right eye. Blood had coagulated around and in his shaved eye. Since a chunk of it was missing and one of his eyelids was gone, it was easier for him to operate. He thrust the blade at the top of Nestor's eye and started sawing through the muscles around it.

Nestor groaned and spasmed. He tried not to scream because he didn't want to make things worse. He felt like he was whirling out of control. He ground his teeth so hard that his enamel cracked. He tasted blood in his mouth. Some of it was his, leaking out of his gums. A few drops had fallen into his mouth from Harrison's hollowed eye socket.

After slicing through the optic nerve, Harrison pulled the mutilated eye out of the socket. Like a red worm, a piece of the optic nerve hung from the back of it.

"You still with me?" the killer asked. Nestor couldn't speak due to the pain but he was conscious. Harrison said, "Nod if you can hear me. Hey, can you hear me?"

Nestor nodded.

"Can you see me?" Harrison asked.

Nestor gave another nod.

With a wry smile, Harrison said, "Watch this."

He shoved Nestor's mutilated eye into his own hollowed eye socket. The right side of his face crumpled as fresh pain exploded in his skull. Sweating profusely, he fought through it. He grabbed his detached eyeball from the nightstand and plugged it into Nestor's hollowed eye socket. It was a tight fit. The whole bed shook as Nestor flinched.

Asymmetric eyes were common, but Nestor's appeared ludicrous, as if he were wearing googly eyes over his real eyes. The size of his eyeballs, his irises, and his pupils were all different. His donated eye was larger than his natural eye. One eye appeared dead and vacant while the other was dim but alive. With different eye colors, he looked like a person with heterochromia.

Harrison said, "You can see what I see now, can't you?"

"I... think... so."

"What do you see?"

"You... Us..."

"That's right. I'm starting to see the world through your eyes, too. The world is clearer than ever. But we can do more. May I continue, brother? May I complete our transformation?"

"Yes," Nestor squeaked out in a stupefied state. "But..."

"*But?*"

"I need you... to help me with something first... while I can still speak."

"Of course," Harrison said as he held the knife up to Nestor's jaw. "I'll do whatever you ask. Then I'll finish our transformation. Soon, we'll be together forever."

28

WE ARE ONE

THE BLUE SUV ROLLED TO A STOP IN THE DRIVEWAY. *Little Saint Nick* by the Beach Boys was playing through the speakers. Sitting in the driver's seat, Marcus Griffin put the car in park. Mina sat in the front passenger seat, arms crossed and concern written on her face. In the back, sitting in rear-facing baby seats, Melody and Kaylee danced and giggled with the music. Chelsea was back there with them, trying to keep them from breaking free from their belts.

"Marcus, can you turn off the music?" she asked.

"Why? Let the kids groove to it."

"You're not the one back here taking care of two kids at one time. They don't need to be this hyper right now."

"C'mon, don't be a Grinch. It's the holiday season."

"Oh *please,* it's not even close to Thanksgiving yet.

Just turn it off, Marcus. This isn't the time for games anyway. This is serious."

Marcus gave Mina an awkward side-eye, as if he had forgotten she was there. She hadn't said a word since they left the Griffin house.

"Right," Marcus said as he turned off the radio.

In the back, the toddlers continued singing along to the song. They followed the melody of the music but recited the wrong lyrics, even making up words while wiggling around in their seats. Although tired of the noise, Chelsea couldn't stop herself from smiling. She preferred their singing to their wailing.

Marcus said, "So, um... Look, I can go check on him alone if you want. He's probably drunk or–"

"I'll go," Mina interrupted.

She got out of the car and started for the house. She stopped in the walkway and looked up at her home. The structure was the same, but she didn't recognize it anymore. It didn't feel like home. It had an intimidating aura. She felt like a kid staring up at the local haunted house. After some bickering with his wife, Marcus exited the SUV and joined her.

"You okay?" he asked.

"Yeah," Mina responded reluctantly.

"You sure? Like I said, I can go talk to him alone. It's no problem, really."

"No, no, I'm fine. I can do this."

"All right, well, Chelsea insists that I go with you. I'll stay close, but I'll give you your privacy. C'mon, let's go check on the guy. We have to pick up Asher from kindergarten soon anyway."

He marched forward with Mina trailing behind him. Chelsea watched them from the car, trying to keep her sanity while keeping the kids occupied.

"You wanna knock or ring the doorbell before going inside?" Marcus asked as he walked onto the porch. "You know, give him a heads-up?"

Mina went straight to the window next to the front door, her brow furrowed. She reached for the security bars but stopped with her fingertips just an inch away from one of the rods.

"What is this?" she asked.

"The bars?"

"We don't have security bars."

"You do now," Marcus said. Squinting, he leaned closer to the bars and asked, "Did he cover the windows with something or is that one of your art projects?"

"Something's wrong."

Mina squeezed past him. She tried to unlock the front door but her key didn't fit. She tried again and again and again, but to no avail.

"He changed the locks," she said, sounding panicky. "Why would he change the locks?"

"Maybe he lost his key or someone tried to break in."

Mina pressed the doorbell five times in quick succession, then pounded the door with the bottom of her fist three times, then rang the doorbell again. She looked at the sidelight, hoping to spot some movement, but that window was covered as well. They didn't hear anything inside of the house, either—not a whisper from a person or a creak from a floorboard or a clank from a pipe.

"Are you sure he's even home?" Marcus asked.

"His car's in the driveway."

"He could have taken an Uber or gotten a ride from a friend. His birthday was coming up, right? Or did it just pass? Either way, maybe he got shit-faced and stayed somewhere else. Why don't you give him a call?"

Mina knew he was trying to comfort her with his optimism, but she could only imagine the darkest outcomes. She was certain Nestor was hurt. However, she wasn't sure whether he had harmed himself or if someone had attacked him. She took her phone out of her pocket and hurried off the porch.

As she jogged around the house, she called Nestor's phone. It went straight to voicemail. She tried her key on the side door but it didn't fit. Upon a quick inspection, she saw the kitchen windows were barred and covered in tape as well. On her way to the back of the house, she dialed Nestor's number again.

Straight to voicemail.

"Shit," she muttered, one hand buried in her hair.

She spun and glanced around, hoping to find her husband somewhere on the lake. Marcus wasn't in a hurry, so he walked around the house. He finally caught up to Mina.

"Anything?" he asked.

"He changed every damn lock."

"What about his phone? Did he answer?"

"No, it's going straight to voicemail."

"Okay, okay, relax. Let me give him a–"

"We don't have time to call him. We have to get inside. Can you, I don't know, break the door down?"

"Break the..."

Bug-eyed, Marcus' voice tapered off before he could finish repeating her request. He looked at the door, then at Mina.

He said, "Listen, that's not as easy as it sounds. It's not like the movies where you just kick the door a few times and it pops open. And that door looks... sturdy."

"Then how do we get inside?"

"I guess you could try to pry the bars off one of these windows. Break the glass, then you're in. But I don't have the equipment to do that. And, honestly, I'm not comfortable doing something like that in the first place. We're talking about destruction of property and breaking and entering here. I'm not a criminal, Mina."

Glaring at him, Mina said, "It's *my* house, too. And Nestor could be in danger. He could be hurt—*seriously* hurt—right now. We have to get in there."

Marcus blew a sigh of frustration, then said, "I understand, but even if I agreed to help you, I'd have to go back and get my pickup truck or head over to my store to get the right equipment. I can't kick the door down or pry the bars off a window with my bare hands. Driving back and forth would take... What? Forty-five minutes? An hour? You're better off calling the cops, no?"

"Every time I call the cops, they take thirty minutes to get here. There has to be an easier way inside."

"The easiest way is letting the cops deal with this. You said he hasn't been himself lately. He needs a welfare check. He doesn't need us smashing windows or breaking down doors."

Mina agreed with him, but she wasn't ready to give up on Nestor. She walked around in circles with her palms against her forehead, mumbling unintelligibly to herself. She went through her options. *Call a neighbor for help?* She wasn't sure if any of her neighbors had the equipment necessary to enter the house. *Ram the garage door with Marcus' SUV?* Although she was close friends with Chelsea, she knew Marcus was never going to let her use his car as a battering ram. Then she stopped pacing and her eyes lit up in a eureka moment.

"Follow me," she said.

"Let's call the cops."

"I will, I promise!" she shouted as she ran off. "Just follow me!"

Marcus grunted before following her back to the driveway. He found her peering into Nestor's car, face pressed up against the driver window. Chelsea was standing outside of their SUV with the door open, keeping one eye on the kids and one eye on the situation unfolding before her.

"What's going on?" she asked.

Ignoring her, Mina said, "Nestor's clicker is still there. Break the window and we can use it to open the garage door."

"Are you serious?" Marcus responded.

"Do it. I'll call the detective on his case and tell him everything. Don't worry about 'destruction of property.' We can replace a car window."

"I don't know about this."

Mina said, "Marcus, if Nestor's hurt in there, if he's..." She paused as she realized she was speaking loudly. Although Melody couldn't understand every word, she was worried the girl could sense her apprehension. Lowering her voice, she said, "Every second could be the difference between life and death. If Nestor's injured in there and we miss our chance to save him... are you going to tell my daughter why she has to grow up without a father?"

Marcus really didn't want to get involved. He liked Mina, he had met Nestor a few times, but as far as he was concerned, the Castles were his wife's friends. He was willing to help Mina out—offer her a place to stay, give her a ride—but he wasn't expecting her to ask him to break down doors and shatter windows. For all he knew, Nestor could have been waiting inside with a loaded gun or he could have booby-trapped the house.

"Just do it, Marcus!" Chelsea hollered, having over-heard the conversation.

"Fine," Marcus said. "But if I do this, I'm not going in there with you."

Mina got her phone out and dialed Dean's number. She had saved it in her contact list. Listening to the ringback tone, she walked onto the lawn and stared up at the second floor of the house.

As he walked over to the trunk of his SUV, Marcus gestured at his wife and said, "Get in, lock the door, and turn up the music. If you want me to do this, I don't want them to see or hear any of it."

Chelsea did as she was told. Since the radio was connected to Marcus' holiday playlist, *Jingle Bell Rock* by Bobby Harris played through the speakers. Oblivious to everything going on outside, the toddlers started giggling, singing, and dancing again.

"Detective Dean Mueller, Cyber Crimes Unit, how may I help you?" Dean answered Mina's call.

"Detective Mueller, it's Mina Castle. I'm Nestor Castle's wife. We were having that, um... 'stalker' problem."

"I remember you, yes. How may I help you, Mrs. Castle?"

"Nestor is... in trouble. I'm at the house now. We need you here as soon as possible. If you need the address again, I can give it to you."

"I remember the place. What's going on over there? Are you okay?"

"I told you, Nestor is... he's hurt, okay?" she said before swallowing back a sob. "We need the police and paramedics and firefighters. Send everyone. Please."

The call fell silent for ten seconds.

Dean asked, "Ma'am, where is your daughter?"

"Melody? She's in the car."

"Away from Mr. Castle?"

"Yes?" Mina answered, wondering where the conversation was heading.

"And are you in a safe location as well?"

"*What?*"

"Has Nestor threatened you or–"

"You're not listening!" Mina snapped. "Nestor's not threatening to hurt us, damn it! *He* is hurt! *He* is in danger!"

"Ma'am, I'm only trying to–"

Mina lowered the phone, gasped, and jumped as a window shattered with a loud crashing sound. Fragments of glass rained down on the driveway, tinkling. The car alarm went off, the *beeps* echoing through the neighborhood. Marcus had struck the driver window of Nestor's car with a lug wrench. He looked back at Mina with an expression that said something along the lines of: *Good enough for you?* She put the phone back up to her ear.

"What was that noise?" Dean was saying. "Mrs. Castle? Mina?"

"Please hurry. He needs us."

She ended the call, then walked up to the side of

the car, glass crunching under her shoes. She reached in through the broken window and used the remote clipped to the visor to open the garage door. It rattled and rumbled as it rolled up. The stench of garbage exited the garage, immediately staining the driveway. The sunlight revealed the black trash bags and cardboard boxes piled up in the corners of the garage.

Marcus asked, "Are you sure about this?"

'*No,*' she wanted to say. '*Please go in for me. Please tell me he's okay.*' But she couldn't turn her back on Nestor. *Not again,* she told herself.

As she walked forward, Mina said, "Watch Melody, please."

———

Mina pushed a door open. An ominous darkness filled the living room. A light in the kitchen was on. An acrid scent—smoky, earthy—filled the first floor of the house. The home was dead quiet. Only the sound of the car alarm blasted through the house. She used her phone's flashlight to navigate the living room. She turned on the lamps on the end tables next to the sofas.

She stopped in front of the window next to the front door, running her light over the strips of duct tape. She held her hand over her mouth and sniffled, tears building up in her eyes. She turned and aimed her light at the other windows in the living room. They were all covered in tape. A terrible sinking feeling brewed deep in her stomach.

"Nestor?" she called out.

She waited for an answer but only heard the car alarm. She walked into the kitchen. Dirty dishes, pans, and pots were piled in the sink. She noticed the stench was stronger near the stove. On a counter, she found an empty can of chicken noodle soup and an empty container of yogurt. None of it explained the pungent scent.

"Nestor?" she said as she turned on the staircase light.

The house responded with a groan. She walked up the steps with caution, as if expecting them to fall apart under her feet. The smell grew thicker and nastier on the second floor—a blend of the smoky stench in the kitchen and the scent of days-old sweat, urine, and feces. The door to the master bedroom was wide open. It was the only room with any light. It called to her.

Arms down to her sides, she walked down the hall. Her heart was beating fast and her breathing was speeding up. Although she knew Melody was safe in the car, she instinctively peeked into the nursery on her way to the master bedroom. Aside from the tape on the window, it looked like the room hadn't been touched since she left the house.

"Oh my God," she whispered as she reached the master bedroom.

Her legs gave out but she caught herself on the doorway. Tears spilled out of her eyes in waterfalls. Her breathing became labored.

There was blood everywhere—the bedsheet, the pillows, the headboard, the nightstands, the wall, the floor. There was a pen and an envelope on Mina's nightstand. They appeared to be the only clean items in the room. Nestor was still handcuffed to the bedposts, limbs outstretched, hands and feet covered in blood-soaked bandages. The bandage had fallen off his mutilated penis, though. His skin was deathly pale. He was motionless. A comforter covered his head and torso.

"Please, no, please," she said as she stumbled over to the side of the bed with her hand cupped over her mouth.

Her stomach turned and her throat closed up as she looked at his injuries. She had explored the deepest depths of mankind's depravity through Nestor's horror books, seen the goriest movies ever made, read the grimmest news articles, but none of it could prepare her to experience it in person. It was hard for her mind to accept the fact that humans could be this cruel. She couldn't imagine what could compel someone to torture another person.

Sobbing and shaking, she grabbed the comforter and held it tightly, trying to find the courage to pull it off the dead body in front of her.

"Please, God," she whimpered.

Mina was praying she wasn't going to find her husband under the comforter. But she wasn't sure if it would have been any better if she found a dead stranger in their bedroom. She needed to see the truth with her own eyes. She yanked the comforter off him, then with her eyes bulging from their sockets, she slapped both her hands over her mouth and staggered back.

Nestor was indeed handcuffed to the bed. However, he was wearing another man's skinned face over his own. It was a face with a butterfly-shaped scar on the left temple. His vacant eyes—one of which clearly didn't belong to him—were fixed on the ceiling. There was a massive hole at the center of his chest. His sternum as well as some of the costal cartilage—which connected the ribs to the sternum—had been removed.

His heart was missing, too. Despite the blood flooding the fleshy cave in his chest, his steady, dead lungs were visible from outside his body.

Mina could only repeat a single word: "What... What... What... What... What..."

Yet, in her head, her thoughts were overlapping in a slew of internal monologues.

Is it really him?

What happened to him?

He's dead!

It's my fault!

Who did this?!

314   JON ATHAN

Scream!

Run!

Do something!

She started retching into her hands while sobbing hysterically. Behind her, the bathroom door swung open slowly. She heard its creak, but she was too busy grieving to check on it. When her crying weakened to some sniveling, she heard someone else breathing in the room. She assumed it was Marcus.

As she turned around, she saw the hallway was empty. But a figure stood at the periphery of her vision. Her eyes darted to the right, then widened again.

Harrison was standing there, nude. He wore Nestor's skinned face over his own. The skin was sewn into his jaw, cheeks, and scalp with surgical sutures. He held Nestor's heart in his right hand. Small chunks of it had been torn off. Fresh blood was smeared on the human mask's lips. Stringy pieces of the heart were stuck between his bloodstained teeth.

"Honey," he said in his best imitation of Nestor's voice. "Welcome back. I missed you so much. How are Chelsea and Marcus? Did you say hello to them for me?"

Mina knew her husband was dead, but Harrison's knowledge concerning her whereabouts had her questioning her own sanity. She slitted her eyes and tilted her head forward, as if trying to read the fine print on a coupon.

Harrison held out his arms for a hug and said, "What's the matter, honey? You look surprised to see me. You must have missed me too, huh? We have so much to talk about. But first, come here. Give me a kiss."

"Oh my *fucking* God!" Mina screamed.

She ran to the door. Harrison dropped the heart and went for a bear hug but his fingers barely grazed her shoulder. He followed her into the hallway, breathing right down the nape of her neck. Halfway down the hall, he wrapped his arms around her, lifted her from the floor, and pulled her back. Mina shrieked while kicking the walls and swinging her elbows at him. She landed a blow to his jaw, loosening the sutures on his mask and sending streams of blood down his neck. He howled and dropped her to her feet but he didn't let go of her.

"Calm down, damn it!" he shouted. "Let me explain! Let me open your eyes!"

Mina turned and elbowed him again, hitting his chest. She reeled forward, but to her dismay, Harrison was holding onto the back of her shirt. She slipped and fell to her knees, bringing him down with her. She quickly got back to her feet, and he jumped after her. Before he could grab her again, she juked into the nursery. With the killer right on her tail, she slammed the door on his forearm. His ulna and radius bones broke with a clear *snap*. The broken bones made a bump on his outer forearm.

"You bitch!" he growled as he tackled the door with his shoulder.

They fell to the floor in the middle of the nursery, Harrison on top of Mina. She scrambled forward. Although it was covered in tape, all she could think about was throwing herself through the window— survival by any means necessary. Harrison jumped on top of her, though, using his body to weigh her down. Only using his left hand, he punched the back of her head. He hit the floor a few times but it didn't hurt him. The punches made Mina dizzy. She put her hand on the back of her head and threw her other arm out in front of her, reaching for anything she could use as a weapon.

"I waited *days* for you, and *this* is how you treat me!" he yelled as he continued punching her. "Why are you making me do this to you?! You could have just listened to me! You could have just read the damn letter! I loved you! Loved you with all my heart! You want me to prove it to you? Do you?! Then I'll shove '*my*' heart down your throat, you little–"

Mina flipped over and swung Melody's toy piggy bank at Harrison's face. Some of the sutures tore. The right half of the human mask drooped away from his head, revealing his own skinned face. She saw his pulpy, fibrous facial muscles. Face flayed to the bone in some sections, she spotted patches of his skull, too. She noticed his right eye had been mutilated. She didn't know it was Nestor's, though. Harrison released a guttural bellow of agony. Mina had an opportunity to run, but the surreal, grotesque sight wiped her mind clean of all rational thoughts. She couldn't comprehend what she was seeing.

A man?

A ghost?

A demon?

While crying, Harrison grabbed her neck with his left hand. Mina swung at his face, but he dodged her. She swung at him again and missed. He tightened his grip. Her eyes watered and she felt painful pressure in her throat. Unable to reach his face, she grabbed his broken forearm and gave it a good squeeze. An electrifying jolt of pain shot through him. He stiffened up and wailed. Nestor's eyeball fell out of his eye socket, landing next to Mina's head. He grabbed his injured arm, jerked it away, then fell off her.

Grasping at her neck and gasping for air, Mina rolled in the opposite direction. Her survival instincts were reawakened. She rose shakily to her feet before stumbling out of the room. She tried to scream for help but could only produce a squeak. Merely attempting to speak, swallow, or breathe made her throat ache. She crashed into the wall across the hall. With the world spinning around her, she was afraid she wasn't going to make it downstairs safely. One wrong step would have sent her tumbling down the stairs, then she would have been at the killer's mercy.

She limped into the bathroom and locked the door

behind her. She turned on the light, then glanced around. There was only one way out, so she immediately went to the window. She tried to open it, but Nestor had taped the windowsill and frame ten times over as well. The tape was too difficult to peel, so she struck the window with her elbow. The glass cracked after a few hits but the tape held it all together. She heard a siren blaring in the distance.

"Help," she said throatily.

She recoiled as the door shook behind her. Harrison was using a console table as a battering ram. Cornered in the bathroom, Mina's fight-or-flight response told her to fight. Searching for a weapon, her eyes went straight to the plunger next to the toilet. Harrison struck the door again. Mina snatched the plunger and held it like a baseball bat. It didn't feel right, though. She dropped it, then searched for another weapon.

The door rattled and groaned again.

Mina took the heavy ceramic lid off the toilet tank. Just as she raised it over her shoulder, the door burst open. Harrison dropped the console table and charged into the bathroom. She hit his shoulder with the lid, but it wasn't enough to stop him. He grabbed her neck and pushed her back, slamming her against the window. It cracked and curved like a dome but, still, the tape kept it from crumbling.

The lid slid out of Mina's hands and landed on her toes. She would have screamed if she wasn't being strangled. Harrison pulled her towards him. They stumbled to the middle of the room. Mina was clawing at his wrist. She heard someone calling her name from downstairs. It was Marcus, but she mistook the voice for Nestor's. Harrison swung her head at the medicine cabinet. The mirror exploded, shards falling into the sink below, and the cabinet door popped open.

The side of Mina's face was badly gashed, fragments of glass sparkling in the deep cuts on her forehead, temple, and cheek. Harrison let go of her neck. Her legs gave way and she fell on top of the sink. Blood dripped from her wounds, plopping on the glass. The killer reached under her and fished for the largest shard. When he found it, he swiped it against her neck. Blood trickled out of the wound, but it was superficial.

Despite that, the stinging pain sent Mina into panic mode. She was certain her throat had been slit and she was going to die soon. She reached up and grabbed a bottle of rubbing alcohol from the medicine cabinet, then swung it at Harrison's face. The rest of the sutures tore. Nestor's skinned face flew off Harrison's head, soaring like a frisbee before landing in the bathtub. Teetering back, Harrison held his hands up to his face and screeched.

Shaking frantically, Mina unscrewed the bottle's cap, then splashed the rubbing alcohol on his skinless face. Harrison felt like his head had been swallowed by a ball of flames. The white-hot agony sunk deep into his skull, the pain spreading through his brain. Debilitated, he fell into the bathtub, bringing the shower curtain down with him. Mina crawled out of the bathroom. Staying on her hands and knees, she made her way to the stairs.

"Mina?" a male voice called out.

"Nes... Nestor," she rasped.

She grabbed the handrail and pulled herself up to her feet. She made it halfway down the stairs before Dean showed up at the bottom of the steps.

"Jesus Christ," he said. He ran up to her, threw one of her arms over his shoulders, then helped her down. He asked, "What happened? Is Nestor still up there?"

"It's... not him," Mina said weakly. "It–It... It was a–a... a monster."

Dean assumed she was talking about Nestor. He had met traumatized victims of domestic abuse who referred to their abusers as monsters. A beat cop met them at the bottom of the stairs. He threw Mina's other arm over his shoulders, then used his radio to call for an ambulance.

"You're okay now," Dean said.

"He took Nestor's face," Mina responded, speaking so fast that some of her words ran together as one. "He killed Nestor. God, he killed Nestor. He–He killed him. God, no, why did he kill him like that?"

"Nestor's dead?"

"He's dead. He's dead. He's dead."

"Okay, we're going to–"

"I'm not dead," Harrison interrupted from the top of the stairs.

Wide-eyed and slack-jawed, the men gazed up at him at a loss for words. They were staring at a naked, one-eyed, faceless man holding a large shard of glass in his left hand. His hands, neck, shoulders, and chest were drenched in blood, too. He was a human monster. Weeping, Mina pulled away from the police and lurched into the living room, unwilling to take any chances around the killer.

Dean drew his handgun from his holster, pointed it at Harrison, and ordered, "Drop the weapon."

"We're alive," Harrison said. "We are one now. Harrison is Nestor. Nestor is Harrison."

"Drop the weapon!" the beat cop barked, finally drawing his pistol and aiming at the killer.

"We just want to be with our true love. Mina... Mina!"

He took a step down.

"Don't move!" Dean demanded.

Hiding behind a sofa, Mina yelled, "Kill him!"

Two more beat cops entered the house through the garage.

Harrison ran down the stairs and yelled, "We loved you!"

Dean and the beat cop ran backwards but they didn't have time to redeploy. They fired their weapons. Dean pulled the trigger twice. The bullets hit Harrison in the abdomen and chest. The rounds stopped in his liver and thoracic diaphragm underneath his heart. The beat cop shot at him eight times. Five of the bullets hit the stairs. One bullet hit the side of the killer's abdomen, the second struck his chest, and the third went through his neck.

Five steps away from the bottom, Harrison collapsed. He rolled down to the bottom of the stairs. He squirmed around a little while the police redeployed, all of them pointing their guns at him and barking orders. The shard had shattered in his hand on his way down, though. The smaller shards had pierced his palm. He curled into the fetal position. His breathing turned hoarse and rattly. After thirty seconds, he stopped moving.

"Show me your hands!" one of the cops yelled.

Two officers grabbed Mina's arms and helped her up. They spoke to her but she couldn't hear them over the commotion.

She said, "Don't let my daughter see me like this. Please don't let her see me like this."

Mina lay in bed under a blue blanket. Her gashed face and sliced neck were bandaged. Her empty gaze was glued to the white wall across from her. The sofa to her left was empty, and the door next to the sofa was wide open. The generic soundtrack of a hospital—beeping, clicking, hissing, whirring, thudding—echoed through the hall endlessly. A local news program played on the TV mounted at the upper corner of the room. The report was about a holiday toy drive in the region.

The smiles and giggles on the TV didn't reflect the bleak reality in most of those hospital rooms, though. No one ever went to a hospital for fun after all. Some patients celebrated life there, welcoming newborns to the world. Others were feeling temporary relief after surviving accidents, illnesses, and severe injuries. But all that joy and relief was going to morph into pure horror once they saw their medical bills. Mina's room, like the rest of them, was garish. And for many patients, the fluorescent lighting at hospitals was the white light at the end of the tunnel.

Someone knocked on the door.

Without moving her head, Mina looked over and saw Dean standing in the doorway.

"May I have a minute?" the detective asked.

Mina wasn't eager to talk to him. She had been in the hospital for two days. Since then, she had spoken to several detectives about the case. She learned about Harrison as well as her husband's suffering. She was also visited by Chelsea, who was taking care of Melody for her until her parents could fly in from Japan. During the first day at the hospital, she blamed the police for everything. She spent the second day blaming herself.

"Yeah," she responded, her voice hoarse from the attempted strangulation.

Dean walked up to the side of the bed and said, "I believe my colleagues spoke to you recently. I don't have much to add. I wouldn't call it an open-and-shut case, though. We're looking into how Harrison Hammer carried out this... attack. I know this might not bring you any comfort, but we want to make sure something like this doesn't happen to anyone else. It should have never happened in the first place, and I'm truly sorry it did."

She believed him. She heard the remorse in his voice and saw the sadness on his face.

"Thank you," she said.

"I'll try not to take more of your time. Like I said, I don't have much more to add, but I brought this for you. Thought you should see it."

He pulled a folded piece of paper out of his coat pocket and wagged it, then put it on the table next to the bed.

"What is it?" Mina asked.

"It's a letter. It was found in your bedroom. This is just a copy. The original is being held as evidence for the time being. I'm not sure if it was written by Nestor or Harrison, but it's addressed to you. I'm not going to lie to you: It's a lot to swallow. But it may give you an idea of what happened in that house. If you want, I can summarize it for you. Or if you don't want it, I can take it back with me and I can make sure you never hear about it again. Just say the word."

"You can leave it."

"Sure, sure. I'll get out of your hair then. You have my number, ma'am. Call me if you need anything."

Mina watched him stroll out of the room, then she stared at the letter for a long, long time. Her eyes misted over as she cast her mind back to the moment she discovered Nestor's butchered body. She remembered seeing his hands swathed in bandages. She believed the letter was written by Harrison, but something inside of her told her it had been dictated by her husband. It seemed like something Nestor would have done.

She grabbed the letter and unfolded it. It was a photocopy of a handwritten letter. Seconds after starting to read it, she began to cry.

29

FINAL CORRESPONDENCE

DEAR MINA,

I'm sorry we have to communicate like this. Unfortunately, I can't feel my hands anymore. On the bright side, it feels good writing a letter again. Dictating, I suppose. You remember when I used to write love letters to you early in our relationship? Every birthday. Every anniversary. Every Valentine's Day. Good times, huh? I would have left you a voice message, but my words have always been better on a page. If you're reading this, you've probably seen what happened to me. I didn't want you to see me like that again, so a video message was out of the question, too. I hope you can erase that image from your mind. Remember me for who I was, not for how I died.

But death isn't the end.

I learned that from Harrison Hammer. He's the man I had been searching for. He was the butterfly I was trying to catch. But I was confused. I thought I was running from someone dangerous, but I was just running from myself. If all goes well, you'll have the opportunity to meet him. It'll be a lot to take in, but you have to let him speak and you have to listen to him. I guess I should say you'd be listening to us. You see, Mina, Harrison and I share a special connection. I know I told you I didn't believe in this sort of stuff, I was never a spiritual person, but this is different. Harrison and I share the same soul.

No, I'm not saying we're soulmates. You and I are soulmates, honey. Two separate people coming together for love. Harrison and I, we were born with half a soul. And when we put our halves together, we make one soul. We make our soul, Mina. Soul, soul, soul... You're probably sick of hearing that word, but I don't know how else to put it without rambling on and on. I'm good at that, I guess. We're good at that. I saw his life in my dreams and used it to write my books. He saw my life, too. He knew all of my hopes and fears. He knew the thoughts I had buried and forgotten in my mind, thoughts I couldn't even remember thinking. We may even share a mother. After all, we don't really know where we came from, right? Life just happens. And get this, we share the same birthday. We were born the same day, and we're going to die on the same day. I know it.

We're going to come together, Harrison and me. The Nestor you know will be nothing more than a husk. You'll meet a new me, the complete me, the real me. I know this sounds crazy, I know what you'll see is going to be scary, but please approach us with an open mind. Fortunately for us, Melody is young. She is perceptive, though. I'm sure when I meet her again, she'll only notice a positive difference. She'll feel that I'm her father, and she'll feel my newfound happiness. If you ever feel any doubt, trust her. She'll guide you. She's a butterfly, too.

I'm getting tired of talking now. We'll speak in person after our transformation is complete. And if anything goes wrong, I don't want you to worry about me. I wasn't scared. No, honey, I'm not scared anymore.

We are one.

We are Butterfly.

We love you.

JOIN THE MAILING LIST

'Shared by Two' is a standalone novel. My next release will be a slasher, but I would like to tackle the themes and ideas in this book from a different angle someday. I already have a few concepts in mind, some that I had planned out years ago but never got around to writing. I always have something new on the horizon, too. I've slowed down in recent years for a variety of reasons, but I'm still working on new stories and breaking new ground every day.

If you want to stay up to date with my newest books, I recommend signing up for my mailing list. With all the doom and gloom about social media now, my newsletter is the best way for us to stay connected. I'll send you an email when I release a new book or when I'm hosting one of my *huge* book sales. I usually only send one email a month, but you might receive two during a busier season or none at all if I have nothing book-related going on. And this newsletter is strictly about my books. I won't spam you with my personal opinions on politics or send you pictures of myself (unless you're willing to pay for them). My newsletter is always free, and it only takes a few seconds to register.

Visit this link to sign up: http://eepurl.com/bNlıCP.

DEAR READER

'*An extreme horror author meets his biggest fan: An aspiring serial killer.*' That was the first note I wrote for this project. Then I jotted down a question for myself: '*What happens when sick readers find pleasure in your extreme horror books?*' I wasn't talking about finding entertainment or relief through a form of exposure therapy, either. I was thinking full-blown—possibly carnal—pleasure. This idea and question came to me after years of receiving requests from a handful of readers. Just a few, really. I was being asked to write 'specific' torture scenes for them.

Now, don't get me wrong. I've received requests from people asking me to write about their greatest fears or their worst traumas, and I completely under-stand that. Extreme horror can be therapeutic. I've also received requests to write sequels to some of my older books, and I love those messages. (I'm still tinkering with ideas for the sequels to *Our Dead Girlfriend* and *Night of the Prowler*, by the way.) But it was the tone of those other requests—from those handful of readers— that made me believe they wanted me to create their personal fantasies.

Eventually, this got me thinking about the relationship between author and reader, boundaries, and the power of words. I suppose you can connect the pieces and see how this original idea evolved into what you just finished reading. I was also still thinking about the themes I had tackled in my previous book, *The President's Son*. If you missed it, it was all about the fine line between fact and fiction—the world's weakening grip on reality. I still wanted to toy with the idea of communicating through fiction.

I thought about writing novels under the pseudonym of Nestor Castle before the release of this book. It was part of my marketing plan. I wanted to release a few books as Nestor Castle, never acknowledge that I was the one writing them, then have him 'disappear.' I was worried that he would have gotten a real fanbase, though, and I would have ended up manipulating so many people. I know extreme horror fans are some of the most caring people in the world, so I would have felt bad making all of you worry for someone that didn't exist for some marketing scheme. Plus, it would have taken years to pull off something like this.

Fun fact, though: I used the titles from some of my canceled projects for Nestor's books in this story. For example, *The Demons We Inherit* was the title for a prequel to my book *A Family of Violence*, one of my first major releases.

Some of the letters in this story were inspired by messages, comments, and even reviews from real readers. I've talked about the harassment I've received from writing *The Groomer* in the past. People like to assume the worst, fabricate my intentions, and attack me *personally* when it comes to this book. I've received harassment for others, too. And, no, I'm not confusing 'criticism' for 'abuse.' I've always welcomed negative reviews. Just look back at my letters in my older books. I'll be honest, I generally don't read my negative reviews these days, but they helped me become the writer I am now.

Anyway, I didn't want this book to be an outright response to all of that, but I wanted to acknowledge it. Not just the harassment *I* receive, either. I wanted to talk about the abuse many authors across many different genres receive from certain readers. Sometimes I have to vent, you know? Although I didn't really think about it before, this kind of circles back to what I was talking about earlier: Communicating through fiction. I'm getting a little better at adding layers to my books, huh?

I incorporate a little bit of myself into every book—

my fears, my goals, my studies, references to the TV shows I'm watching and the movies I love, and stuff like that. Parts of Nestor's life are obviously inspired by mine. We're both extreme horror authors, right? I wouldn't call myself a recluse, but I am an introvert. But don't worry, unlike Nestor, *I* adore my readers and appreciate every interaction we share. I also don't live in a lake house because, unfortunately, I'm not rich. I don't have an agent, either. I enjoy receiving praise, too, so... y'know... you can shower me with compliments if you want.

I'm writing this letter on December 2nd, 2022. This book took me a lot longer to finish than I was expecting. My personal life has been hectic. I've spoken about my issue with migraines over the past few years before. Well, from the end of October to around Thanksgiving, I had the worst migraines of my life. I'm talking four or five days a week of painful tension in my head, especially in my right eye. I felt like the side of my head was going to explode. I had days where I thought I was better tearing my own eye out. (That's where the 'razor to the eye' idea in this book came from.) I've been seeing a neurologist since September. The good news: I already had an MRI on my head, and they didn't find any issues with my brain. I've been taking serotonin since my first visit. It appeared to be working for the first month and a half, then I got hit with that month-long wave of migraines. My next appointment is on

December 12th, so we'll see if I can get some help. I'm sharing this simply to explain why my writing has slowed down recently. Again, the extreme horror community has always been caring to me, so I figured this is something you should know about.

What else has been going on in my life? Hmm... Oh yeah, I'm going to be a dad. My wife and I will be having our first baby in March 2023. Our estimated due date is March 13 to be exact. So, this book—which is scheduled to be released on March 30th, as of right now—will be released after she arrives. I suppose that means you probably already know about this since I might have announced it on social media. I've been lucky enough to join my wife during her appointments and watch our baby grow through 3D and 4D ultrasounds. It's been an amazing journey. And it's given me *a lot* to think about. I'm sure you'll see this experience seep into some of my future books. I don't expect a radical change, but I am growing as a person. Those of you who have been reading my books since I was 22 or 24 (depending on if you started with my short stories or my novels) have been witnessing my growth already.

This is a good place to segue into what's coming next. I announced a book called '*Blender Babies*' over a year ago, I think. If you read my letter at the end of '*The President's Son*,' then you know '*Blender Babies*' was supposed to be my next book. It was actually scheduled to come out between January and March 2023. Of course, shortly after publishing my last book, I found out my wife was pregnant. I'm not a very superstitious person, but it didn't jibe well with me to release a book like '*Blender Babies*' on the month of my daughter's birth. So, I delayed it. It is still coming out, though. Right now, I have it locked in for a September 7th, 2023, release. Before that, I'm planning on releasing '*Do Not Disturb 3: Goldbrush*' in June 2023. I have a fourth book planned for 2023 as well, but I don't want to announce that yet. And to be honest, these dates might change. I have no idea what it will be like to write after I become a father. I still have a lot of great extreme horror books on the way, though.

If you enjoyed this book, please don't forget to take a minute to leave an honest review on Amazon. Reviews on Goodreads, TikTok, Instagram, Facebook, and your blogs and vlogs are also greatly appreciated. Even though I don't get to respond to everything, I'm always happy to see your reviews and it makes my day better to see you sharing my writing. It's always great when I stumble upon a nice, civil conversation about my work on social media. I'm still a fully independent author. Every expense comes straight out of my pocket, so I don't have the biggest budget or a big publisher to help me advertise my books. Your word-of-mouth has always been key to the success of authors like me.

If you need help writing your review, you can answer questions like these: Did you enjoy the story? Were the characters interesting, relatable, or memorable? Did you like the ending? Would you like to read another extreme horror novel with similar themes from Jon Athan? I'm not writing a sequel to this book, but I may tackle these themes again in the future. Good or bad, your reviews help other readers find my books, they help me improve, and they help me plan my future novels. Thank you for taking time out of your day to help me out.

And thank you for reading my *55th* novel. It's been a dark but amazing journey so far. I've written in so many different subgenres over the years: revenge, political, psychological, supernatural, slasher, cannibal, coming-of-age, body horror, urban legends reimagined. I still have a lot more to explore, too. I might even get around to doing an epic period horror piece. If you're interested in horror with an *extreme* edge, please visit my Amazon's author page and check out the rest of my work. You'll have 54 other novels waiting for you. My previous book, 'The President's Son,' examined conspiracy theories, misinformation, and disinformation. Think of it like 'American Psycho' meets 'Forrest Gump.' I'll share more on my upcoming books soon. Thanks again for reading and hope you're all staying healthy!

Until our next venture into the dark and disturbing,
  Jon Athan

P.S. If you have any questions or comments, feel free to contact me directly using my business email: info@ jon-athan.com. You can also contact me via Twitter @Jonny_Athan, my Facebook page, or Instagram @AuthorJonnyAthan. I can't promise that I'll reply right away, but I always try to respond. Thank you for your patience!

Printed in Great Britain
by Amazon

37547708R00199